THE **TOKYO**
ZODIAC MURDERS

SOJI SHIMADA

PUSHKIN VERTIGO

THE TOKYO
ZODIAC MURDERS

TRANSLATED BY ROSS AND SHIKA MACKENZIE

JOHN PUGMIRE, EDITOR

Pushkin Vertigo
Somerset House, Strand
London WC2R 1LA

Senseijutsu Satsujinjiken © 2013 Soji Shimada.
All rights reserved.
Publication rights for this English edition
arranged through Kodansha Ltd., Tokyo.

Translation by Ross and Shika Mackenzie

First published in Japanese as
Senseijutsu Satsujiniken in 1981 by Kodansha Ltd.

First published in English in 2004 by IBC Publishing

First published by Pushkin Vertigo in 2015

11

ISBN 13: 978-1-782271-38-3

Text designed and typeset by Tetragon, London
Printed and bound by Clays Ltd, Elcograf S.p.A.

www.pushkinpress.com

CONTENTS

DRAMATIS PERSONAE
(in alphabetical order)

1936

Akiko Murakami	*Masako's daughter*
Ayako Umezawa	*Yoshio's wife*
Bunjiro Takegoshi	*Policeman*
Genzo Ogata	*Mannequin factory owner*
Gozo Abe	*Painter*
Heikichi Umezawa	*Artist*
Heitaro Tomita	*Yasue's son*
Kazue Kanemoto	*Masako's daughter*
Kinue Yamada	*Poet*
Masako Umezawa	*Heikichi's second wife*
Motonari Tokuda	*Sculptor*
Nobuyo Umezawa	*Yoshio and Ayako's daughter*
Reiko Umezawa	*Yoshio and Ayako's daughter*
Tae Umezawa	*Heikichi's first wife*
Tamio Yasukawa	*Mannequin craftsman*
Tokiko Umezawa	*Heikichi and Tae's daughter*
Tomoko Murakami	*Masako's daughter*
Toshinobu Ishibashi	*Painter*
Yasue Tomita	*Gallery owner*
Yasushi Yamada	*Painter*
Yoshio Umezawa	*Writer (Heikichi's brother)*
Yukiko Umezawa	*Heikichi and Masako's daughter*

Crazy man, mannequins, etc.

1979

Emoto	*Kiyoshi's friend*
Fumihiko Takegoshi	*Policeman (Bunjiro's son)*
Heitaro Umeda	*Theme-park employee*
Kazumi Ishioka	*Illustrator and amateur detective*
Kiyoshi Mitarai	*Astrologer, fortune-teller and self-styled detective*
Misako Iida	*Bunjiro's daughter*
Mr Iida	*Policeman (Misako Iida's husband)*
Mrs Kato	*Tamio Yasukawa's daughter*
Shusai Yoshida	*Fortune-teller and doll-maker*

Dog, *maiko*, mannequins, shop owner, tourists, waitresses, etc.

FOREWORD

To the best of my knowledge, the case of the serial murders which took place in Japan in 1936—popularly known as "the Tokyo Zodiac Murders"—is one of the most peculiar and most elusive mysteries in the history of crime. No one involved in the case at the time could even imagine such a crime occurring, and finding the murderer—or murderers—was believed to be absolutely impossible.

The precise record of the case had been made available to the public in the hope that the mystery of these murders would be solved. This book opens more than forty years after the incident, when the case still remained an utter mystery.

Readers may like to attempt to unravel the puzzle themselves, just as we—my good friend Kiyoshi Mitarai and I—set out to do on that fateful day in the spring of 1979.

I can assure you that I have included all the necessary clues—the same clues we had to work with.

Kazumi Ishioka

PROLOGUE

Azoth

I am not writing this to be published. However, as it is taking form, I have to consider the possibility that someone will discover it. Therefore, let me start by saying that although this document constitutes my last will and testament, it also happens to be an accounting of my fascination with women. If my work should be found more interesting after my death, such as Van Gogh's was after his, I hope that those who read this document will understand my final wishes and that my legacy will be extended to generations to come.

Heikichi Umezawa
Friday, 21st February 1936

Last Will and Testament

I have been possessed by a devil, an evil spirit with thoughts of its own. It plays vicious tricks on me. I am in agony. Under the devil's control, my body is a mere puppet. One night, a huge clam, as big as a calf, appeared under my desk. It extended its foot, slid across my room, and left a trail of mucus on the wooden floor. Another evening, I noticed geckos hiding in my room, their bodies in the shadow of a lattice. I tried to kill them, but found that I was powerless.

One early spring morning, I awoke chilled to the bone. The devil was trying to freeze me to death! In time, my youth left me, and so did my physical strength, allowing the devil to possess me even more easily. Celsus said: "To exorcize the demon from a person possessed, you should starve him. Feed him but bread and water, and then beat him senseless with a club." In the Gospel of St Mark there is corroboration of this method: "Master," a parent says to Jesus, "I bring my child possessed by a demon to you. My child occasionally frothed at the mouth and clenched his teeth, and now he is emaciated."

During my own childhood, I realized I was possessed. In order to exorcize the devil in me, I tried everything I could think of. I found this bit of information in another book: "In the Middle Ages, people burned strong incense in front of someone possessed. When the patient fainted, they yanked out some of his hair, put it into a bottle, and capped it. It was believed that the demon could thus be trapped and the patient allowed to recover his senses." I begged my friends to try this on me, but they scoffed and called me deranged. I tried to pull out my hair myself, but I fainted from the pain. My friends, watching, thought me either crazy or epileptic.

You cannot imagine what I have been through. I have lost all sense of pride; I have been so overwhelmed that I feel a mere transient in this world. With my person, the devil took the shape of a ball, which must have been akin to the "hysteric ball" of the Middle Ages. Usually it stayed in my lower abdomen. Sometimes it crawled up through the stomach and oesophagus, and then into my throat. This always happened on a Friday. Just as St Cyril described it, my tongue is taut with tension, my lips tremble, and my mouth produces foam. The demon explodes with laughter, and nails are driven into my body. Maggots, snakes and toads emerge before me, one after another; dead men and animals strut around my room; wet reptiles gnaw at my nose, ears and lips. The odour is so incredible it sizzles! Now I understand why reptiles are used in the ceremonies of witchcraft.

Recently, it is rare if they attack; but the thought of them never leaves me. My scars, which are sacred, bleed each Friday. I have begun to indulge in religious exaltations as if I were Catharine Cialina in the seventeenth century or Amelia Bicchieri of Vercelli in the thirteenth century.

The devil is relentless, urging me constantly to obey him. To achieve this end, he has created an almighty woman, a goddess, a Helen of Troy—or perhaps a witch. She appears nightly in my dreams, where all manner of black magic can reside. I ingest medicinal plants, as Plinius prescribed; before I go to bed I take the ashes of lizards, mix them with a fine wine, and apply the concoction to my nipples and over my heart… but to no avail.

While being manipulated like a puppet, I dream of the perfect woman. I am mesmerized by her beauty, her psychic power, her vigour. I know I would be incapable of painting her on a canvas. Would I be able to bear seeing her with my own eyes? My desire is so overwhelming, it is slowly killing me. I would gladly give up my wretched life if this perfect woman were to become a reality.

Following the terminology of alchemy, I shall call her Azoth, which means "from A to Z"—the ultimate creation, the universal life force. She fulfils my dreams completely.

According to my understanding of the human body, there are six different major body parts: the head, the chest, the abdomen, the hips, the thighs and the legs. In astrology, the human body—a bag-shaped object—is a reflection of the universe in miniature. Each part of the body has its own planet that rules, protects and empowers it:

- The head is protected and dominated by Mars, the ruling planet for Aries, which Mars also empowers.
- The chest is the territory of Gemini and Leo, protected by Mercury and also the sun. If I were to substitute the breasts of women for the chest, then they would come under the control of Cancer. The moon rules Cancer.
- The abdomen is for Virgo, ruled by Mercury.

17

- The hips are designated to Libra, ruled by Venus. However, I could substitute the womb for the hips. Scorpio, ruled by Pluto, controls the sexual organs.
- The thighs are in the territory of Sagittarius, ruled by Jupiter.
- The legs are Aquarius, ruled by Uranus.

As I have said, each of us has a part of our body that is given strength by our ruling planet. Those born under Aries, for example, find strength in their head, and Librans have theirs in their hips. A person's astrological identity is determined by the alignment of the sun and the planets at the exact moment of birth. One's sign and correlating part of the body determines who he or she is. No one can be perfect, because everyone has a gift from the ruling planet in only one part of their body. So I thought to myself: if I were to take the perfect head, the perfect breasts, the perfect hips and the perfect legs, and then combine them into a female body, I would have the perfect woman! She would be a goddess. And if I were to put six virgin parts of the body together, their combined beauty would be supreme.

Thereafter, my only focus in life was this goddess, and, as fate would have it, what one concentrates on usually manifests itself. One day, I realized that six virgins of different zodiacal signs were living near me—my daughters and nieces! I chuckled to myself at life's so-called "coincidences", grateful for my knowledge of astrology. My knees grew weak as my fantasies assumed a reality.

People may be surprised to hear that I am the father of five daughters. The eldest one is Kazue, followed by Tomoko, Akiko,

Tokiko and Yukiko. The three eldest ones are stepdaughters from my second marriage, to Masako. Tokiko is from my first wife, Tae, and Yukiko is my daughter with Masako. Tokiko and Yukiko were born in the same year. My wife Masako, who used to be a ballet dancer, teaches ballet and piano to our daughters, and Reiko and Nobuyo have joined them. These two girls, who moved out of their small house to live with us, are the daughters of my younger brother Yoshio.

Kazue (Capricorn, born 1904) has lived alone in her own house since her divorce. So there are now these six young women in my house: Tomoko (Aquarius, born 1910); Akiko (Scorpio, born 1911); Yukiko (Cancer, born 1913); Tokiko (Aries, also born 1913); Reiko, one of the nieces (Virgo, also born 1913); and Nobuyo, Reiko's sister (Sagittarius, born 1915).

Thus, I found my fate sealed. The devil was telling me to sacrifice these young women. Kazue (thirty-one) is much older than the others, so I excluded her from the group. I would take the head from Tokiko, the chest from Yukiko, and the abdomen from Reiko. The hips would come from Akiko, the thighs from Nobuyo and the legs from Tomoko. Then I would fashion these parts together to make one woman. It would be desirable if the hips were from a Libra and the chest from a Gemini virgin, but one cannot be so greedy. Since Azoth is female, her chest can be represented by breasts and her hips by a womb. Because the devil is generous, I know my plan will work!

I shall follow the rules of alchemy strictly, however, in order to create eternal life. The six virgins will serve as metallic elements, and I will refine these base metals into gold. When my work is accomplished, blue sky will appear through dark clouds, setting me free from agony and torture.

Ah, how my body trembles! I want to see what Azoth will look like! I want to see my thirty years of devotion bear the fruit of my diligence. This shall be my art from the devil's workshop. Throughout history, no one has ever had the same idea as mine—a Black Magic Mass, a philosopher's stone and all the sculptures ever made in an attempt to capture the beauty of women would all pale before Azoth.

Of course, the six young women will have to die. Their bodies will be cut into three pieces (into two in the cases of Tokiko and Tomoko). Azoth will be constituted of the selected pieces, and the rest of the bodies properly disposed of. The young women will die, but their body parts will live on for ever in Azoth. If only they could know why they must die, I am sure they would be satisfied with their fate.

I shall proceed in accordance with the principles of alchemy:

- I should start my work while the sun is in Aries. Tokiko, who offers her head, is an Aries. Thus, she should be killed by ♂, which stands for Mars and also represents iron in alchemy.
- Yukiko, who offers her chest, is a Cancer. Thus, she should be killed by ☽, which stands for the moon and also represents silver in alchemy.
- Reiko, who offers her abdomen, is a Virgo. Thus, she should swallow ☿ to die. The symbol stands for Mercury and also represents mercury in alchemy.
- Akiko, who offers her hips, is a Scorpio. Its ruling planet is ♇, Pluto today. But I would follow the tradition of the Middle Ages, so ♂ will be desired for her death.

- Nobuyo, who offers her thighs, is a Sagittarius. Thus, she should die of ♃, which stands for Jupiter and also represents tin in alchemy.
- Tomoko, who offers her legs, is an Aquarius, which has Uranus as its ruling planet. In the Middle Ages, however, Uranus had not yet been discovered, so ♅ was used. Thus, Tomoko can die of ♄, which stands for Saturn, and also represents lead in alchemy.

I will purify their bodies and mine with a mixture of wine and an assortment of ashes. Next, I will remove the desired body parts from each young woman with a handsaw. These parts will be carefully assembled onto a carved wooden cross on which I will create Azoth. I could use nails to affix Azoth to the cross—in the same way Christ was—but I do not want to incur damage from the nails. The body I will decorate with small lizards, as it is said in the oracle of Hecate. Then, I shall prepare the "hidden fire". Hontanus interpreted the term as an actual fire, as did many alchemists… only to see their experiments fail. "Hidden fire" or "fire that burns without flame" really refers to a certain kind of salt ⊖ and incense. To this mixture is added the flesh of a sheep, a cow, an infant, a crab, a lion, a virgin, a scorpion, a goat and a fish—all astrological symbols. Frogs and lizards will be added as well. And I will prepare the type of furnace that alchemists call an "athanor".

I will intone from an invocation written in the ancient *Philosophoumena* of Origen of St Hippolytus:

Viens, infernal terrestre et céleste Bombô,
déesse des grands chemins des carrefours,

toi qui apportes la lumière, qui marches la nuit,
ennemie de la lumière, amie et compagne de la nuit,
toi que réjouissent l'aboiement des chiens et le sang versé,
qui erres au milieu des ombres à travers les tombeaux,
toi qui désires le sang et qui apportes la terreur aux mortals,
Gorgo, Norno, lune aux mille formes,
assiste d'un oeuil propice à nos sacrifices.

The mixture will then be removed from the furnace and sealed within a "philosopher's egg". It will be incubated until it becomes a panacea. With this panacea, each part of the body will be glued to form a whole, to become an eternal life. And when the perfect woman appears in the light, I will become an adept.

This is the "magnum opus" of so-called "Alchemy". It is often referred to as witch's work, even though it cannot be denied that alchemy contributed greatly to the progress of chemistry, just as astrology was the foundation of astronomy. I think it is absurd that people should deny the significance of their ancestors' beliefs. The goal of alchemy is more profound than what many people may think today: its aim is to embody the true nature of things, such as "supreme beauty" or "supreme love". Our consciousness tends to be vulgarized by daily life. But through the process of alchemy, we can purify our soul and rise above worldly things. In the East, Zen is the correspondent to this. The true aim of alchemy is the creation of an "eternal circle" or universal relief.

Some people have attempted to create gold with alchemy, but more likely this was done as a joke or a trick. Many have searched in underground mines for the "first element", but elements are not necessarily metal or mineral. Paracelsus said:

"You can find it everywhere, and children are playing with it." My belief is that it resides in the bodies of women. Where else could it be?

I am well aware of my reputation as a lunatic. I may be different from others, but that is what makes me an artist. Art is not to copy the work of another; real art exists only in difference. Although it would be easier, I could never follow in the footsteps of someone else. I prefer to make my own path! I am not a violent man, but I admit to extreme excitement when I witnessed the dissection of a human body for the first time. I am unaccountably attracted to the distortion of human bodies. I love seeing a dislocated arm, and how a dying man's muscles go through changes. I wish I could have a chance to draw such things. I am sure that many other artists share my leanings.

Now I want to tell you about my past. I discovered the marvels of astrology when I was a teenager. Astrology was not common in Japan back then, and the man who introduced me to it was the first astrologer in Japan. My mother had learnt of his reputation and desired his insight. I was reluctant to go with her, but she took me along. As I watched this fortune-teller in action, I was astonished. He could see into a person's past as well as their future! I was fascinated, and later I became his student. Originally, this man had come from Holland as a missionary, but he had been dismissed because of his negligence towards his mission. From that point on, fortune-telling became his sole work.

I was born in Tokyo at 7.31 p.m., on 26th January 1886. My sun is in Aquarius, and my ascendant is in Virgo, which is ruled by Saturn. Therefore, Saturn, the symbol of my life, holds my destiny. It was Saturn that guided me to alchemy.

Saturn represents lead, one of the basic chemical elements. This understanding caused me to believe that alchemy would hone my craft. Saturn implies challenges and perseverance. The fortune-teller told me that I would struggle with my inferiority complex all my life, and that I would suffer from poor health, especially in childhood. I was advised to be careful of getting burnt. His advice was correct, if unheeded. In elementary school, I fell on a brazier, and my right foot was severely burnt. I still have the scar.

The fortune-teller also predicted that I would be involved in an illicit love affair; and, in fact, I have two daughters born of different mothers in the same year. He also predicted marriage complications: although my Venus is in Pisces and, therefore, I am naturally attracted to Piscean women, I would in fact marry a Leo, and my family obligations would increase when I was twenty-eight. Tae, my first wife, was in fact a Pisces. I took to painting ballet dancers, influenced by Degas. Masako, a married woman, was one of my models. Almost by force, I made love to her. We had an affair, and Yukiko was born—at around the same time that Tae gave birth to a daughter. I divorced Tae and took custody of the baby, Tokiko. Then I married Masako. This all happened when I was twenty-eight!

Today, in Hoya, Tae sells tobacco at the house I purchased for her. At the time of our divorce, I was concerned about Tokiko, who would live with the other girls in my home. But she seemed to get along with them without any problems. Twenty years have passed since the divorce, but still I feel guilty about Tae. If Azoth becomes the masterpiece of my life, I intend to give the fortune I will make to Tae to assuage my guilt.

My horoscope, according to the fortune-teller, also suggested a tendency towards secrecy and loneliness, and the possibility of being locked up in a hospital or an institution—in other words, I would spend a life apart from others. And today, in fact, I seldom see my family, who live in the main house. I spend most of my time in my studio, which I converted from the old storehouse in the backyard.

I have two planets—Neptune and Pluto—in the ninth house, which is rare. Moreover, planets in the ninth house have a greater influence than planets in other houses. The latter half of my life has been dominated by these planets. The ninth house implies mystical power and a fascination with paganism. The fortune-teller said I would become involved in witchcraft and roam foreign countries. He said that, given the movement of the moon, my departure from Japan would occur when I was nineteen or twenty years of age, and that the trip would mark a turning point in my life. As it turned out, I left for France at the age of nineteen, and it was there that I was drawn to mysticism.

I had not given myself over to astrology, but everything the fortune-teller said came true. I even tried to go against his prophecy, but to no avail. My family seems also to be manipulated by fate—especially the women, who have had little luck in love or marriage. Tae is divorced from me, and now that I have chosen to kill myself, Masako will be widowed soon. My mother failed in her marriage, as did my grandmother. Kazue, Masako's first daughter, was recently divorced.

Tomoko is now twenty-six, and Akiko twenty-four. They live in the spacious main house and are close to their mother. If necessary, they can make a living by teaching piano and ballet, so they have the option of remaining single. With tensions between Japan and China heightening, young men will soon be drafted. Masako dislikes soldiers, and she will see to it that her daughters remain virgins.

Everything seemed to be going along fine, but then Masako and her daughters started having ideas about doing something with the family property, which has a total area of 2,400 square metres. They kept barging into my studio, urging me to build an apartment building. "You can do whatever you want after I die," I told them.

It is not really fair to my brother Yoshio that I control the Umezawa family land just because I am the eldest son. He and his wife have always been welcome to live in our main house, but they have politely declined my invitation even though their daughters moved in. Perhaps there is incompatibility between Masako and Ayako, Yoshio's wife. If an apartment building is built after I die, however, Yoshio and Ayako would gladly live there, saving money that would otherwise go to rent elsewhere. Anyway, I am the only one who is consistently opposed to this plan. Masako—the ringleader—and her daughters have become frustrated in the extreme. I worry that if this situation continues they will cause me bodily harm; perhaps they will poison me. Recently, I have been thinking a lot about Tae. She is a modest, obedient woman; she does not excite me, but she is an angel compared to Masako.

The reason I keep turning them down is my love for my studio, which is in the north-west corner of the yard. After I inherited this property in Ohara—in Meguro Ward in Tokyo— from my mother, I renovated the old storehouse and made it into a studio. I spend most of my time here. It's surrounded by trees, so my privacy is protected. If we built an apartment building, the studio could be left as it is, but the trees would have to be cut down. My studio would no longer be a hideaway. How could I concentrate on my work with tenants coming and going around me? It would be impossible.

Ever since I was small, I have loved the gloom of this storehouse. It is where I often played. My preference for closed-in spaces did not change until recently. In order to get more light into the studio, I had two large skylights put in. For security, I put iron grilles under them. I put grilles inside the windows on the ground floor, too. I love the skylights. In afternoons in autumn, I can see leaves falling onto the glass. The grille and falling leaves create shadows on the studio floor that look like musical notes. They are so beautiful that I am moved to sing my favourite songs—'Isle of Capri' and 'Orchids in the Moonlight'. I also installed a bathroom and a kitchen. I sleep alone on a military bed. It has casters, so it can be rolled anywhere I want in the room.

I took out the first floor, doubling the height of the ceiling, and the studio became very spacious. Now I can store large paintings and the space also allows me to view my artwork from a distance. Because they faced a stone wall, the windows on the north and west side of the studio did not get much light, so I sealed them. Now I can stand paintings against the walls. I have eleven large paintings standing there now. They are part of my series called "The Twelve Signs of the Zodiac". The sketch for the twelfth, *Aries*, is almost done. I will start to create Azoth very soon. When I complete her, I will depart from this world for ever.

I went to Paris in 1906. I was young and restless. Japanese tourists were scarce back then. My meagre knowledge of French deepened my loneliness, and I felt as if I was the only man living in the world when I took a walk under the moonlight. As my language ability gradually improved, my loneliness lessened and I began to feel more comfortable. I began to visit the Latin Quarter. Autumn in Paris was stunning. I loved the rustle of fallen leaves being blown by the wind, and the contrasting colours of the leaves were very beautiful against the grey stones. The curtains drawn around my heart slowly parted to reveal the dramatic stage set of Paris.

I discovered the works of Gustave Moreau. I remember the gold plate bearing the inscription "14" on his house in Rochefoucauld Avenue. I added him to my list of greatest artists, along with Van Gogh. Moreau influenced me tremendously.

One day in late autumn, at La Fontaine de Médicis, one of my favourite places, I saw a young woman. In the cold air, the trees were extending their bare branches under a dark sky. They reminded me of the blood vessels of old men. Winter was just around the corner. What I didn't realize at first was that spring was right there in front of me, leaning on the metal handrail and deep in thought. Realizing that she was also Asian, I walked up to her. She looked timid. I sensed the same kind of shyness that many Japanese girls have, but I could not be sure. She might have been Chinese. However, she seemed relieved to see me. Taking a chance, I spoke in French, saying it seemed that winter was on its way: "*On dirait que l'hiver arrive.*" In Japan, one would rarely approach a stranger this way, but speaking in a foreign language made me bolder. She didn't seem to understand me. With a look of depression, she shook her head and started to leave. I decided to ask if she was Japanese: "*Kimi wa nihonjin desu ka?*" She stopped and turned back, and her sullen expression turned into a beautiful smile. We fell in love immediately. Her name was Yasue Tomita.

After that, we met each other every day, and our loneliness turned into true happiness. In winter, there were always vendors selling roasted chestnuts near the fountain. *"Chaud, chaud, marrons chauds!"* they would cry. Yasue and I would often buy some chestnuts and then try to imitate the vendors, falling into each other and laughing as if we were drunk.

Yasue was born in late November in the same year as me, but because my birthday is in January she was almost a year younger. She had also gone to Paris to study art, so she must have come from a wealthy family like myself. We returned to Japan together several years before Europe was overwhelmed by the First World War. I was then twenty-two. We thought we would marry, but our plans didn't materialize. Life in Tokyo was not the same as our romantic days in Paris. Yasue filled her days socializing with old friends, and eventually the modern girl's attentions turned away from me. We didn't see each other for a while. I heard later that she had married.

When I was twenty-six, Yoshio introduced me to Tae and we got married. He was at Tokyo Metropolitan University, and he happened to know her because she worked at a kimono shop nearby. Although the introduction was very casual, I decided right away I would marry her; I was so lonely after my mother's death. I had inherited her property, so I must have seemed a good catch for Tae, although women never spoke of such things back then.

Ironically, several months after I married Tae, I ran into Yasue in Ginza, holding her son's hand. She told me she was divorced and owned a cafe gallery in Ginza. "And guess what!" she said with a grin. "It's named after a memorable place." "La Fontaine de Médicis?" I said immediately. "Yes!" We both smiled. After that, Yasue became the one and only dealer of my paintings. My work didn't fetch much, but Yasue always encouraged me to use her space for exhibitions. I had several shows there, but the results were not very good. I think it was because I had chosen not to enter competitions and had few prizes on my curriculum vitae, and I was not an aggressive businessman. I painted Yasue whenever she visited my studio, and I always included paintings of her when I showed at "De Médicis". Yasue was a Sagittarius, born on 27th November 1886. Heitaro, her son, was a Taurus, born in 1909. Sometimes Yasue would imply that I was his father. She might have been kidding, but it could have been true. In fact, she used the same kanji character "hei" from my name for his name. If Heitaro really was my son, it would have been destiny!

I would say that my taste in art is rather conservative. Abstract painters like Picasso and Miró have never appealed to me particularly. But I love Van Gogh and Gustave Moreau. I suppose my taste is rather old-fashioned, but I prefer art that gives off strong energy in a direct way. If a painting has no energy within, then I feel it is just a piece of canvas smeared with paint. In that sense, I suppose I have to admit some of Picasso's works do have energy and I admire them for that. I also think that Fugaku Sumie, who throws his body against a canvas, is rather good. However, I believe that creation of any good art has to be done with a certain amount of technique. If you just fling mud at a wall and call it art, I would maintain that a young kid could probably do better.

To me, so-called "avant-garde" art is very mediocre compared to what we see in real life. I would rather look at a traffic accident—I can see explosive energy in the skid marks of the tyres and in the blood splattered on the road. The thin white chalk lines are a quiet contrast to all that brutality.

I like sculpture, but I have never found abstract sculpture very interesting. I want sculptures to look real. I suppose that is why I am more attracted to dolls than modern sculptures. I found a very attractive woman when I was young. Actually she was not a human but a mannequin in the window of a boutique near Tokyo Metropolitan University. I was infatuated with her. I went to see her every day, sometimes five or six times a day. When I went into town, I always made a detour to see her. This went on for a year. As the seasons changed, I saw her in summer dresses, winter coats and spring blouses. I wanted to ask the shopkeeper if I could buy her, but my shyness wouldn't allow me to do such a thing.

I called her Tokie, because she looked like an actress I adored who had that name. I grew obsessed with Tokie. I dedicated poems to her. Her face was always in my mind. And I drew portraits of her from memory. That was really the beginning of my life as a painter. I would stand just to the side of the shop window and pretend I was watching the unloading of raw silk at the wholesale store next door. Secretly, of course, I was staring at the doll. She had frizzy brown hair, delicate fingers, and slender legs that I could see below the hem of her skirt. Her face had a certain elegance. Even now, I can recall exactly what she looked like.

One day, I happened to see Tokie naked while the shop-keeper was changing her clothes. My knees trembled and I almost fainted. No other woman has ever left me feeling that way. The experience had a tremendous effect on my sexuality. Female sex organs covered with pubic hair lost all their attraction. And I began to prefer women with coarse, curly hair. I also started taking an admittedly perverse interest in mute girls and female corpses.

But my love affair with Tokie came to a sudden end. One warm spring morning, when I arrived at the boutique, she was gone from the window. My feelings could not be put into words. I was heartbroken. It was 21st March, and the cherry blossoms were about to bloom.

I'm not so fond of noisy nightclubs filled with cigarette smoke, but recently I started going to a bar called "Kakinoki"—the Persimmon Tree. I enjoy talking to one of the regular customers; he is, in fact, the owner of a mannequin factory. One day, after a few drinks, I told him about my love affair with Tokie and he kindly invited me to visit his factory. But there was no doll like Tokie to be found there.

Probably nobody could understand my feelings towards Tokie. She was very special, and no other doll could compare to her. She was like a precious pearl, whereas all the others were mere grains of sand.

My first daughter was born on 21st March—the same date that Tokie disappeared. So I called her Tokiko. It had to be fate: Tokie had been reincarnated as a human being called Tokiko. I was convinced that Tokiko would look more and more like that doll as she grew up. However, she was not blessed with good health.

As I write this, I am astonished to see where my ideas come from. Tokiko is my favourite child. I wanted her to have a perfect body, and so my subconscious must have suggested that I create

Azoth. Perhaps my love for Tokiko is something more than a normal father's love. People born under the sign of Aries tend to be cheerful and vigorous, but Tokiko's birthday is close to the cusp of Aries and Pisces. I think that is what causes her mood swings. When I see her depressed, I think of her delicate heart condition and then my love for the poor child surges.

I have often used my daughters as models, sketching them half-naked. Tokiko is rather skinny and has a birthmark on the right side of her belly. When I first saw how thin she was, I regretted she did not have a perfect body to match her very pretty face. I don't mean that her body is inferior—in fact, come to think of it, I suppose Tomoko, Reiko and Nobuyo are all even thinner than she is. But since Tokiko—along with Yukiko—is my real daughter, I have always wanted her to be perfect.

Several years ago, I visited Europe again. I didn't find the Louvre very exciting, so I took a trip to Amsterdam to see an exhibition of the work of André Milhaud. I was so overpowered by his work that for a while I could not go back to my own. It could be titled *The Art of Death*. In a deserted building that once housed an aquarium, he had constructed several tableaux. Among them was the corpse of a man hanging from a pole, and the corpses of a mother and daughter abandoned on a street. Their bodies were rotting, and the stench was terrible. The corpses were fake, of course, but I didn't realize that for a whole year. Their faces were distorted by fear, and their muscles were wrenched with the agony of death. The most shocking exhibit was a man dying in water. His hands were handcuffed behind him as another man shoved his head underwater. There were tiny bubbles coming out of the drowning man's mouth. This was taking place in a glass case, lit from the inside.

33

I could think of nothing to measure up to Milhaud's work, let alone surpass it. After spending a whole year producing nothing, I decided to create Azoth. I decided that nothing but Azoth could supersede his work!

Nobody will know where I create Azoth, but I must be careful of dogs. They can hear the screams of the dying. Humans cannot pick up a sound when its frequency exceeds 20,000 cycles per second, but dogs can. In the aquarium of Milhaud's exhibition, I saw a lady with a Yorkshire terrier in her arms. Its ears trembled as it listened to the sounds of death.

The place for the creation and assembly of Azoth will be determined by mathematical calculations. I could do this work in my studio, of course, but it would be very suspicious if six young women disappeared suddenly. The studio would obviously come under investigation. And even if the police didn't suspect me, Masako could come to the studio. Therefore, I must have another venue for this work, somewhere I can store my creation. So I have bought a house in the countryside at a very good price. However, because this document may be found before my death, I dare not mention the exact location. I will only say that it is somewhere in Niigata Prefecture.

I will leave this note next to Azoth. After her creation, the parts of the girls' bodies that have not been used should be delivered to various locations that relate to their respective zodiacal sign. The ideal correlation will be a place where a specific metal is mined. For example, gold relates to Leo, iron to Aries and Scorpio, silver to Cancer, and tin to Sagittarius and Pisces. Thus, the remains of the bodies will be disposed of as follows:

- Tokiko (Aries), in a place that produces iron
- Yukiko (Cancer), in a place that produces silver
- Reiko (Virgo), in a place that produces mercury
- Akiko (Scorpio), in a place that produces iron
- Nobuyo (Sagittarius), in a place that produces tin
- Tomoko (Aquarius), in a place that produces lead.

Once the bodies have been returned to where they belong, Azoth will emerge with supreme power. Then the magnum opus shall be completed!

I am creating Azoth not only for myself, but for the sake of the Empire of Japan. The country has followed a misguided path, and our history is marred with unfortunate incidents. Lest Japan be destroyed, we must assume the responsibility of our ancestors. The day approaches. Azoth shall guide us. Azoth shall save our nation.

In ancient times, the Goddess Himiko reigned over our country. Her realm of Yamatai was glorious. Astrologically, the islands of Japan belong to Libra, where people tend to favour social gatherings. The Japanese people believed in God and loved feasts and festivals. However, when Korean forces over-powered Japan and Confucianism was imported from China, our people changed. Their souls lost their freedom and they became self-suppressive. Then they imported Buddhism from China, but that didn't take root, either. What the Japanese learnt was not real Buddhism, but Buddhism as misinterpreted by the Chinese. We should revert to what this country was originally—an empire ruled by a goddess.

For that reason, Azoth should be placed in the very centre of Japan, so that she can play the part of the Goddess

Himiko. Today, our standard time is determined by the Akashi Observatory at longitude 135° E, but I think this is wrong. The real centre of the Japanese Empire is longitude 138° 48′ E. The Japanese archipelago has a striking bow-like shape, but it is not easy to determine the country's northern and southern borders. From my point of view, it would be appropriate for the north-eastern border to be either the Chishima Islands or the Kurils, which are located next to the Kamchatka Peninsula. The southern border would have to be Iwo Jima, which is located south of the Ogasawara Islands. Although Hateruma Island, one of the Sakishima Islands of Okinawa, is located at a lower latitude, Iwo Jima is to be preferred because it has the shape of an arrowhead.

The physical geography of the Japanese Empire has a characteristic beauty. That convinces me that the country's ruling planet is Venus, which falls under the sign of Libra. We would never find such geographical beauty in any other part of the world. The Japanese archipelago reminds me of a well-proportioned female figure. Then there is the Fuji volcanic zone resembling an arrow held against a bowstring. Iwo Jima, as I have said, looks like an arrowhead. Some day, Japanese people will realize how that island has contributed to our country's history. The arrow was shot once. It passed Australia and Cape Horn, and hit Brazil, where the largest population of Japanese immigrants in the world resides.

I can pinpoint the exact north-easternmost spot in the Japanese archipelago. Most parts of the Kurils should be regarded as part of Japan. Many claim that the islands of Paramushir and Onekotan belong to Japan, but I think they should be excluded. They are so large and close to the Kamchatka

Peninsula, they rightfully belong to the continent. The centre of the Kurils is where Rasshua and Ketoi are located, but I believe that Japan can go further and include Kharimkotan and other southern Kuril islands in its territory.

Those tiny islands, scattered in the far north and the far south, sandwich the main islands of Japan, making it look like a giant bow hung from the continent with tassels. The easternmost tip of Kharimkotan Island is at longitude 154° 36′ E, and its northernmost tip is at latitude 49° 11′ N.

Next, the central point of the north-east–south-west axis. The westernmost tip of Japan is Yonaguni Island, which is located at longitude 123° E. The southernmost tip of the Empire, I repeat, should be Iwo Jima. The southernmost tip of Hateruma Island, located south-east of Yonaguni, is at latitude 24° 3′ N whereas the southernmost tip of Iwo Jima is at latitude 24° 43′ N. However, the central point between Kharimkotan Island and Yonaguni is at longitude 138° 48′ N. This line is the central axis of the Japanese Empire, which starts from the edge of the Izu Peninsula and goes all the way up to the Niigata Plain, where the land extends north. A part of Mount Fuji is also on this line. Therefore, this line must have played an important role in the history of the Japanese Empire, and I foresee that it will continue to do so.

The line of longitude at 138° 48′ E is full of meaning. Mount Yahiko is located at the northern end of this line. That is where Yahiko Shrine is located. It is the key to the myth. There must be a saint stone. Mount Yahiko is the navel of Japan, the exact centre of the country. No one should ignore this holy place; the future of Japan depends on it. It is the one place I would like to visit before I die. I must, and I will! If I fail to do so because of my death, I want my children to visit there on my behalf. Mount Yahiko has mystical power.

Four, 6 and 3 are the numbers on the line dissecting the middle of Japan. These three numbers add up to 13, which is the devil's favourite number. Azoth will be placed in the centre of 13...

ACT ONE

The Unsolved Mystery,
Forty Years On

Footprints in the Snow

"What the hell is all this?" Kiyoshi exclaimed. He closed the book, threw it to me, and lay down on the couch.

"Did you read the whole thing?" I asked.

"Well, Heikichi Umezawa's story, at least."

"And what did you think?" I asked.

Kiyoshi, who had been in the doldrums recently, said nothing. After a long pause, he replied, "Well, it was like being forced to read the Yellow Pages!"

"But what about his take on astrology? Was there anything unusual?"

Kiyoshi's an astrologer, so the question seemed to flatter him. "Well, some parts are based on his own interpretation," he said. "In astrology, you see, the ascendants characterize the body parts rather than the solar signs, so I would say his interpretation was a bit broad. Other than that, his knowledge was pretty solid. I don't think he had any crucial misunderstandings."

"What about his ideas on alchemy?"

"Completely wrong. That kind of thinking was typical among the older generation. It's like baseball. When it first came to Japan in the 1880s, people thought it was a way to discipline the mind, American-style, but they went too far. They took it so seriously that if they didn't get a hit, they were ready to commit hara-kiri. Heikichi Umezawa was like that, but I suppose he knew more than those people who think alchemy is a way to turn lead into gold."

My name's Kazumi Ishioka. I'm a huge fan of mysteries; in fact, they're almost an addiction. If a week goes by without reading a mystery, I suffer withdrawal symptoms. Then I wander around like I'm sleepwalking and wake up in a bookshop, looking for a mystery novel. I've read just about every mystery story ever written, including the one about Yamatai, the controversial ancient kingdom, and the one about the bank robber who stole 300 million yen and was never caught. But it's not an intellectual pursuit; it's more like me getting my fill of gossip.

But of all the mysteries I've read, *The Tokyo Zodiac Murders* was, without a doubt, the most intriguing. The murders actually happened—in 1936, just before the Second World War, at the time of the abortive military uprising on 26th February known as the "2-26 Incident".

The story was extraordinary—incomprehensible, bizarre and with unbelievable depth. The mystery swept the country like a swarm of locusts. And ever since then—for over forty years—numerous intellectuals and would-be detectives have been trying to figure it out. Of course, to this day, the case remains unsolved.

Documents of the case and the last will and testament left by Heikichi Umezawa were compiled into a book. It came out around the time I was born, and immediately became a bestseller. Part of the bigger picture at the time was that the failure to solve the murders seemed to symbolize the darkness surrounding pre-war Japan.

The most horrible and baffling thing about the case was that six young women were killed exactly as described in Heikichi's notes. Moreover, they were buried in six different places, each body had a different part missing, and metal elements were buried with them.

The bizarre thing was, Heikichi was killed prior to the deaths of the young women, who were, in fact, his daughters and nieces. Several people's names were mentioned by him, but they all had alibis. Of course, all the alibis were checked out thoroughly and all the possible suspects were cleared. Heikichi himself seemed to be the only person with a strong motive, but since he was already dead when the murders took place, he was beyond suspicion.

Consequently, the conventional wisdom was that the killer was someone outside the family. The public came up with hundreds of theories, which led only to chaos. Every conceivable motive had already been suggested; things looked like they were at a dead end.

From the late 1970s, a number of books were published that tied the murders to the occult. Most of them were rather crude and shoddily constructed, but they sold very well. So, naturally, more books of the sort were published; it was like a gold rush.

I remember some of the more ridiculous ideas put forward: the Chief of the Metropolitan Police was involved; the Prime Minister had a hand in it; the Nazis wanted the girls for biological experiments; and—the best one in my opinion—cannibals from New Guinea wanted the body parts for eating. These theories were more like a bad joke, but people began to enjoy them. When a gourmet magazine published an article on the fine art of eating human beings, things were clearly out of control. The last crazy idea was that aliens from outer space had done it.

It seemed to me that all these ideas missed two critical points: how could an outsider have read Heikichi's note, and why would someone want to carry out his plan anyway?

The police focused on the fact that the eldest daughter, Kazue, had Chinese connections and might have been a spy. So there was speculation that a secret military agency might have assassinated the Umezawa girls.

My own far-fetched theory was that someone found Heikichi's note and then used it as a cover-up for his own crime. The fellow might have been romantically involved with one of the girls—she broke up with him, so he took his revenge. And if he killed all six girls, his motive wouldn't be obvious. But this theory didn't quite fit with the fact that, according to investigators, the Umezawa girls were strictly guarded by their mother and didn't have any boyfriends. Having a date without parental permission was out of the question in the 1930s. And if one of the girls did have a boyfriend that she jilted, surely he could have chosen an easier method of killing her. And again, he wouldn't have had access to Heikichi's note.

Nothing made sense. Eventually, I stopped thinking about the bizarre murders.

Kiyoshi Mitarai was usually a very energetic fellow, but in the spring of 1979 he was coming out of a bout of depression. He was not in the best condition to solve such a mystery. Many artists have idiosyncrasies, and Kiyoshi was no exception. He would suddenly become happy with the pleasant taste of toothpaste, or he would suddenly get depressed when his favourite restaurant changed the colour of the tablecloths. Once his mood turned bad, it would last for several days. So he was not an easy man to be around. I'd become used to his mood swings, but they seemed to be worse than ever. When he went to the kitchen or to the toilet, he moved like a dying elephant. Even when he saw his clients, he looked sick. He was normally bold and cheeky towards me, but right now he wasn't. To tell the truth, I preferred it that way.

Kiyoshi and I had met the previous year, and since then I had spent much of my free time in his astrology classroom. I would help out when students and clients visited his office. One day, a Mrs Iida came by and said matter-of-factly that her father was involved in the famous Zodiac Murders case. She handed us a piece of evidence, which apparently no one else had seen, and said something to the effect that maybe we could solve the case with it. Kiyoshi was not famous, although he had the respect of his peers. That this woman would entrust such important evidence to him caused him to rise in my estimation. I felt important being associated with him.

It had been a long time since I'd thought about the murders, but it didn't take me long to recall them. Kiyoshi, on the other hand, didn't know anything about the case, even though he was an astrologer himself. I had to find *The Tokyo Zodiac Murders* on my bookshelf, wipe off the dust and explain everything to him.

"So, you're saying that the writer of this note, Heikichi Umezawa, was killed?" Kiyoshi asked, stretching out on the sofa.

"That's right. You'll find the details in the second half of the book."

"I'm tired. This small type is killing my eyes."

"Oh, come on, stop complaining!"

"Can't you just give me a rough idea?"

"All right. I suppose you want an outline of the crimes first?"

"Yes."

"Ready?"

"Just do it…"

"Well, the so-called 'Tokyo Zodiac Murders' actually consist of three separate cases. The first was the murder of Heikichi Umezawa; the second was the murder of Kazue Kanemoto, his stepdaughter; and the third was the Azoth multiple murders. Heikichi was found dead in his studio on 26th February 1936. His note, which seemed a very bizarre story on the face of it, was dated five days before his death. It was found in his desk drawer.

"Kazue was killed at her house in Kaminoge, Setagaya Ward, which was quite far from the Umezawas' house and Heikichi's studio in Ohara, Meguro Ward. She had been raped, so the deduction was that her killer was male, and probably a burglar. It may have been pure coincidence that Kazue was killed at almost the same time as Umezawa and the others.

"Right after Kazue's death, the serial murders took place, just as spelt out in Heikichi's note. They were called 'serial murders', but in fact the victims weren't killed serially, one after the other—they were all killed at more or less the same time. Somehow, the Umezawa family was cursed. By the way, does the date 26th February 1936 mean anything to you?"

Kiyoshi's answer came quick as a flash: "The 2-26 Incident."

"That's right," I said. "I'm very impressed with your knowledge of Japanese history! Heikichi's death was on the very same day. Oh, that's what the book said? Well, good. Anyway, let's take a look at their family tree. Their ages were charted as of that day, 26th February 1936."

"And their blood types?" Kiyoshi asked.

"Yes, their blood types too. The information in the note was all correct and true. But he didn't write about Yoshio, his

Family Trees
(Ages as of 02/26/1936)

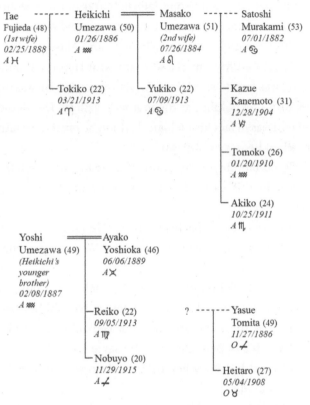

Tae ----- Heikichi === Masako ----- Satoshi
Fujieda (48) Umezawa (50) Umezawa (51) Murakami (53)
(1st wife) *01/26/1886* *(2nd wife)* *07/01/1882*
02/25/1888 *A* ♒ *07/26/1884* *A* ♋
A ♓ *A* ♌

└Tokiko (22) └ Yukiko (22) ┌ Kazue
03/21/1913 *07/09/1913* Kanemoto (31)
A ♈ *A* ♋ *12/28/1904*
A ♑

├ Tomoko (26)
01/20/1910
A ♒

└ Akiko (24)
10/25/1911
A ♏

Yoshi ===Ayako
Umezawa (49) Yoshioka (46)
(Heikichi's *06/06/1889*
younger *A* ♐
brother)
02/08/1887
A ♒

├Reiko (22) ? -----┬--- Yasue
09/05/1913 Tomita (49)
A ♍ *11/27/1886*
O ♎

└ Nobuyo (20) └ Heitaro (27)
11/29/1915 *05/04/1908*
A ♐ *O* ♉

All dates are given in the American month / day / year format

younger brother, so let me tell you something about him. He was a writer who wrote essays for travel magazines, serialized novels for newspapers, features, etc. When his elder brother was killed, he was up in the north-east in Tohoku, doing research for an article. His alibi checked out, but it would be worth reviewing. Anyway, we'll get back to Yoshio later.

"Next, Masako, Heikichi's second wife. Her maiden name was Hirata. She was from a wealthy family in Aizu-wakamatsu. Her first marriage was to one Satoshi Murakami, an executive in an import–export company; it was an arranged marriage. They had three daughters—Kazue, Tomoko and Akiko."

"I see," said Kiyoshi. "Now what about Heitaro Tomita?"

"He was twenty-six at the time of the murder. He was unmarried, and was helping at his mother's gallery, De Médicis. If Heikichi was in fact his biological father, he must have fathered him when he was twenty-two."

"Could blood type determine if he really was the father?"

"Not in this case. Heitaro and his mother were type O. Heikichi was type A."

"Now we know Heikichi and Yasue, Heitaro's mother, broke up in Tokyo and then met up again later. Were they seeing each other in 1936?"

"Most likely," I replied. "When Heikichi went out to meet someone, it was usually her. It seems he trusted her because they shared the same art interests. Heikichi wasn't close to Masako or his stepdaughters in the same way."

"Why did he marry her, then?… Anyway, did Masako and Yasue get along?"

"I don't think so. They would say hello to each other, but Yasue seldom went to the main house when she visited Heikichi. He spent most of his time in his studio anyway. Now I think about it, Yasue could easily have visited him there without anyone knowing. Heikichi might still have loved Yasue. He married Tae because he was lonely after his mother's death. Then he was drawn into an affair with Masako—yeah, 'drawn' might be the right word to explain his character."

"So, presumably, Yasue and Masako would never have joined forces…"

"It seems highly doubtful."

"Did Heikichi see Tae after they divorced?"

"Never. But their daughter, Tokiko, often visited Tae in Hoya. She worried about Tae, who was operating a small cigarette shop by herself."

"Heikichi was cold-hearted, then?"

"Well, he never visited Tae, and she never visited him."

"Tae and Masako didn't get along either, did they?"

"Of course not. Masako took Tae's husband away from her. Tae must have hated her. That's a woman's nature."

"So, Kazumi, you know all about the psychology of women!"

"What?… No!" I mumbled.

"But if Tokiko was so worried about her mother, why did she stay with the Umezawas? She could have lived with Tae, couldn't she?"

"I have no idea. I'm not an expert on female psychology!"

"What about Yoshio's wife, Ayako? Was she close to Masako?"

"They got along well enough."

"But even though Ayako let her two daughters live with Masako, she chose to stay away herself."

"There might have been some hostility between them."

"Back to Yasue's son, Heitaro. Did he and Heikichi often see each other?"

"I have no idea. The book doesn't have information going back that far. Heikichi often went to the De Médicis gallery in Ginza. He must have seen Heitaro there from time to time. They might have been friendly."

"Hmm. Heikichi's unusual behaviour—which is not so

uncommon among artists—certainly created complicated relationships."

"Yes, it did," I said. "A good moral lesson for you, isn't it?"

"What kind of lesson?" Kiyoshi asked, missing my sarcasm. "I have a keen sense of morals—unlike him. Enough of the general introduction. Let's get down to the details of Heikichi Umezawa's murder."

"Certainly. I'm an expert on that!"

"Are you indeed?" said Kiyoshi with a grin.

"Yes. I learnt everything by heart, so you can have the book... Oh, wait... Keep the page that has the floor design."

Kiyoshi yawned. "Ah, I just wish I didn't have to keep listening to your boring lecture, but go on, go on..."

That was typical Kiyoshi. I ignored him and continued. "At noon on 25th February, Tokiko left the Umezawa house to visit her mother. She returned around 9 a.m. the next morning, the 26th. Now please keep in mind the fact that on that day in history—besides the attempted coup—there was a record snowfall in Tokyo, the heaviest in thirty years. After Tokiko got home, she prepared breakfast for her father. He always ate whatever she cooked, because he trusted her and, among other things, she was his real daughter.

"Tokiko carried breakfast to the studio a few minutes before 10 a.m. She knocked on the door, but he didn't answer. She walked to the side of the studio and looked through the window. She could see her father lying on the floor in a pool of blood.

"Tokiko was horrified. The door was locked, so she rushed back to the main house and got the other women to help break the studio door down. Heikichi was dead. The back of his head had been crushed by a blunt object, possibly a frying pan. It was determined that his death was due to brain contusion. Bleeding could be seen from his nose and mouth. There was some money and valuables in his desk; but nothing seemed to have been stolen. His bizarre note, which was written in a notebook, was found in the drawer.

"Eleven paintings—which Heikichi called his life's work—were standing against the north wall. There was no damage to any of them. A twelfth painting remained unfinished on an easel. Coals were still glowing in the heater when his daughters broke into the studio. Detective stories were popular at the time, so they knew not to disturb the crime scene. The police soon arrived.

"As I said, Tokyo the previous night had had the heaviest snow in thirty years. Now please look at the second illustration."

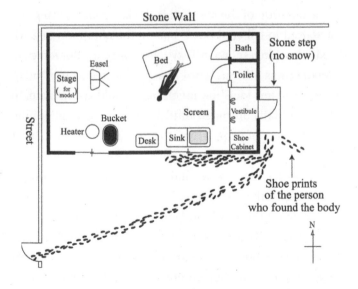

"Between the studio and the gate, some footprints in the snow were clearly visible. They were the shoe prints of a man and a woman—or at least a man's shoes and a woman's shoes. Whatever their gender, it would seem the two people did not walk out from the studio together. And they certainly didn't walk side-by-side. Their prints overlapped.

"True, they might have left the studio at the same time, one following behind the other. But the man's shoe prints led out of the studio to the window above the sink on the south side, where it appeared he walked back and forth, while the woman's shoe prints lead straight from the door to the gate. If the two people left the studio at roughly the same time, the man left the studio slightly after the woman. In fact, he stepped over her prints. Beyond the gate to the property, the street was paved. At the time the police arrived, both sets of prints ended there.

"The duration of the snowfall is the key point. In Meguro, snow started to fall at about 2 p.m. in the afternoon of 25th February. It seldom snows in Tokyo, and the system for forecasting weather was obviously not as sophisticated as it is today, so no one had any idea how much snow would accumulate. In fact, the snowfall continued until 11.30 p.m.—a total of nine and a half hours of snow. Then, the next morning, at 8.30, it snowed again lightly for about fifteen minutes.

"You can see how the second snow would have left only a light dusting on the shoe prints. Therefore, the two people had to have entered the studio at least thirty minutes before the snow stopped at 11.30; and the woman, followed by the man, left sometime between 11.30 at night and 8.30 in the morning. The reason I say they entered the studio thirty minutes before the snow stopped is because their prints were covered with snow but not fully obscured."

"Uh-huh."

"Now, there had to have been three people in the studio that evening: whoever left the man's shoe prints; whoever left the woman's shoe prints; and Heikichi Umezawa himself. It seems highly unlikely that the man killed Heikichi after the woman had left. But if the man did kill him, the woman must have seen who he was. Likewise, if the woman killed him, the man would have seen who she was—but it couldn't have happened that way, because he left the studio after her. Presumably he wouldn't have watched her kill Heikichi, nor would he have remained in the studio after the murder—nor would he have been walking back and forth between the south window and the door.

"But, supposing that the two were accomplices, there is the odd detail of the sleeping pills found in Heikichi's stomach. The dose was far from a fatal one, so he must simply have taken the pills to fall asleep. Then after he took the pills, he was killed. But would he have taken the sleeping pills while entertaining his two visitors? Unlikely, eh?

"So could the crime have been committed by the man after the woman left? That, too, isn't likely. Heikichi was not very comfortable around men; he had no close male friends. He felt secure around women, and if he was going to take some pills in the presence of anyone, it'd be a woman. And that didn't happen because the woman would have already gone. In any case, no one's been able to make any sense of the sleeping pills.

"What we come down to is this: whoever it was that left the man's shoe prints was the killer, and whoever it was that left the woman's shoe prints witnessed the killing. So, Kiyoshi, who do you think was the person in the woman's shoes?"

"His model?"

"Yes, very good! She could well have been a model, and she could well have witnessed the killing. The police made several public announcements, asking the model to come forward, promising her privacy would be protected. She never appeared. Nobody knows who the model was, even today, forty years later.

"But if a model was in Heikichi's studio at 11.30 at night, then another mystery presents itself: would a model be working as late as that? If she was, then she must have been very close to Heikichi. No woman would work that late otherwise; in those days even daytime jobs for women were scarce. Of course, she might have been waiting for the snow to stop. And it's true that there was no umbrella in the studio. But Heikichi was certainly capable of walking to the main house to get one.

"Many, however, have doubted the existence of the model at all. The police couldn't produce her, that's for certain; what's more, they think the shoe prints were just a ruse. The only established fact was that whoever left the shoe prints walked from the studio to the street, not the other way around. That was determined by the way the snow was disturbed. And the prints were made in one pass. The possibility that someone could wear a pair of shoes on his or her hands and walk like a dog was also examined. The conclusion: impossible. The uneven distribution of the weight would have made it obvious.

"Anyway, enough about the question of shoe prints—which is far from the most interesting aspect of Heikichi's murder. As he mentioned himself, he'd installed iron bars over his windows and skylights. He was a cautious man. The bars had not been tampered with in any way. For security purposes, they had been designed to be removed from the inside.

"Therefore, there was only one way to enter the studio, and that was through the door. The killer had to come and go through the door. Actually, the door was unusual in itself: it was a Western-style, single-panel door that opened outwards, and it had a bar to secure it inside. Apparently, Heikichi had seen doors like that at hotels in the French countryside and he had ordered one for his studio. To lock the door, you had to slide the bar and insert it into a hole in the door frame. The bar had a small tongue that had to be turned downwards over a projection on the door. This projection had a ring, fastened by a padlock."

Kiyoshi suddenly opened his eyes wide, raising himself up on the couch. "Really?" he said.

"Yes. And Heikichi was killed behind a locked door!"

SCENE 2

The Twelfth Painting

"No, that's not possible," Kiyoshi said. "The killer would have had to escape through a secret passage!"

"You're right. But the police checked everywhere. There was no other way out, short of the killer diving into the toilet and exiting through the pipes! Also impossible.

"Now, in the studio itself, two curious things were discovered. First, Heikichi's bed was not against the wall as shown in the illustration. We know he liked to move his bed around, so that in itself was not so unusual—but it could still be an important clue. The other thing was that Heikichi had always had a beard. But when his body was found, his beard was partly cut off. From the look of things, he didn't do that himself; it was done by another person—with a pair of scissors. Some whiskers from his beard were found near the body, but there were no scissors or razor in the studio.

"Now Heikichi and his brother Yoshio looked so much alike they could have been twins, and there was a rumour that the dead man was really Yoshio. Perhaps—for whatever reason—Heikichi had invited his brother to his studio, killed him, and then left, or vice versa. However, no one takes this idea seriously. Yoshio, moreover, never grew a beard. Yet it is still possible that family members misidentified the corpse. They had never seen Heikichi without a beard, and his head had been crushed. So misidentification can't be excluded altogether. Heikichi was such a maniac about his art, it seems he would have done anything to create Azoth.

"Well, that's all that's known about the circumstances. Shall we move on to the alibis of the possible suspects?"

"Just a minute…"

"What?"

"Your explanation is too fast! You've given me no time to contemplate the facts."

"You're kidding me!"

"No. I want to know more about Heikichi being locked in. Has as much thought been given to that as to the mystery of the shoe prints?"

"Well, forty years' worth anyway."

"Tell me more about the studio."

"OK. I hope I can recall all the details. The roof of the studio was as high as a two-storey house, so even if the bed was stood on end, no one could reach it. What's more, the skylights had iron bars over them. There was no ladder. The heater had a tin chimney, but it was too fragile to climb up—even Santa Claus couldn't have done it! Besides, the coals were still burning in the heater. There was a hole in the wall to attach the pipe, of course, but it was smaller than your head. That's about all I remember. There really was no other way out of the studio."

"Were there curtains on the windows?"

"There were some, yes. And a long pole used for opening and closing them was found near the bed at the north side of the studio, a long way from the window."

"Uh-huh. And the windows were locked?"

"Some were, but some weren't."

"How about the window above the spot where the man's shoe prints were found?"

"It wasn't locked."

"I see. And what else was there in the studio?"

"Not much else, as you can see from the illustration. A desk, some paints and pigment, some pens, the notebook that Umezawa wrote his note in, a wristwatch, some cash and a map. I think that's all. There were no books, magazines or newspapers, and no radio or phonograph. When he was in his studio, Umezawa didn't want any worldly intrusions."

"I see the wall of the property had a gate. Was it locked?"

"It could be locked from the inside, but the lock had been broken. It could be wrenched and opened easily from the outside."

"Not very safe."

"No, not safe. Oh, and at the time he was killed, Heikichi was emaciated. He suffered from insomnia and didn't eat much."

"Hmm. He was weak and in a locked room... And he was killed from behind by someone who didn't even try to make it look like a suicide. Now, Kazumi, why do you think the killer locked the studio?"

I was prepared for this question. "Well, think about the sleeping pills," I replied. "When Heikichi took them, he had either one or two visitors. So you have to figure that at least one of them was not a stranger."

"Hmm. Did he have any friends?"

"There were a few artists he met in the De Médicis gallery and some customers at the small bar called Kakinoki. He went there quite often and got to know two regulars: Genzo Ogata, who was the owner of a mannequin factory, and Tamio Yasukawa, one of Ogata's employees. But they were not particularly close friends. Another acquaintance sometimes visited the studio, but you couldn't call him a close friend, either."

"What about Yoshio? Or Heitaro? They knew Heikichi pretty well."

"Their alibis checked out, although they didn't have many witnesses. On the night of the 25th, Heitaro played cards with his mother Yasue and some friends who came by after the doors of the gallery were closed. The guests left at 10.20, and mother and son went to their bedrooms upstairs at about 10.30. If Heitaro was the killer, he would've had to speed over to Heikichi's studio in thirty or forty minutes to do the deed. Even without snow, it's hard to get from Ginza to Meguro that fast; in heavy snow, it's impossible. However, if Heitaro had conspired with Yasue to kill Umezawa, they might have bolted out of the gallery right after their friends left. So they could have made it within the presumed time frame of the murder. But what would have been their motive? Heitaro might have resented Heikichi—if he was his father—for his irresponsibility and the agony he had caused Yasue. Yasue, on the other hand, had no reason to hate Heikichi; she was quite close to him, and they were business partners. And she was his art dealer. Heikichi's paintings sold for very high prices after his death, especially after the end of the war. Yasue had no contract with Heikichi, so she didn't profit—and wouldn't have profited—from his death."

"Uh-huh."

"As for Yoshio, Heikichi's brother, he left for Tohoku on 25th February, and came home on the 27th around midnight. At the time of the murder, he was on his way to meet friends in Tsugaru; there was no doubt that he had travelled there. It's a long story; I'll spare you the details. He had an alibi, but—as with several other possible suspects, especially the females—it wasn't airtight. Yoshio's wife, for example. While her husband was away and her two daughters were staying with Masako, she was alone. She had no alibi."

"What if she was the model?"

"She was forty-six at the time. Would Heikichi have been inclined to paint a middle-aged housewife?"

"Hmmm…"

"Then there was the eldest daughter, Kazue. She was divorced and living alone in Kaminoge, which was a rather remote town at that time. She also had no alibi. Masako was in the main house having dinner with Tomoko, Akiko and Yukiko—her daughters—and Reiko and Nobuyo—her nieces. At 10 p.m., they all went to bed. And Tokiko was at her mother's house in Hoya.

"Now the main house had six bedrooms, in addition to the kitchen and living room, which is where the daughters practised their ballet and piano. Masako, Tomoko and Akiko had their bedrooms on the ground floor. Upstairs, Reiko and Nobuyo shared the room nearest the stairs, the next was Yukiko's, and the other one Tokiko's. Heikichi essentially lived in his studio.

"Any one of the women could have sneaked out of her room at night, but there were no shoe prints around the main house. If they had gone out to the street from the front door, they could have walked around the property and entered through the back gate. Tomoko rose early on the 26th and said she shovelled the snow off the stone steps. She said there were only the shoe prints of the newspaper delivery boy, but there were no other witnesses to prove that. Masako testified that when she awoke that morning, there were no shoe prints outside the kitchen door. Also, there were no shoe prints near the wall, which surrounded the property and had barbed wire on top of it—making it virtually impossible to walk along it or climb over it.

"Heikichi's ex-wife Tae and her daughter Tokiko testified for each other. Tae claimed that Tokiko was with her on the 25th. Among the daughters, only Tokiko had an alibi that someone else could attest to, but because it was her mother, her alibi was not absolutely reliable, either."

"I see. So they were all suspects. Now, what about the mysterious model who never came forward?"

"Well, the police suspected that the woman's shoe prints could have been left by a model. Umezawa often hired his models through the Fuyo Model Club in Ginza, or else he'd go through one of Yasue's contacts. But nobody could be found who had worked for Umezawa on the 25th. Moreover, according to Yasue, Umezawa was very excited about having found a model who was exactly right for what he wanted to paint. Apparently, she fit the image of his dream girl, and he was very happy. He was going to dedicate all of his energy to that painting, because it would be the last chance for him to do something so large."

"Uh-huh," Kiyoshi grunted. His eyes were closed, and he was slumped on the sofa.

"Are you listening to me?" I asked him. "I'm only going through all this for your benefit! Come on."

"Of course I'm listening! Please carry on."

"It seems that the model Umezawa wanted to paint was an Aries, the same sign as his last motif, you'll remember. Now he could have used his daughter Tokiko, who was an Aries, but police deduced that Heikichi got someone else because the model would have had to be naked."

"Fair enough."

"So the police went to every agency in Tokyo, seeking a model who looked something like Tokiko. The investigation took a month, but they found no one. In the aftermath of the 2-26 Incident, the police became too busy to continue, so the Heikichi murder case was closed. They concluded he must have picked up a girl on the street or in a bar. Perhaps she needed money desperately and was willing to pose naked but wanted to keep it a secret. She could have been a married woman. Anyway, she never came forward."

"Of course she wouldn't if she was guilty!" Kiyoshi piped up.

"Huh?"

"Well, let's say the model killed Heikichi," he continued. "She could have covered her own shoe prints with a man's shoes, right? Therefore..."

"That supposition has already been ruled out," I interrupted. "If she had brought a pair of men's shoes with her, she must have expected it to snow. But no one knew it was going to snow before it actually started to snow at 2 p.m. that afternoon. And Heikichi's daughters said that from around 1 p.m. the curtains of the studio were closed, normally a sign that their father had someone with him. The model could have worn Heikichi's shoes, of course, but the two pairs he kept in his studio were found in their usual place in the vestibule. It would not have been possible for the model to walk back to the studio to return them."

"If there *was* a model, that is."

"Right, if there was a model."

"The killer could have walked away in a man's shoes while making the prints of a woman's shoes."

I nodded. "Well, yes, that's possible."

"But wait… It doesn't make sense. If a female killer wanted to pretend to be a man, she would have needed only the shoe prints of a man. Why did the person in the man's shoes need to make those prints of a woman? Good grief!"

"What's wrong?"

"You're giving me a headache. You're like that snowstorm on the 25th—coming and going, starting and stopping. Just give me the facts."

"I'm sorry. Do you want to take a break?"

"No thanks," Kiyoshi said, rubbing his temples with both forefingers.

"All right. The facts. Well, there was no evidence left at the scene. Heikichi was a chain-smoker, so there were cigarette butts in the ashtray. And there were fingerprints—some his, some his brother's, others unidentifiable, maybe from the models he used. There was no sign of any attempt to wipe off fingerprints."

"Uh-huh."

"And no murder weapon was found. Nothing in the studio suggested it had been used for the deed."

"Was there anything that could imply a dying message from Heikichi?" asked Kiyoshi. "For example, there were those paintings of the astrological signs, right? He could have pulled one of them down when he was dying and tried to show what sign the killer was."

"He probably had no time."

"Uh-huh. Or he might have been trying to say something by cutting off his beard…"

"They reckoned he died instantly."

"Instantly?"

"Yes," I replied. "Well, I've told you all I know, so now it's time for you to start on your deduction!"

"Hmm. All the seven daughters and nieces were killed after that, yes?"

"Yes."

"So that excludes them from the list of suspects."

"Be careful not to confuse Heikichi's murder with the others."

"Ah, yes. But from the point of view of motive, what do we have so far? Well, there were the family members who wanted—or didn't want—the apartment building built. Or the daughters might somehow have got wind of Heikichi's crazy idea for creating Azoth and murdered him before he murdered them. Or some art dealer might have believed that something sensational like this would drive up the price of Heikichi's paintings. Or… what else?… Kazumi, how much did his paintings sell for after the murder?"

"The large oil zodiac paintings were each worth about the price of a house."

"Ha! So eleven paintings could have turned into eleven houses?"

"Yes, but all that didn't happen until more than ten years later. First, the Sino-Japanese War broke out, and then there was Pearl Harbor, and then the Second World War. So there wasn't much selling of paintings going on in those days. After that, *The Tokyo Zodiac Murders* was published, and it became a bestseller right away. Tae got a lot of money from that; Yoshio, too, probably. And that's when the price of the paintings shot up."

"I see. The story has so much of the occult about it. It must have made quite a sensation."

"Yes it did. In fact, there was such a big fuss that a book could be written about the fuss alone! One elderly scholar said that Heikichi's thinking was sickening—it was enough to make even God angry, and his violent death was a display of that anger. Morality was hurled all over the place. Some zealots burst into the Umezawa house. The police had to be called in. People from all walks of life—preachers, psychics, channellers—came from every corner of Japan."

"That's amazing!" Kiyoshi exclaimed, excitement momentarily showing on his face.

"So, what do you think? Based on what you know now, how do you think Heikichi's murderer did it behind a locked door?"

"Oh, that's easy," replied Kiyoshi, stretching his arms above his head. "Whoever did it hung the bed from the ceiling and dropped it on his head!"

"And how did you deduce that?"

"Well, the murder weapon was flat," Kiyoshi continued. "A panel of wood would have done the job, or even the surface of the floor. And there's no magic about that padlock if Heikichi locked the door himself. The police found his note in which he talked about suicide, which would have been convenient for the murderer—or murderers—but in fact he died from a blow to the back of his head, which rules out suicide. So it's got to be like I just said."

"That's right! You're great, you know! The police took a long time to figure it out."

"You mean the police thought about the bed? Oh, I'm tired of talking…" Kiyoshi sighed, disappointed.

"All right," I said, "let me explain the theory to you. Umezawa's bed had casters. Four people got onto the roof, removed the glass plate of the skylight, dropped a length of rope with a hook at the end into the room, hooked the bed frame, and manoeuvred the bed into position. They knew Heikichi—who was already in the bed—would be in a deep sleep from the sleeping pills. They dropped three more lengths of rope, secured the bed, and began to pull the bed up towards them. When Heikichi was in their hands, they were going to poison him with potassium cyanide, or cut his wrists, or something else that suggested suicide. But they screwed up. It turned out that pulling the bed up wasn't so easy; they couldn't maintain the balance. And from about fifteen feet up, Heikichi fell on his head and died."

"Yeah, that's it."

"You're such a good detective, Kiyoshi. It took the police a month to work that one out."

"Uh-huh."

"But what about the prints in the snow? Have you got any ideas about those?"

"Hmm…"

"Well?"

"It isn't such a big deal, is it? The shoe prints were clustered under the window because that's where they put the ladder. Four people were needed to pull the bed up—at least. There might have been another person on the ground, making five. That would account for so many prints in that spot. They were all ballet dancers, right? That means they could walk on their toes, stepping carefully into the prints made by the first person. Inevitably, their prints showed a tilt. So the last person stepped on each print wearing a man's shoes. Naturally, that limits the suspects, doesn't it?"

"You're a genius! It is a huge loss to the nation that you decided to become a suburban fortune-teller!"

"You see," he went on, "criminals almost always leave traces."

"So that's why there were all those prints and the prints of the man's shoe covered up all the others, as well as the prints of the ladder. You're good, Kiyoshi, very good indeed. I hate to say this, but in fact all you've said has already been suggested. The real mystery starts from there…"

My words seemed to hurt Kiyoshi's feelings. "Oh, really?" he said, curling his lips. "Hmm. Well, I'm hungry! Let's go downstairs and have something to eat."

A Vase and a Mirror

The next morning, I had breakfast and then hurried to Tsunashima, where Kiyoshi's office was located. When I arrived, he was eating ham and eggs, which he'd apparently prepared himself. The place looked like a disaster area.

"Morning! Sorry to disturb your meal..."

"Oh, you're early today," he said, moving his shoulder over his plate. "Don't you have any work of your own?"

"No, I'm off today. Wow, your breakfast looks really delicious!"

"Kazumi," he said solemnly, "what else can you see on the table?"

There was a small package.

"Yes, you guessed..." he said. "Freshly ground coffee beans. What I would really appreciate right now is some nice, hot coffee!"

"Right, how far did we get yesterday?" Kiyoshi asked me, once he had the cup of coffee in his hand. His depression seemed to have vanished. He seemed to be full of energy again, and that meant I would have to start enduring his sarcasm once more.

"The murderer—or murderers—were pulling Heikichi's bed up to the skylight."

"Ah, yes. There are still some parts that don't make any sense, but I don't quite remember what they are... I'll tell you when my memory comes back."

I started without hesitation. "There's something I forgot to tell you yesterday, about Yoshio—you know, Umezawa's younger brother, who was in Tohoku on the day of the murder."

"He and Heikichi looked like twins," added Kiyoshi. "But Heikichi had a beard. OK, I remember all that."

"Well, I think those two facts complicate the story."

Kiyoshi stared at me. "In what way?"

"It's important, isn't it? What if the victim was really Yoshio, not Heikichi?"

"It's not worth talking about. After Yoshio came back from Tohoku on the 27th, his life continued as usual, right? His family saw him and so did people at the publishing companies. Neither Heikichi nor Yoshio could have deceived people who knew them that well."

"You may be right, but everything concerning the Azoth murders might make you want to rethink this question: could Heikichi Umezawa still be alive? People, in fact, are often falsely identified. As an illustrator, I frequently meet with people at publishing companies. When I see them after I've been up all night, they say I look like a different person."

"But do you really think the same trick would work on your family?"

"I don't know, but it could work on editors if I changed my hairstyle, wore a pair of glasses, and met them only at night..."

"Did Yoshio start wearing glasses after the murder?"

"I didn't find any record of it."

"Well, you might possibly deceive everyone at a publishing company if they were all severely short-sighted and also hard of hearing, but not your own wife—unless she was your accomplice. But would Ayako have helped her husband even though their two daughters were among the victims?"

"Hmm… Yoshio might have had to deceive his daughters as well… Wouldn't that be a reason to kill them? He had to kill them before they discovered the truth."

"Look, don't say the first thing that comes into your head. Think! What would Ayako want, then? Would she want to sacrifice her family just for a space in a new apartment building?"

"Hmm…"

"There's an illogical leap in your reasoning, Kazumi. Or perhaps you think that Heikichi and Ayako were lovers?"

"No."

"Did Heikichi and Yoshio *really* look alike? People tend to exaggerate details just to feel important, you know. After all, how could anyone believe that Heikichi was still alive?"

I had nothing to say.

"I don't think there was any confusion between the brothers," Kiyoshi continued. "I'd sooner believe that Heikichi was killed by God. He might conceivably have found someone else who looked like him and then killed him—but no, that's crazy, too! Let's build a firm alibi for Yoshio and then we won't need to think about this any more."

"You're sounding so confident! But that will change when we start talking about the Azoth murders."

"Oh, I'm looking forward to it!"

"You don't know how much is involved… Anyway, let's look at Yoshio's alibi."

"The police knew where Yoshio stayed in Tohoku, didn't they? So his alibi could easily have been checked."

"Not so easily. He took a night train to Tohoku on the 25th. The next day he said he walked beside the ocean to take photographs and didn't see anyone until he checked into a hotel. He hadn't made any reservations, because winter was the off-season. So he would have had enough time to kill his brother, provided he left Tokyo in the morning of the 26th and arrived at the hotel in Tsugaru that night. Yoshio's photography was well known, and a collector visited him at the hotel on the morning of the 27th. It was only their second meeting. Yoshio spent some time with him and then left for Tokyo alone in the afternoon."

"I see! So the pictures he took at that time would have confirmed his alibi."

"That's right, along with that collector. It was Yoshio's first visit to Tsugaru in 1936. Therefore, if his pictures were not taken at that time, they would need to have been taken the year before."

"If Yoshio took the pictures himself."

"Yes, but he had no friends who could take them and send the film to him."

"What about the collector?"

"If someone did that, surely he, or she, would have told the police. There was nobody who would risk jail to hide the truth for Yoshio. In any case, investigators discovered a house in Yoshio's photos that wasn't completed until October 1935, so his alibi was confirmed. Isn't that dramatic? It was one of the highlights of the case."

"Hmm, then Yoshio's alibi is firm. He wasn't killed in place of Heikichi."

71

"Well, you can say that for now. Let's go on to the next murder. Masako's first daughter, Kazue, was killed in her house in Kaminoge between 7 p.m. and 9 p.m. on the night of 23rd March, a month after Heikichi's death. She appeared to have been beaten to death with a glass vase. I say 'appeared' because the blood on the vase had been wiped off. Compared to Heikichi's case, hers was less mysterious. It may seem awful to say this, but it looked like a run-of-the-mill murder, probably by a burglar. Her rooms had been ransacked, and valuables and money had been stolen from her drawers. Even though the killer seemed oblivious to details, he had wiped her blood off the vase with a cloth or a piece of paper. If he had wanted to destroy evidence, he could have taken the vase with him, but it was left on the floor in the next room to where she was found."

"Uh-huh. And what did the police and all the amateur detectives have to say?"

"They thought that he tried to wipe off his fingerprints."

"I see. But what if the vase wasn't used as a weapon?"

"There's no possibility of that. The indentation on Kazue's head fit the shape of the vase perfectly."

"You suggested it was a man, Kazumi. But perhaps the killer was a woman. It would be more natural for a woman to clean the blood off unconsciously, and return the vase to its original place."

"Ah, but there's strong evidence against that!" I replied. "The killer was definitely a man, because Kazue had been raped."

"Umm…"

"It seems that she was raped after she was killed. The semen found in her vagina was from a man with blood type O. Among the people closely related to the case, only two were males: Yoshio, who was blood type A, and Heitaro, who was in fact blood type O. However, Heitaro had an alibi between 7 p.m. and 9 p.m. on 23rd March.

"So the case would appear to have been an unrelated crime that happened to take place between Heikichi's murder and the Azoth murders. Boy, were the Umezawas cursed! It gives me the chills."

"Heikichi didn't mention Kazue's murder in his note, did he?"

"No, he didn't."

"And when was Kazue's body found?"

"Around 8 p.m. on 24th March. That afternoon, a housewife from the neighbourhood visited Kazue with an information board about some upcoming events in the community. Kazue's front door was unlocked, so she entered into the vestibule and called out Kazue's name. She got no answer, so, assuming Kazue had gone out shopping, she left the information board and went home. Later that day, the housewife learnt that the information board had not been passed on to the next house, so she went back to Kazue's. It was dusk, and the house was dark. She became suspicious. Kaminoge is a remote town along the banks of the Tama River, so she left quickly, waited until her husband came home, and then went back to Kazue's house with him. That was when they found the body."

"Kazue was divorced, right?"

"Yes, she'd been married to a Chinese man. His name was Kanemoto."

"And what did his family do? Some sort of trading business?"

"They had several large restaurants in exclusive areas of Tokyo. They must have been very wealthy."

"So Kazue lived in a big house."

"No, it was a modest one-storey house. Some people wondered why such a rich family would own such a small house. Some people thought Kazue must be a Chinese spy!"

"Did Kazue and Kanemoto marry for love?"

"I think so. Masako strongly opposed her daughter's marriage into a Chinese family. Because of political events then, she had good reason, of course. Kazue and the Umezawas didn't see each other for a while, but later they reconciled. Kazue's marriage, however, only lasted for seven years. She and Kanemoto divorced about one year before her murder. There was a lot of tension between Japan and China in the air, so the Kanemotos sold their restaurants and went back to China. The war may not have been the only problem; there must have been something else since Kazue didn't even try to return with him. She stayed in the same house they had lived in, keeping her married name to avoid the tiresome paperwork."

"Who inherited the house after her death?"

"Probably the Umezawas. None of the Kanemotos had remained in Japan. Kazue had no children, and, after the murder, nobody wanted to buy the house. It must have stood empty for a while."

"An empty house in a remote area… near the Tama River… it would be the perfect secret place for creating Azoth, wouldn't it?"

"Right. At least, most of the amateur detectives thought so."

"Even though Heikichi said in his note that it was in Niigata?"

"Yes."

"Did they think that the same person killed Heikichi and Kazue and then created Azoth in her house?" Kiyoshi asked.

"Yes, and with some reason. If you look at the Azoth murders, you can see that the killer acted according to a precise plan. So Kazue's case must have also been planned. But the police only investigated the Kaminoge crime scene once! The neighbours stayed away, and so did the Umezawa women; they were all still shaken by Heikichi's death—something that the killer might have anticipated. Things get a little confused here, though. Suppose the same killer—a man with blood type O— also committed the Azoth murders. It's hard to imagine that someone outside the family would do it. It makes more sense if the culprit had a strong motive. Among the men, only Heitaro was blood type O, but, as I said, he had a solid alibi. At the time of Kazue's murder, he was with three friends at De Médicis and a waitress testified to that. It's also highly unlikely—given the scenario you've worked out—he could have killed Heikichi behind a locked studio door. He might have visited him to talk about business, and he might have threatened him, forcing him to swallow the sleeping pills. But if Heitaro really is a suspect, how did he manage the padlock trick? Anyway, we've already determined that Heitaro couldn't be the killer. We have to think about the possibility of someone outside the family committing the crimes. I know that's not very exciting, but I suppose we have to admit that the case doesn't exist just for our entertainment."

"Right."

"I think—or perhaps I want to think—that Kazue's murder occurred by coincidence."

"You don't think that her house was used as a studio?"

"No, I don't... Although I suppose it does have the makings of a great horror novel: a deranged artist creating Azoth in a haunted house in the dark of night. Very Gothic! But, practically speaking, he couldn't work in the dark. If he worked by candlelight, the neighbours would know something was going on and report it to the police. If I was the artist, I'd find a different house—one that was unknown and didn't have a reputation. Otherwise, I wouldn't be able to concentrate and wouldn't be able to enjoy my wonderful creation!"

"I agree," Kiyoshi said. "But many people still believe that Azoth was created in Kazue's house, don't they?"

"Yes, they believe her murder was part of the plan."

"But if the killer's blood type was O, and he wasn't Heitaro, he had to be someone outside the family... So, presumably, Kazue's case wasn't solved?"

"That's right."

"Why couldn't the police catch a burglar?"

"It's not so unusual, if you think about it. Suppose we went to Hokkaido, killed an old lady and stole her money. The police would probably never find us because we have no connection to her. Many such cases remain unsolved. On the other hand, suspects of premeditated murders have motives that can be examined, so it comes down to confirming alibis. One reason why these murders remain a mystery is that nobody had a motive for the Azoth murders except Heikichi—who had already been murdered himself. I don't want to believe that the crimes were committed by an outsider. It's not at all exciting."

"So that's why you believe Kazue's case was a coincidence? I see. Anyway, please describe the circumstances of her case."

"OK. Look at the plan of her house."

"Not much needs to be explained, really; the case seemed very simple. Kazue was found lying on the floor. She was dressed in a kimono, but she wasn't wearing any underwear."

"No underwear?"

"That wasn't so unusual. Women didn't wear panties under their kimono back then. The room was a mess. The drawers were all pulled out and her effects were scattered all over the room. If she had kept any money in the house, it was gone. Her three-mirror dresser was untouched. The vase that was determined to be the murder weapon was found on the floor in the next room beyond the *fusuma* sliding doors. Kazue's body was found as shown, but of course she may have been killed somewhere else. There was an absence of bloodstains in the house, although you would imagine blood must have splattered around when she was hit. The killer might have moved the body to rape her."

"Hmm. You said he raped her *after* he murdered her. Are you sure of that?"

"That's what I heard."

"Hmm. I don't get it. She was found dressed in a kimono. If the killer was merely a burglar who apparently didn't care about leaving his semen as evidence, would he really have bothered to dress his victim up again after killing and raping her?"

"That's a good point."

"Anyway, please continue."

"Strangely, the police couldn't determine exactly where Kazue was killed. It had to have been somewhere in the house, not outside. According to the investigation, a small amount of blood was found on the mirror and it was identified as Kazue's."

"Could she have been attacked when she was applying her make-up?"

"She only had a little make-up on. The police supposed she was combing her hair when it happened."

"Because she was facing the mirror?"

"Right."

"But I still don't get it. There were *fusuma* doors on one side of the dresser. If she was sitting at the dresser, and combing her hair facing the mirror, then the *shoji* doors—which opened on to the corridor—were right behind her. The *fusuma* and the *shoji* were the only ways into the room. If the burglar entered the room through the *shoji* doors, Kazue would have seen him in the mirror, and she would have tried to escape. If he entered through the *fusuma*, she would have seen him in one of the side mirror panels. At the least, she would have sensed that someone had come in and turned her head towards him. Was she hit on the front part of her head as she faced the assailant?"

"No, I don't think she was… Wait a second… No, she wasn't. According to the report, she was hit on the back of her head while she was seated with her back to the killer."

"Hmm, the same way Heikichi was murdered. Interesting. I don't think it was a burglar at all. It was more likely an acquaintance, someone she knew. She never tried to protect herself; she just sat there, facing the mirror. She didn't move even though she saw the killer approaching her. That suggests the killer was someone she knew very well. Yes, I'm sure it wasn't a careless burglar. A burglar would never think of wiping the blood off the mirror. The reason the killer carefully wiped off the blood was to hide his relationship with his victim. Kazumi, this is a great lead! The victim and her killer might even have been intimate enough to be lovers, because, generally speaking, women don't look into a mirror and show their backs to a member of the opposite sex—at least they didn't in those days. Yes, the killer must have been her lover. But wait… Why did he rape her after she was dead, when they could have had sex while she was alive?"

"Beats me. The book doesn't give any reason. It just says she was raped. I agree with you—it's weird."

"That would make him a necrophiliac. Anyway, he must have been intimate with her already. Kazue did have a boyfriend, didn't she?"

"Sorry, but according to the police she had no known lover."

"Hmm, so much for that theory! No, wait… Her make-up. You said she had only a little make-up on?"

"Right."

"A woman in her thirties, getting ready to see her man, with hardly any make-up on... Ah, now I see. That changes the picture entirely. Do you know what I think, Kazumi? The killer was a woman! Oh, no, it couldn't be—not if the victim was raped and there was semen inside her! But the whole thing would make more sense if it was a woman who did it. Kazue could easily have been looking into the mirror, showing her back to a woman, especially if she knew her well. And if it was a woman, Kazue wouldn't care that she only had a little make-up on, would she? The female killer approached the victim with a smile on her face, and then—whack!"

"What about the semen?"

"Hmm. Well, what if the female killer brought a supply of semen along with her? Yoshio's wife could have done that easily, using her husband's... No, that doesn't work. Yoshio's blood type was A."

"The police could check how old the semen was. It would've been clear if it was one-day-old stuff."

"Absolutely right. As they get old, sperm lose their tails. Now, Kazumi, I must ask you to give me the alibis for everyone who was related to the Umezawas."

"Well, none of them had strong alibis, except for Heitaro. His mother, Yasue, had been at her gallery, but she was out in Ginza at the hour of the murder. At the Umezawa house, Masako, Tomoko, Akiko and Yukiko were all in the kitchen together. Tokiko was with Tae in Hoya again. Therefore, all the women had alibis, even though they were vouched for by family members. Reiko and Nobuyo had no alibis. They claimed they went to see a film, *The Age of Aerial Revue*, in Shibuya. The film finished at around 8 p.m., and then they returned to their parents' house at about 9 p.m. So those two could be suspects. Kaminoge is not so far from the Municipal High School Station on the Tokyo–Yokohama train line. But those two young women couldn't have had much of a motive. Ayako and Yoshio had no firm alibis, either, but again we can't find much of a motive for murder there. They knew Kazue, of course, but they were never close to her. Yasue and Heitaro had never met Kazue. And why would the Umezawa daughters want to kill their eldest sister?"

"Did Kazue often visit the Umezawas?"

"Well, sometimes. But none of them seemed to have a motive; that's why I began to suspect a burglar. But we shouldn't forget that we just got a new clue from Mrs Iida. So why don't we move on to the Azoth murders?"

SCENE 4

Poisoned Fruit Juice

Kiyoshi wanted to hear more about Kazue's case, but I'd had enough of that for a while and insisted we get on to the Azoth murders.

"As long as we come back to it later," he said.

And so I began.

"Right after the murders of Heikichi and Kazue, the notorious Azoth murders occurred—perhaps the most grotesque and bizarre murders in Japanese history. After Kazue's funeral, the Umezawa women all journeyed to the shrine at Mount Yahiko in Niigata Prefecture. They were hoping their visit would have the effect of purifying them. If you remember, it was the shrine that Heikichi had wanted to visit, and the family hoped that the journey there would put his soul to rest. In fact, they were afraid of being cursed by him."

"Whose idea was it originally?"

"Probably Masako's, but she said that they all had the same feeling. On 28th March, Masako and the six young women left Tokyo—Tomoko, Akiko, Yukiko, Tokiko, Reiko and Nobuyo. They were travelling together just as if they were on a school excursion. There was even a slight feeling of recreation among them. They arrived at their destination that night and stayed at the Tsutaya Hotel. They climbed the mountain the next day."

"Did they visit the shrine?"

"Of course. From Yahiko, they took a bus to Iwamuro hot spring in Sado Yahiko National Park. That's where they spent the night of the 29th. The surroundings were beautiful, and the young women said they would like to extend their stay. Masako wanted to visit her parents in Aizu-wakamatsu, which was not so far from Yahiko. She didn't want to take all six girls with her, so she agreed they could stay on longer. The girls decided they would spend another night at the hot spring and then return home to Tokyo on the 31st. Masako left Iwamuro on the morning of 30th March, arriving at Aizu-wakamatsu that afternoon. She spent two nights with her parents and then left for Tokyo on the morning of 1st April. She arrived back in Tokyo that evening, expecting to find the girls already at home."

"And did she?"

"No. When Masako got home, no one was there. In fact, they never showed up. By that time, they were all already dead. In time their bodies were found exactly as described in Heikichi's note: each one in a different location, and each one missing a certain part. It was horrific. Masako was arrested on suspicion of murder."

Kiyoshi sank into thought. He was clearly perplexed. "But why Masako? It wasn't because they thought she might have killed Kazue, was it?"

"No. In fact, they arrested her as a suspect in the murder of Heikichi."

"So the police had figured out how the killers pulled the bed up to the skylight?"

"They didn't figure it out by themselves. Many people wrote to them, suggesting it."

Kiyoshi snorted with superiority. "Well, Kazumi, that proves that amateur detectives can prove useful now and then! I would have done the same thing. Anyway, let me get this straight. The police had gone to the Umezawa home, found no one there, and concluded that the women had all fled. Then, when Masako arrived home alone, she was arrested as a suspect in the killing of Heikichi—and presumably also held for the apparent disappearance of the six girls." Kiyoshi was about to add something, but he swallowed his words. He thought for a moment and then asked, "Did Masako confess to the crime?"

"No, she maintained she was innocent right up until she died in prison in 1960 at the age of seventy-six. They used to call her the 'Lady Monte Cristo of Japan'. In the Fifties and Sixties, she was the subject of sensational reportage in the media. That was one reason why trying to solve the Zodiac Murders became such a fad. Can you imagine the fame that would be bestowed upon the person who cracked the case?"

"Hmm. And was she a suspect in the Azoth murders, too?"

"The fact was, the police didn't really have a clue. They arrested her because she seemed suspicious, and then beat a confession out of her—which she later recanted."

"Ah, they're savages, those cops! How could they get an arrest warrant based on sheer guesswork?"

"I have no idea."

"They must have been desperate to make any kind of arrest. But what did the prosecutors say? Did they make a clear case?"

"Not as far as I know."

"What was the verdict?"

"Guilty. She was sentenced to death."

"Was that the decision of the Supreme Court?"

"Yes. Masako asked for a retrial over and over again."

"And the courts rejected her each time?"

"That's right."

"Well, Kazumi, from what I've heard, I don't believe Masako was capable of killing her own daughters. Only a witch—an *onibaba*—could do that!"

"But she might have been capable of it. She did have a reputation for being cold-hearted."

"Maybe. But if we think in purely practical terms, did she really have enough *time* to commit the murders?"

"That was thrown around for a long time, of course, with quite a lot of faulty reasoning. But it does appear that really she couldn't have killed them, no matter how much she juggled the train schedules. Employees at the Tsutaya Hotel testified that Masako and the six young women stayed there just as she claimed. No one saw the girls after they left the hotel.

"The times of death were not so precise, because of the time it took to find the bodies. Tomoko was found much earlier than the others, and is believed to have been killed between 3 p.m. and 9 p.m. on 31st March. Given the circumstances, it's highly possible that the others died at the same time and the same place.

"Masako's alibi was weak. Her parents said she was with them in the house on the evening of 30th March, but family members are never considered 100 per cent reliable. To make matters worse, Masako hadn't left her parents' house the whole time she was there. Her face was well known from Heikichi's murder, and she didn't want to be an object of attention. So she stayed indoors all day on the 31st and saw no one. That meant she couldn't prove that she hadn't gone back to Yahiko early on the 31st."

"Uh-huh. But the bodies were found in different places, weren't they? If Masako couldn't drive, she couldn't possibly have done it."

"Right. Few women had driving licences back then—it was comparable to having a pilot's licence today. In fact, among all those involved in the case, only Heikichi and Heitaro had one."

"So, by that reasoning, if the crime was done by only one person, it's unlikely it was a woman."

"You're right."

"Can't we trace the path the girls took at all? There were really no witnesses? The six of them were travelling together. Someone must have seen them, surely?"

"No. No one saw them."

"They were supposed to be back home in the evening of 31st March; maybe they changed their mind and stayed another night?"

"The investigators enquired at all the inns and hotels in Iwamuro, Yahiko, Yoshida, Maki, Nishikawa, and then extended their search to neighbouring areas. None of them had had a group of six girls as guests. So there was even speculation that some of the girls were killed before the 31st."

"The six stayed at the Tsutaya Hotel on that day, didn't they?"

"Yes. If one of them had suddenly disappeared, you'd think the others would have reported it to the police—which suggests that the killer must have killed them all at once!"

"Maybe the girls took the ferry to Sado Island?"

"I don't think so. The police checked that out, too. The ferries to Sado only went from Niigata or Naoetsu, both of which were quite a distance from Iwamuro."

"Well, we're sure about one thing: the girls had no reason to hide themselves while travelling. So someone must have seen the six of them travelling together, wherever they had gone."

"That's right."

"The police must have found something after interrogating Masako, even if they didn't have any hard evidence."

"Yes, they found some rope with a hook tied onto it in her house."

"What? Rope?"

"Yes, but only one piece. I imagine it wasn't meant to be left in the house."

"I don't believe it. She must have been framed."

"Well, that's what she said, but she had no idea who might have done it."

"Hmm. That's strange. Now, let's go back to the skylight. When the police checked it out, was there any indication that the glass had been removed?"

"Yes, in fact there was. Several days before the murder, the glass in one skylight had been damaged—perhaps by kids throwing stones—and it was replaced. It was put back on with putty. So when the police got around to examining the glass, they couldn't make a clear determination as to whether the glass had been removed during Heikichi's murder or not. Anyway, over a month had already passed."

"Very clever!"

"Clever?"

"I suspect it was the killer who threw the stones."

"What do you mean?"

"I'll explain later. The police should have thought of that. There must have been a lot of snow on the roof that night. If they'd climbed up a ladder to check the roof, they would have found shoe prints, handprints or something. Oh, wait a minute!" Kiyoshi exclaimed.

"What is it?"

"The roof must have been covered with a layer of snow. When Heikichi's body was found, the studio must have been dark, with no light. But if the glass had been taken out of one skylight and then put back in, it would have had less of an accumulation of snow. And more light would have been coming into the studio from that one skylight. Anything in the record about that?"

"No. Both skylights were covered with snow."

"Well, I suppose the killer, being so devious, would have been smart enough to cover the glass with snow after it was put back in the frame... Did the Umezawas own a ladder?"

"Yes. It was kept alongside the wall of the main house."

"And had the ladder been moved?"

"It was hard to tell. It was kept under the eaves, where there was no snow. We do know that the repairmen used it when they replaced the glass, but, as I said before, the police didn't conduct a full search of the property until over a month after the murder."

"If Masako and her daughters killed Heikichi, they would have had to use the ladder, but you said there weren't any prints in the snow..."

"There were ways around that. They could have taken the ladder through the main house, gone out from the front door, and gone around the property to the back gate."

"Yes, that's possible. They could have done that *if* they killed him."

"You think it was someone else? Then how do you explain the arsenic compound in the house?"

"Arsenic compound? What are you talking about?" Kiyoshi asked, surprised.

"Arsenious acid was used to kill the six girls: 0.2–0.3 grams of the stuff was found in the stomachs of all six of them."

"What? There's something's not quite right here. According to Heikichi's note, every girl was supposed to be killed with a different metal. And a bottle of poison being in the house doesn't make sense—weren't the girls killed elsewhere before Masako got home?"

"Ironically, that was the excuse the police used to detain her. The poison enabled them to acquire an arrest warrant. As for the metals described in Heikichi's note, different metals were indeed detected in the victims' mouths and throats, but they were not what killed them. It was definitely arsenious acid that did it—a lethal dose is just 0.1 grams. Among murderers, potassium cyanide is the poison of choice, but that requires 0.15 grams. Arsenious acid is more toxic. Arsenic trioxide dissolves in water to become arsenious acid. The more alkaline the water, the easier it is to dissolve. The equation is $As_2O_3 + 3H_2O \Leftrightarrow 2H_3AsO_3$. By the way, the antidote for arsenic poisoning is iron oxide hydrate."

"Thank you. I guess that could be valuable to know."

"The victims drank fruit juice that had been laced with the poison. Now fruit juice was not sold in markets at that time, so the killer must have prepared it himself—or herself. All six girls drank from the same batch, because exactly the same amount of poison was detected in them all. So it's reasonable to assume that they were killed when they were all together."

"I see."

"Then the killer put different metal elements into each one's mouth. Tomoko, the Aquarius, had lead oxide in her mouth. It's a yellow powder which doesn't dissolve in water easily, and it's also a deadly poison. But that wasn't what killed her. Presumably the killer couldn't use different metal elements as poison if the girls were all to be killed at the same time."

"You may be right."

"Akiko, the Scorpio, was found with red ochre in her mouth. It's a kind of red mud that is often used in paint; it isn't toxic, and it's a very common substance. Yukiko, the Cancer, had silver nitrate in her throat; it's colourless and toxic. Tokiko, the Aries, was decapitated, but red ochre was smeared all over her body. Reiko, the Virgo, was found with mercury in her mouth. And Nobuyo, the Sagittarius, had tin in her throat.

"One question that arises is: where did the killer get the chemicals? Mercury can easily be obtained from thermometers, of course, but the other chemicals are not so easy to acquire, unless you're connected to the medical field or a university lab or a pharmacy. You'd also need some working knowledge of chemicals. Heikichi was clearly passionate enough about these killings to acquire the necessary knowledge and materials."

"Did the police find any chemicals in his studio?"

"No."

"Yet they were willing to believe that Masako could collect all those chemicals and spike the juice?"

"Apparently, yes. Anyway, the killer followed the interpretation of alchemy in Heikichi's note to the letter, thereby fulfilling
his grotesque plan. But why?"

"Yes, why indeed? What did the public think of Masako?"

"They thought she was innocent."

"So everyone but the police thought she was innocent?
Hmm." Kiyoshi was quiet for a moment. "Kazumi, was Heikichi
really dead?" he asked, staring at me.

I burst into laughter. "Of course he was dead! I knew you'd
come up with a crazy idea like that!"

Kiyoshi looked vaguely embarrassed. "Well, it's just that
from a different point of view…"

"What's your theory, then?" I was hoping he'd have to admit
he was lost, although I doubted he would.

"No, you go on first. Please finish the story," he said, stall-
ing. "I'll tell you my theory after you've told me everything you
know. Now, where did they find the bodies? Which one was
found first? The one buried closest to Tokyo?"

"No. In fact, Tomoko's body was found first, at the Hosokura
mine in Miyagi Prefecture. It was wrapped in oilpaper and both
legs had been cut off at the knees. It was found in the woods
just off a walking path. It wasn't buried. She was wearing the
same clothes she'd been wearing at Yahiko. She was found on
15th April by someone who lived in the neighbourhood, so
fifteen days had passed since she was last seen with her sisters
on the morning of 31st March. The Hosokura mine produced
zinc and lead, which was in keeping with Tomoko's astrological
sign, Aquarius. The police immediately began to suspect that
Heikichi's plan was being put into action and that the other
girls might have met a similar fate.

"Now, if you remember, several metallic elements were specified in Heikichi's note, but no locations. So the police started searching at mines around the country according to the metals he had mentioned. Needless to say, it took a great deal of time and resources. When the bodies finally turned up, they were all buried, wrapped in the same kind of oilpaper, and wearing the same clothes they had been last seen in."

"Buried? So you mean Tomoko was the only one not buried?"

"That's right. And that brings us to another very interesting point. Each girl was buried at a different depth. What would you say about that from an astrological point of view?"

"Hmm. How deep were they buried?"

"Well, Akiko was found at a depth of about 50 centimetres, Tokiko at 70 centimetres, Nobuyo at 1.4 metres, Yukiko at 1.05 metres and Reiko at 1.5 metres. Neither the police nor the brigades of would-be Sherlock Holmeses could come up with a reasonable explanation for that!"

"Aha!"

"Of course, it might have been entirely random. The killer may have had nothing particular in mind: if the ground was firm, he didn't bother to dig deep; if it wasn't, he dug deeper."

"Maybe. But you can barely cover a body at 50 to 70 centimetres. There was actually a big difference in depth. The deepest burial was 150 centimetres—a short person could be buried standing up in a hole like that! Let's see… Akiko was a Scorpio, and the depth was 50 centimetres… Tokiko was…"

"An Aries, buried at 70 centimetres; the Scorpio at 50 centimetres; the Virgo at 1.5 metres; the Sagittarius at 1.4 metres; and the Cancer at 1.05 metres. Here's the chart with them all indicated."

HOKKAIDO

Kosaka Mine ⛏
☽ Yukiko (10/02/1936)

⛏ Kamaishi Mine
♂ Akiko (05/04/1936)

Kosokura Mine ⛏
♄ Tomoko (04/15/1936)

⛏ Gumma Mine
♂ Tokiko (05/07/1936)

HONSHU   ✕
Tokyo

Ikuno Mine ⛏
♃ Nobuyo (12/28/1936)

⛏ Yamato Mine
☿ Reiko (02/10/1937)

SHIKOKU

KYOSHU

"I see. So only the Aquarius wasn't buried. Hmm. To be honest, I can't figure out any relationship to the astrological element. I can't see any rhyme or reason to it."

"What about the one 1.05 metres deep? Do you think that means anything?"

"The killer got tired? Anyway, after Tomoko, whose body was found next?"

"Akiko's. It was found on 4th May by police dogs in the mountains near the Kamaishi iron mine. A part of her hip—about 20 to 30 centimetres long—was missing. Masako, who was being detained by the police, identified both bodies.

"After that, the police mobilized their canine units. Their search for Tokiko took them to Nakatoya in Hokkaido, Chichibu in Saitama Prefecture, Kamaishi again, and then the big iron mine in Gumma Prefecture. That's where they found her body three days later, on 7th May. It was headless, so it was Tae—Tokiko's real mother—who had to positively identify it. It had the legs of a ballet dancer and also a birthmark on the right side of the stomach—as described in Heikichi's note.

"It took longer to find the other missing girls because they were buried much deeper. Police searched the Koh-no-mai and Toyoha silver mines in Hokkaido, the Kamioka mine in Gifu Prefecture, and the Kosaka mine in Akita Prefecture—Yukiko was found there on 2nd October. Her body was partly decomposed after the hot summer, and her chest had been cut out. It was a ghastly sight. She was the one buried at 1.05 metres. Masako identified her.

"Then Nobuyo's body was found on 28th December. The metal elements for Sagittarius and Virgo are tin and mercury, which are only produced in a few areas. On Honshu, only the

Yamato mine in Nara Prefecture produces mercury, and only the Akenobe and Ikuno mines in Hyogo Prefecture produce tin. Without those clues, the last two bodies would probably never have been found, because of the depth at which they were buried. Nobuyo was discovered in the mountains near the Ikuno tin mine. Her body was missing both thighs, so the torso had been buried with the legs cut off at the knees. Nine months had passed since she was killed, so the corpse was partially skeletal.

"The last one found was the body of Nobuyo's sister, Reiko. That was on 10th February 1937, almost a year after Heikichi's murder. It was in a hole 1.5 metres deep in the mountains near the Yamato mine, where mercury is extracted. Her abdomen was missing. Her remains were almost skeletal as well, and in fact Ayako couldn't positively identify either of her daughters."

"Hmm. So, if their faces weren't recognizable, and their clothes were the only clue, it was possible that they weren't really Reiko and Nobuyo."

"That's possible, yes, but there were some irrefutable facts. The police relied on blood type and skeletal structure; they even reconstructed their faces with clay. But the most revealing factor was a distinctiveness in the leg musculature and toes that's particular to ballet dancers. Something about dancing on pointe. Given that there were no other ballet dancers missing, it seemed safe to conclude that the bodies were indeed those of the Umezawa girls."

"Accepted," Kiyoshi said.

"However, none of their belongings were found, and that may be an important point. The calculated time of Tomoko's death was between 3 p.m. and 9 p.m. on 31st March 1936. The rest of the girls were presumably killed at the same time. Some sleuths have thought they were killed in early April, but I don't think so."

"Anything else?"

"No, I don't think so. We can only guess what happened to Nobuyo and Reiko. The forensic medicine specialists couldn't agree on the time of their deaths, especially as so much time had passed."

"All right. Now I want to know about everyone's alibi on the afternoon of 31st March. This was a genocide of the Umezawa family. The idea of Azoth could just have been camouflage for an act of revenge. And from that point of view, the first person to come to mind is Tae, Heikichi's ex-wife."

"But she couldn't have been the killer. She sat in her cigarette shop all day, and her neighbours saw her sitting there as usual on 31st March. We don't know where she was when Heikichi was killed, but she was certainly in her shop when the girls disappeared. There was a barbershop across the street, and the barber testified that Tae was sitting in the shop window all afternoon until she closed up at 7.30 that night. Her shop was open every day of the year. Also, would a forty-eight-year-old woman really have been able to carry six bodies to six different places all by herself? She didn't drive, and Tokiko, her daughter, was among the victims. It seems to me highly unlikely she was the killer."

"But are you sure that her alibi was good?" Kiyoshi asked, picking up his coffee cup. Seeing it was empty, he put it back down again.

"Yes."

"On the other hand, Masako was detained because of her weak alibi. But that didn't happen to Heitaro or his mother, did it?"

"I think all the suspects were held for a certain period. Police could detain any suspects without arrest warrants back then and keep them detained for just as long as they wanted. Detention was applied to everyone who was stopped and questioned. Yoshio was certainly held for several days."

"Even a lousy shot will eventually hit the mark if he tries often enough!" Kiyoshi said sarcastically.

"Maybe so. Yasue and Heitaro were able to prove they were at De Médicis on 31st March. Customers, acquaintances and a waitress testified that the Tomitas were never out of sight for longer than thirty minutes until the gallery closed at 10 p.m. at night. Friends testified to being with them until midnight.

"As for Yoshio, he was able to prove he was meeting with his publisher in Gokokuji in Tokyo from 1 p.m. until 5 p.m., and he returned by train to his home in Meguro with Mr Toda, his editor. They drank together until a little after 11 p.m. We don't know what Ayako, his wife, was doing at 6 p.m., but she had a conversation with a neighbour at around 4.50. Her alibi wasn't quite firm, but if she was the murderer she would have had to be in Yahiko early that day. She wouldn't have had time to bury the bodies and get home that evening. Besides those five, there were no other suspects."

"Masako had an alibi, too, didn't she?"

"Unfortunately, she only had the family testimony. And since a bottle of arsenic was found in her house, the other five were presumed innocent."

"Uh-huh. But suppose Masako and her daughters had conspired to kill Heikichi and they had worked together to pull his bed up to the skylight, I can't believe that a month later she would suddenly decide to kill them all!"

"What do you mean?" I asked.

"I'll explain later. Anyway, the murderer—an artist of quite epic lunacy—acquired the ingredients that he—or there's a slight chance it might be a she—needed to make Azoth. So the next question is: did the lunatic succeed in creating the monster?"

"Well that is really the ultimate mystery of the case, isn't it? Probably not. Certainly, Azoth has never been found. So no one knows whether he succeeded or not. Some people say that the body parts were made into a stuffed specimen—a piece of grotesque taxidermy—that is kept somewhere. While we look for the killer, we may also want to find Azoth. According to Heikichi's note, it was to be placed in the 'centre of 13', the very centre of Japan—whatever that may mean. As the killer seems to have followed his plans precisely, all we have to do is figure out what the 'centre of 13' is—which is what Azoth hunters have been trying to do for the last forty years. Tae offered a lot of her inheritance as a reward to whoever found Azoth. I believe the reward is still available."

"Let's stick with finding the killer first."

"You seem very confident, Kiyoshi. But let me repeat: everyone related to the Umezawas—including Masako, who was convicted, however unjustly—had an alibi. So either it was done by someone outside the family, or we have to find Azoth to get a clue."

"Heikichi didn't have an apprentice… but he did know people at De Médicis, right?"

"Yes. He associated with five or six people there and at Kakinoki, but they were not close friends. They didn't even know where his studio was, except for one person who visited him. Another person was invited, but never went.

"I'm sure Heikichi would never have talked about Azoth to those people. And he mentions none of them in his note. It's hard to imagine anyone committing the murders for him, unless there was a strong bond between them, or a brother-hood or something."

"You're right…"

"The only other possibility is that Heikichi got drunk and someone stole the key to his studio, sneaked in and read his note. Pretty far-fetched, but there's not much else to go on."

"Hmm. It's certainly a mystery! Could you show me the dates when the bodies were found again? Maybe there's some kind of pattern there."

"All right, here's the table."

DATE FOUND	PLACE/PREFECTURE	DEPTH	NAME	YEAR OF BIRTH	SIGN
15th Apr 1936	Hosokura, Miyagi	0 cm.	Tomoko	1910	Aquarius
4th May 1936	Kamaishi, Iwate	50 cm.	Akiko	1911	Scorpio
7th May 1936	Gumma, Gumma	70 cm.	Tokiko	1913	Aries
2nd Oct 1936	Kosaka, Akita	105 cm.	Yukiko	1913	Cancer
28th Dec 1936	Ikuno, Hyogo	140 cm.	Nobuyo	1915	Sagittarius
10th Feb 1937	Yamato, Nara	150 cm.	Reiko	1913	Virgo

Kiyoshi pored over the details for a few moments.

"Look, it may seem only natural," he said, "but the deeper they were buried, the later they were found. The one that was abandoned on the ground was found first. Perhaps that was the killer's intention? I think that the bodies were found in the order that the killer planned. Now what could he have meant by that? Hmm... There are two possibilities: one, it would have helped the culprit cover his crime; two, the order might have been related to astrology or alchemy, which Heikichi was obsessed with. The first was Aquarius, the second Scorpio, then Aries, Cancer, Sagittarius, Virgo... No, I take that back. There doesn't seem to be any astrological order... or any relationship between the order and the geography... Wait, wasn't the one buried closest to Tokyo found first? No, I'm wrong... It seems there's no meaning to the order after all."

"I must admit I don't think the order is important, either," I said. "The killer could have been planning to bury all six bodies, but got tired. The holes he dug got shallower and shallower, and finally Tomoko was thrown out on the ground. Couldn't we trace the killer's trail from that point of view?"

"The deepest ones were in Hyogo and Nara—which aren't so far apart—but another deep hole was found in Akita, and that's a long way away."

"Yeah, that throws a bit of a wrench in that theory, doesn't it? If Yukiko wasn't buried so deep in Akita, things would be simpler... First, the killer goes to Nara and Hyogo to bury Reiko and Nobuyo. Next, he goes up to Gumma and buries Tokiko. Then he goes straight up north to Aomori and buries Yukiko at Kosaka, on the border with Akita. From there, he goes south to Iwate and buries Akiko, and then he gets tired and doesn't bother burying the sixth victim, Tomoko. He just throws her body on the ground and goes back to Tokyo."

"It's possible that he might have been worried that the corpses would be found before he got back to Tokyo, rather than that he got too tired of digging."

"Yes, that could be true. But Yukiko was buried deep in Akita, while the nearest body, Tokiko, was buried shallow. The order is deep, deep, shallow, deep, shallow, not buried. In fact, there's no order to it. Was it one killer travelling from east to west, or—something we haven't considered yet—two groups of the military secret service doing the whole thing at the same time? As I recall, there were organizations like that in Tokyo then. One group could have gone west to Nara and Hyogo and then come back to Gumma; the other group could have gone to Akita, Iwate and Miyagi in the east. Each group could have buried the first victims deeper. That makes more sense. But that would eliminate the theory of a single killer."

"By that thinking," Kiyoshi commented, "Tokiko would have been left on the ground by the group in western Japan."

"Hmm. It's hard to believe that the secret service had a role in it. In fact, there was someone knowledgeable about military internal affairs who testified that the secret service would never do anything like this."

"Ah-ha!"

"The secret service might have been covering it up!"

"I wouldn't trust the testimony of an insider."

"Well, if Yukiko was deeply buried, we could infer the possibility that the killer lived in Kanto, in eastern Japan. If he lived in Aomori, Yukiko, who was the last to be buried, would have been left on the ground without a care."

"You may have something there," Kiyoshi allowed. "But aren't there any other clues? There are a lot of mines on the islands of Kyushu and Hokkaido, but the bodies were only found on Honshu. There were no tunnels connecting the islands in those days, so perhaps the killer was limited to disposing of the bodies on Honshu. Did the killer bury the girls in the order of their age? Let's see… Tomoko was twenty-six… Akiko was twenty-four… Yes! At least they found the oldest first and then on down to the youngest last. What could that mean?…"

"I think that's just coincidence. Some people did think that was a clue, but they couldn't make it mean anything."

"Maybe… maybe not."

"I think that's about it," I said. "So what do you think?"

"Well, it's much more difficult than I expected," he responded, knitting his brow and pressing down on his eyelids. He seemed depressed again, or maybe he was just acting. "I won't be able to solve it in one day. It'll take me several days at least."

"You can solve it in several days?!" I thought he was joking.

"Everyone had an alibi for the Azoth murders," Kiyoshi began, as if talking to himself. "The murders seem to have been carried out randomly, the only logic or purpose being the note left behind by Heikichi. But it seems there was no one close to him who would have reason to execute his plans. And no one could have read the note. The secret service couldn't have read it, and why would they be interested in this Azoth business anyway? So far, Kazumi, we're stuck!"

"That's right. So why don't we move on and figure out the next part of the mystery—the numbers 4, 6, 3 and 13?"

"Ah, yes. Heikichi said Azoth would be placed at the centre of Japan."

"So you remember."

"Of course I do. The centre between east and west—on longitude 138° 48′ E. Am I right?"

"Absolutely. Very impressive!"

"So Azoth would have to be somewhere on that line. Why don't you take a walk along it and find it?"

"Not feasible. The distance is about 355 kilometres, almost the same as from Tokyo to Nara. The line is interrupted by the Mikuni Mountains, the mountainous terrain of Chichibu and the forest around Mount Fuji, so that would render an automobile or motorbike useless. Moreover, Azoth could be buried; it's impossible to dig like a mole for 355 kilometres! We need to figure out where to dig."

Kiyoshi snorted. "Oh, that's not so difficult. I'll let you know tomorrow morning…"

His voice had fallen so low that I couldn't catch the last part of his sentence.

SCENE 5

Latitude and Longitude

I suddenly got busy the next day at work, and I wasn't able to see Kiyoshi until the evening. He didn't contact me, either. Perhaps he was concentrating on the mystery of the numbers. As a freelance illustrator, I sometimes resented my situation because it left me no freedom of choice. I wanted to continue my discussions on the murders, but turning down my clients would mean I might lose them for ever.

I once complained to Kiyoshi, "If I switched over to a nine-to-five job, my life would be easier."

"Dangle a carrot before a horse, and he will run!" Kiyoshi said, standing up abruptly. "There's a man in the rose bushes. Cutting them down with a hatchet, he thrashes through to reach the house. Do you get the picture?"

I had no idea what he meant, but I nodded as if I did.

"His devotion to that seemingly long journey is not as worthwhile as it might seem. If he had only climbed the fence and looked around him, he would have seen that the goal was actually very close."

My ignorance must have been apparent.

"What a shame!" said Kiyoshi with a sigh. "If you don't understand, then even a Picasso masterpiece will lose its value."

I only figured out what he was saying later. He was suggesting that working like a dog is ridiculous. But I think he also meant that he didn't want to be alone; he would miss my company if I got a regular job. His pride was so great that he couldn't tell me the truth in a straightforward way.

After my busy day, I went round to see Kiyoshi. He seemed to be in a cheerful mood. Usually when we met he was lying on the sofa as if he was drifting about on a raft in the ocean. But on this occasion he was up and roaming around like a bear, mimicking the electioneering speeches blaring out from the sound trucks outside.

"Let's fight together," he squeaked in a high-pitched, tremulous voice, perfectly imitating the female candidate Otome, "or we Japanese citizens will be in dire financial straits!" Suddenly his voice dropped low, and he proclaimed, "Kanno! Kanno! Kanno! Mansaku Kanno promises you the health care you deserve!" Obviously, something good had transpired. He turned towards me, waving his hand and smiling broadly. Then he announced, "I have solved the 4-6-3 mystery! Those sound trucks were driving me crazy, but I managed to figure it out."

With a cup of coffee in hand, he began to explain.

"It's like this, Kazumi. We knew where the centre of the north-east–south-west axis of Japan was. But we didn't know where the centre of the north–south axis was. According to Heikichi, the northernmost tip of Japan is Kharimkotan at latitude 49° 11′ N, and the southernmost tip is Iwo Jima at latitude 24° 43′ N. That makes latitude 36° 57′ N the centre point. Cross that with the central east–west axis, at longitude 138° 48′ E, and you come out somewhere around the Ishiuchi ski area in Niigata.

"Heikichi also declared the island of Hateruma, which is at latitude 24° 3′ N, to be the real southernmost tip of Japan, so I tried to find the centre between Kharimkotan and Hateruma. It was latitude 36° 37′ N. This line crosses the longitude 138° 48′ E line somewhere around the Sawatari hot springs in Gumma Prefecture. The locations of Ishiuchi and Sawatari are about 20′ apart. This statistic could be important.

"Heikichi described Mount Yahiko, at latitude 37° 42′ N, as the bellybutton of Japan. Mount Yahiko and the Ishiuchi ski area are exactly 45′ apart, but still there was nothing of the numbers 4, 6 or 3 anywhere. The distance between Mount Yahiko and Sawatari is 65′—again, not a number we're looking for.

"So I lay down on the floor for a while, and then a brilliant idea flashed through my mind. I looked up the longitude and latitude of the six mines where the six girls' bodies were found. I made a list. Look at this…" Kiyoshi said triumphantly and threw a sheet of paper at me. This is what was written on it:

☽	Kosaka Mine	Akita	Long. 140° 46′ E	Lat. 40° 21′ N
♂	Kamaishi Mine	Iwate	Long. 141° 42′ E	Lat. 39° 18′ N
♄	Hosokura Mine	Miyagi	Long. 140° 54′ E	Lat. 38° 48′ N
♂	Gumma Mine	Gumma	Long. 138° 38′ E	Lat. 36° 36′ N
♃	Jkuno Mine	Hyogo	Long. 134° 49′ E	Lat. 35° 10′ N
☿	Yamato Mine	Nara	Long. 135° 59′ E	Lat. 34° 29′ N

"When I averaged these longitudes, I got a shocking result: 138° 48′ E. Do you know where that is? It is the exact same location that Heikichi designated as the east–west axis. So those six mines were no coincidence! Next, I averaged the latitudes of the six mines, and the result was 37° 27′ N. This crosses 138° 48′ E somewhere in western Nagaoka. If you compare this location with the centre of the north–south line between Kharimkotan and Iwo Jima, they're only 30′ apart. Between 37° 27′ N and Mount Yahiko, the distance is only 15′.

"So now we have four points, including Mount Yahiko, lining up on 138° 48′ E. Going from south to north: first, there's the central point between Kharimkotan and Hateruma; 20′ north from there is the central point between Kharimkotan and Iwo Jima; 30′ north from there is the average latitude of the six mines; and, finally, 15′ north from there is Mount Yahiko. Four points are placed on the line of 138° 48′ E with intervals of 20′, 30′ and 15′. Divide these distances by five, and you get 4, 6 and 3; add them up and you get 13!

"When those four points are added together and then divided by four, the result is 37° 9.5′ N. This point crosses longitude 138° 48′ E somewhere on the mountain in the town of Toka, in Niigata Prefecture. That must be where Azoth is! You know, Kazumi, the coffee I brew is always good, but today it is the best ever! Can you taste the difference?" And with that he burst out laughing.

"Um, yeah, it tastes all right…"

"Huh? Is that all? Hey, I've solved the mystery of 4, 6 and 3! I even drew a map for you. Here."

"Well, yes, you're great," I replied reluctantly. I didn't want to hurt his feelings, but what he didn't know was that this same conclusion had been figured out by several other diligent amateur detectives, too. "It's really admirable. You got this far in just one night; that could be a record…"

"What? You mean someone else has done this before?"

"Well, forty years have passed since the murders, Kiyoshi. Even an ordinary man can build a pyramid in that time."

This rather blunt kind of response was something that I had learnt from Kiyoshi, and I was just giving it back to him. He was not amused. He kicked the sofa and shouted angrily,

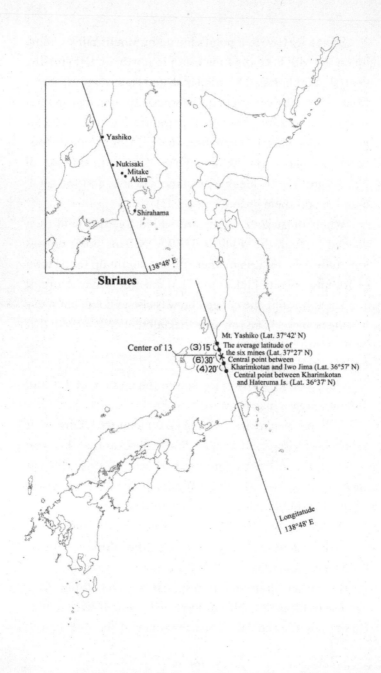

Shrines

Yashiko

Nukisaki
Mitake
Akira

Shirahama

138°48′ E

Center of 13

(3)15′ — Mt. Yashiko (Lat. 37°42′ N)
The average latitude of
the six mines (Lat. 37°27′ N)
(6)30′ — Central point between
Kharimkotan and Iwo Jima (Lat. 36°57′ N)
(4)20′ — Central point between Kharimkotan
and Hateruma Is. (Lat. 36°37′ N)

Longitatude
138°48′ E

"I've never been involved in this kind of nonsense before! What am I doing? Just following someone else's well-worn path? You already know all the answers, and you're just testing me! Why are you wasting my time like this?"

"No, Kiyoshi, no…"

He stood by the window, refusing to turn around, refusing to respond.

"Kiyoshi, I just…"

"I know what you meant," he said, turning to face me. "I don't think I'm extraordinary. We all live on the same planet, we all share the same consciousness and emotions—but does that make us all equal as human beings? Look at the Tokyo businessman, look at the man from Thailand growing rice, look at the artists and the bankers. Sure we're one consciousness, but our present and past karma are different. We have knelt at different graves and walked through different gardens. Our lives are but a burst of stardust, or a passing cloud. I'm not a freak, but others are. I feel like I'm living on Mars. When I look at the existence of other people and try to understand their lives, I feel dizzy!"

He was being quite serious.

"Kiyoshi, you haven't been in very good condition lately… You've been thinking too much… You'll drive yourself crazy… Why don't you sit down and relax?"

"I don't get it at all!" Kiyoshi shouted, not listening to me at all. "We're all struggling so hard, heading in the wrong direction. All our efforts are in vain, Kazumi. They come to nothing! Our pleasure, our sorrow, our anger—it all comes and goes like a typhoon or a squall or cherry blossoms. We are all being pushed by our petty feelings and carried away to the same place. None of us can resist it. Do whatever you think is idealistic? But it's not. It's just petty! We only end up knowing that our efforts were in vain!" He collapsed on his sofa.

"Yes, I know what you mean…"

Kiyoshi stared at me. "You do? How could you?" he said. Then, apologetically, he added, "Sorry, it's not your fault. Please forgive me. You don't think I'm a lunatic, do you? Thank you. You might be one of those people who think they're normal, but you're much better than most of them. All right, let's get back to the drawing board. So has anything been found at the place you mentioned before?"

"What? What place?"

"Come on! I'm talking about the 'centre of 13', north-east of the town of Toka. Amateur detectives swarm there like bees, I bet."

"Yes, I suppose that little town must be quite a tourist spot by now."

"They're probably selling cookies shaped like Azoth."

"Most likely."

"Did they find anything there?"

"No."

"Nothing? Absolutely nothing?"

"Nothing."

"So what all this means is that even though Heikichi only left those mysterious numbers—4, 6 and 3—the killer seems to have known the exact place they suggested. I wonder if those two people are the same person."

"Exactly! That's what I've been thinking!"

"The killer might have had to change his plans for some reason, or maybe he found a better place… or maybe he buried Azoth very deep. Did anyone dig in the area?"

"Sure, they did. They dug everywhere. The place looked like it had been bombed just like Iwo Jima."

"Like Iwo Jima, eh? Heikichi mentioned that somewhere… But nothing was found? What about the geographical features of the area? Is there any place they left unscratched?"

"I don't think so. The land is relatively flat. People have been digging in the area for forty years."

"Hmm. So maybe Azoth was never created."

"But there's no doubt that the girls' bodies were cut up."

"Maybe the decomposition process was faster than he expected, which means he'd have had to rely on taxidermy. Would he have known anything about that?"

"He could have studied it."

"You think so?"

"Heikichi never mentioned it in his note, but the idea isn't illogical. If the killer had to assemble different parts of bodies, they'd start rotting in a day. It would be more satisfying if he gave new life to Azoth. I think he must have done something to preserve it, even if it wasn't perfect."

"Heikichi believed that Azoth would last forever, like Hitler's Third Reich."

"He couldn't have been serious," I replied. "Well, he might have been. He was a lunatic."

"Yes, he was… I have another idea, Kazumi."

"What's that?"

"Heikichi's whole story could be one great big fiction."

"No, I don't think so. It's not feasible."

"Really? Why do you say that?"

"Because there must be something about longitude 138° 48′ E."

"What do you mean?" Kiyoshi asked.

"Well," I replied, "this may be a bit off the subject, but Heikichi wasn't the only one who had it on his mind. The mystery writer Seicho Matsumoto wrote about it in his book *Longitude 139 Degrees East*. You may not be as well versed in mystery novels as I am. Have you ever heard of it?"

"No."

"Well, it seems to support Heikichi's view of history. You see, there were two kinds of fortune-telling techniques in ancient Japan—*kiboku* and *rokuboku*. Ancient psychics burned the shoulder blades of deer and then stuck iron skewers in them to make them crack. They read the cracks to foresee what the hunting and the harvest would be like each year; that was known as *rokuboku*. Eventually, they used turtle shells instead of deer bones, because turtles were easier to catch, and that was known as *kiboku*.

"Now there were only two places where *kiboku* was performed. One of them was Yahiko Shrine, near the Japan Sea. The other was Shirahama Shrine on the Izu Peninsula, near the Pacific Ocean, directly south of Yahiko. Between those two shrines are three others: Nukisaki Shrine in Gumma Prefecture, and Mitake Shrine and Akiru Shrine—both in Tokyo. The five shrines are located in a straight north-to-south line at longitude 139° E, and they were the only ones that performed either *kiboku* or *rokuboku*."

"Wow!"

"And then someone turned up this very revealing fact: in the ancient Japanese language, when you pronounced the numbers 1, 3 and 9, it came out as *hi*, *mi* and *kokonotsu*, which is abbreviated as *ko*. Put them together, and you have 'Himiko', the mythical empress of Japan!"

"Very interesting. But that's merely a coincidence, surely? The concept of longitude and latitude is based on modern science, with measurements centred on Greenwich in England. On the other hand, the supposed empire of Himiko was two thousand years ago. There can be no relationship between the two."

"Matsumoto didn't dispute that. But given the fact that Himiko was a great shaman, I would think it quite possible. I think she must have used *rokuboku* and *kiboku* during the Yamatai Empire."

"You mean that the Yamatai Empire was on longitude 139° E?"

"No, but—as the story goes—the post-Yamatai regime moved, or was forced to move, to that area. According to one Chinese history book written in the middle of the third century, the Yamatai lived in Kyushu. There's nothing about the Yamatai in any Japanese documents, only about the Yamato Empire, which was formed in the eighth century. No one knows what happened to the Yamatai. Some say they were destroyed by the counterforce, Kuna, or by a race that came from the Chinese continent. Heikichi belonged to the latter school. Historians think that the Yamatai Empire was destroyed or merged with the central government.

"According to Matsumoto's novel, the government forced the Yamatai population, including the offspring of Empress Himiko, to move east. This policy was sort of reflected in the Nara period, when the government decided that Kanto in eastern Japan—including Kazusa, Kozuke, Musashi and Kai—was where Korean refugees would be located. Matsumoto thought that the Yamatai might have been the first case of compulsory immigration in the history of Japan. Interesting, huh?"

"Hmm."

"Let's get back to the mystery of longitude 139° E, which obviously caught the imagination of Matsumoto, too. As I said, there were five shrines along the longitudinal line from Yahiko to Shirahama, which is very close to longitude 138° 48' E that Heikichi mentioned in his note. The line happens to be midway between longitude 124° E—where the Sakishima Islands of Okinawa are located—and longitude 154° E, where Shiashkotan Island is located—adjacent to Kharimkotan Island—which he defined as the easternmost tip of Japan. We don't know if the fortune-tellers of old intentionally chose the centre of the country as the place for making their prophecies, but it now seems that Heikichi's ideas were not totally absurd."

"No, obviously not."

"Then there's the novel *A Golden Key*, by Akimitsu Takagi."

"Which has something to say about this same longitude?"

"Well, it's a little bit complicated. The novel focused on the fall of Edo. At the time, two politicians were in charge—Katsu Kaishu and Oguri Kozukenosuke. Katsu was the cautious one, but Oguri, despite Edo's weak army, was ready to attack the allied forces of Satsuma and Choshu. Katsu's caution won out, but when Saigo Takamori, the Satsuma general, learnt about Oguri's strategy later, he shuddered. Oguri's strategy went like this: Edo would pull its army back to Hakone and Odawara, letting the allied forces advance to the east on the Tokaido coast. At Hakone, where Edo's modern battleships were waiting near the shore, Edo would make its stand, pushing the enemy back to Okitsu, a town on a narrow strip between a mountain ridge and the sea. When the Edo ships attacked, the allied forces would have had no place to hide.

"Shogun Tokugawa Yoshinobu was reluctant, so Oguri's plan was not put into practice. If it had been, the Edo government might have secured its regime. But this isn't a history lesson.

From a geographical perspective, the towns of Hakone and Okitsu are located equidistant, to the east and the west, of longitude 138° 48′ E. Also, the village of Gonda, where Oguri was born, is located at longitude 138° 48′ E. Oguri was later caught there by the enemy, beheaded and buried—all at longitude 138° 48′ E. Reportedly, Oguri buried a considerable amount of the government's treasury on Mount Akagi, at longitude 139° 12′ E. Akimitsu says the place Oguri chose must be somewhere between Matsuida and Gonda. If he's right, that would be very close to longitude 138° 48′ E."

"The coincidences don't stop, do they?"

"No, they don't. Akimitsu also wrote about how, in the final phase of the Second World War, Japan—expecting that the US forces would be landing *soon*—made plans to move its military headquarters from Tokyo to Matsushiro, south of Nagano. Matsushiro was famous for the battle at Kawanakajima, where two samurai forces led by Takeda Shingen and Uesugi Kenshin fought a bloody battle. Takeda, drawing on his strength and a bit of good fortune, was victorious. The government of Japan, knowing they would be fighting with their backs to the wall, hoped to have the same good fortune as Takeda. The US forces were expected to land at Kujukurihama Beach and Sagami Bay in order to occupy the Kanto area first. Then they would move their troops inland to attack the Japanese headquarters at Matsushiro. The Japanese military hoped to fortify this by placing several units along Nakasendo Road, which lies between Annaka and the Usui Pass, where the most intense fighting was predicted. Anyway, the point I've been trying to get to is this: Matsuida is located halfway between Annaka and the Usui Pass on longitude 138° 48′ E."

This was a lengthy digression, and Kiyoshi's blank expression reflected that. "Well, it might be fun to explore that area," he said absent-mindedly.

"Actually, some people do explore it. They regard it as one of Japan's ley lines."

"Ah, ley lines? Like the ley lines in Britain?"

"So you've heard of them?"

"Yes, of course. They're the phenomenon of ancient sites located in a straight line."

"Well, we have the same things in Japan. Along latitude 34° 32' N, for example, there are many shrines and ancient sites lined up straight for seven hundred kilometres."

"Hmm."

"Also, north-east of the Imperial Palace in Tokyo, there are shrines in a line, including Yasaki Inari, Hie, Ishihama and Tenso. Also—and this is where it starts getting good—there are several shrines that worship gods related to metals located on a north–south line connecting Tsurugaoka Hachimangu in Kamakura and Toshogu in Nikko."

"Aha!"

"So the ancient Japanese, just like the ancient Brits, must have had some kind of geographical theory for the placement of their sacred sites."

"And crazy old Heikichi must have known all about that."

"I believe so. Anyway, I think I've now explained everything I know about this case to you. With the new piece of evidence from Mrs Iida, all you've got to do now is solve the three cases…"

—

You might wonder what it was that had led us to get so serious about the Zodiac Murders. Well, in fact, it was the visit of a woman named Misako Iida. She came to see Kiyoshi one day at his office without an appointment.

I had never thought that Kiyoshi had many customers. His office was always quiet, except when his students of astrology came by. But there were some clients, mostly female, who had heard of his reputation from friends and visited him to have their fortunes told. Mrs Iida was one of those. But her request was very, very unusual.

"This may be strange…" she began slowly. "It's not actually about fortune-telling that I've come—although that could perhaps help me, even though it's not about me… It's about my father."

From her demeanour, she seemed genuinely serious. Kiyoshi was sitting as still as if he was fishing in a pond. He was too depressed to encourage her to talk, but she was waiting for him to say something. It was the kind of pause where you light a cigarette, waiting for the other person to continue. But in fact Kiyoshi was a dedicated anti-smoker, so he just sat there looking rather foolish.

"To tell you the truth," Mrs Iida continued, "I ought to report it to the police, but our situation doesn't allow us to… Mr Mitarai, do you remember Ms Mizutani? I believe she came to see you about a year ago."

"Ms Mizutani?…" Kiyoshi's eyes blinked quickly. "Oh yes. She came to us about some harassing phone calls she was getting."

"Well, she's a friend of mine. She told me that you are extremely talented, not only as a fortune-teller but also as a detective. She really admires you."

"Ah…" Kiyoshi allowed himself to be flattered.

After a pause, Mrs Iida said abruptly, "May I ask your first name, Mr Mitarai?"

Kiyoshi was badly shaken by the question; it was one he hated to be asked. "Would there be any connection between my name and your story?" he said, raising an eyebrow.

"No, it's just that Ms Mizutani was wondering why you never mentioned your first name."

"Mrs Iida, did you come here just to ask my first name?"

"It's Kiyoshi," I interrupted quickly. "Kiyoshi Mitarai. As a matter of fact, in Chinese characters his name means 'clean toilet'. I'm not kidding!"

Kiyoshi made a sour face.

Mrs Iida looked down for a moment, trying hard to hold her laughter. "Oh, how unusual!" she exclaimed, looking up. Her cheeks were slightly flushed.

"The person who named me had an unusual sense of humour," Kiyoshi responded immediately.

"Was it your father?"

The look on Kiyoshi's face grew more severe. "That's right. He paid for it by dying young."

There was another moment of silence, but the ice seemed to have been broken.

When Mrs Iida started speaking, her words flowed smoothly. "The story includes some facts that could be rather shameful for my father. He died last month, and I'm afraid that things could escalate into criminal liability if the authorities start to ask about his involvement. My husband and elder brother could get into big trouble because—like my father was—they are police officers. I don't mean that my father was a criminal.

He was a very honest man. He received awards and was given a testimonial dinner when he retired. He was always punctual and never missed a day at the office. However, I happened to find out about a shocking incident which he was involved in a long time ago.

"I have come here of my own accord. My husband is a rather conservative man like my father was, but my brother is not. He has an aggressive streak, and he can be ruthless and cold-hearted. Thinking of what my father must have gone through, I can't let him handle this. The case is notorious enough. If someone can solve this case without my father's honour getting smeared, it would be the best for everyone."

She paused for a moment and took a deep breath.

"My father was being used by some criminals," she continued. "I'm sure you've heard of the Tokyo Zodiac Murders, a serial murder case that happened before the Second World War."

Kiyoshi said he knew nothing whatsoever about it, which caused Mrs Iida to stare at him in shock. She couldn't believe it, and neither could I. The case was not only very famous but also concerned astrology.

"I see," she said hesitantly. "Then I should tell you about it, shouldn't I?"

She began to relate the story of Heikichi's death, but I interrupted her, saying that I knew the story quite well and would fill in the details for Kiyoshi later. She nodded, and then went on to summarize the whole story anyway.

Then she added, "My maiden name is Takegoshi. I am the daughter of Bunjiro Takegoshi, who was born on 23rd February 1905. When Mr Umezawa was murdered, my father was thirty-one and working at the Takanawa police station.

I hadn't been born yet; there was only my brother. They were living in Kaminoge when my father got involved in the case.

"After my father passed away, I was cleaning his bookshelves and came across this note. It was in his own handwriting on official stationery, the kind used by detectives in the police department. When I read it, I was stunned. I couldn't believe that my father had done such a thing. He was a very straight, conservative man. He must have endured terrible pain and hardship, and I felt so sorry for him... I made up my mind to do something. In the note, he confesses to his mistake, which, of course, a police officer does not have the luxury to make. That's why I'm here. Could you please solve this case so that he can rest in peace? Here is the note. Please read it. You will see that my father died in remorse, anger and shame... If it's impossible to solve the case entirely, then could you at least try to find a reasonable explanation for my father's involvement?"

"I understand," Kiyoshi replied, saying nothing more.

On my part, there were no words to express how excited I felt. I thanked God that I knew Kiyoshi Mitarai.

After Mrs Iida had gone, we carefully read her father's note together.

ENTR'ACTE

A Police
Confession

A Final Confession

After serving thirty-four years as a policeman, nothing but pain is left. I have a framed testimonial and the title of superintendent, but they are just pieces of paper that mean nothing to me. However, I shall not think of myself as a victim. The deeper the pain you have, the more you hide it. I am sure I am not the only one who has suffered. The bitter truth is often covered with fake smiles.

When I accepted the benefit retirement plan at the age of fifty-seven, my subordinates showed their disbelief. Some might have thought that it was the attraction of the 50 per cent increase in retirement money, but that was not true; nor had I lost interest in my job. I took the offer because I wanted to quit. I was waiting for my retirement day like a girl dreaming of her wedding day.

I realize that making a written confession is risky, but "that incident" has never left my mind in all these years. I wouldn't be able to die in peace without bringing it to an end. So I will write about it, knowing that I can burn this note at any time.

I was always scared. The higher my position got, the more paranoid I became. When my son started to climb the ladder of success as a policeman like myself, my fear became almost unbearable. I had no way out. If I quit the job, my colleagues would have been very suspicious. If the facts had been uncovered, I would have been arrested immediately. Nor would my resignation have changed my son's situation.

What I call "that incident" was the Umezawa serial murders. Japan was infested by crime during the post-war confusion. There were serial murders and many terrible homicides. We saw more of them in rural areas, and some cases were never solved. The Umezawa case was being investigated by the Sakuradamon police station. At the time, I was the chief detective at the Takanawa station. In those days, detectives were given a bonus depending on how many suspects they brought in to be prosecuted. I was competent enough to be promoted to chief at the age of thirty. I bought a house in Kaminoge, and my wife and I had our first child. I was filled with hope. But then, out of the blue, I got involved in that horrific incident. I am still hesitant to describe it, but I must be brave.

When I was a young detective, I sometimes got up earlier than my wife, went to work, and came home after she had gone to bed. At the time of the incident, I had been promoted to section chief, so I would leave for the office at six every morning and return home a little after seven every evening by the same route. One day, I got off work as usual and, arriving in Kaminoge, began my walk home. After about five minutes, I saw a woman in a dark kimono walking ahead of me. There was nobody else on the street. Suddenly she squatted down. She was holding her stomach, so I asked her if she was all right. She said she was in acute pain, so I helped her get home, which was not far from there. When I was about to leave, she asked me to stay with her for a while because she was alone. She lay down on the floor, twisting her body in agony. Her kimono got bunched up around her knees, exposing her thighs. I could see between her legs; she wasn't wearing any underwear. Honestly, I had never had an extramarital affair and I had no intention of having one with this woman, but, to my shame, I could feel myself losing control.

She leant on me and held me, repeatedly whispering how lonely she was. In a sad voice, she asked me not to turn on the light. When we were done, she apologized over and over again. Then she said, "Please leave the light off and go home. Your wife will worry if you come home late. I was just feeling lonely. Please forget about me. I won't tell anyone about you." I put my clothes on in the dark and left.

Walking home, I thought about what I had just done, but everything was like a dream. Acting sick was a popular trick of female pickpockets, but nothing had been stolen from me. So the woman's faked illness might just have been a ploy to entice me into having sex with her. I didn't feel guilty. Actually, I felt rather good for having given her a good time. My wife would never know about the encounter. And even if she found out, it wouldn't hurt my social position. I got home at about 9.30. My dreamlike adventure had lasted less than two hours.

Two days later, I read in the morning newspaper about the murder of the woman I had the sexual encounter with. The article filled about a quarter of a page and included a picture of the victim. Her name was Kazue Kanemoto. It was an old photo that had probably been retouched. She looked rather different, but there was enough resemblance. The newspaper reported the time of death to have been between 7 p.m. and 9 p.m. on the night of the 23rd, which was exactly when I was with her. I had met her on the street around 7.15 and left her house a little before 9. The culprit, presumably a thief, must have entered the house right after I left, or he might have already been in the house, hiding until I left. It said the woman had been killed while she was combing her hair. I could visualize the entire scene clearly. I left my house quickly, went to the office and pretended I hadn't heard about the murder. Although the woman's house was not very far away, it was not particularly close. I could have gone to the site before going to the office, but I didn't want to.

The initial investigation determined that the victim had been raped, which alarmed me. The rapist had blood type O, the same as me. I became too scared to read the newspapers. The victim's kimono and a vase, which I had seen in her house, were being kept as evidence. I couldn't believe that she was thirty-one. She had seemed younger; maybe she had made herself look younger for a chance romantic encounter. I felt very sorry for her. What must have gone through her mind when she looked at herself in the mirror after having sex with me? I felt great anger at the killer.

The case was not under the jurisdiction of our station. Having no way to join the investigation, I waited to see what would happen. Several days later, I received an express letter, postmarked "1st April, Ushigome, Tokyo". The letter was stamped confidential, and the sender told me to burn it after I read it, which I did. As far as I can remember, the letter read something like this:

"We are secret agents of the Emperor. It has come to our attention that you are the murderer of Kazue Kanemoto. It is regrettable and unforgivable that you, a police officer, should have committed such a crime. However, given the fact that our country is in a critical phase, it is not in our interest to

126

bring disgrace to a citizen who has until now led an upright life. Therefore, we will make allowances for the circumstances you find yourself in and will pardon you for your crime if you help us accomplish our goal. Your cooperation will be required only this one time and never again in the future. You will be required to dispose of the bodies of six women who were Chinese spies. They were assassinated in order that war between China and Japan might be avoided. So that the utmost secrecy is maintained, no one from this agency will have any direct involvement in the execution of your mission. You must acquire a vehicle to dispose of these bodies at the designated places in the designated manner within a certain time frame. If you are apprehended, you will be held fully accountable. The corpses can be found in the storeroom of Kazue Kanemoto's house. You must begin your assignment on 3rd April and complete your task within one week. You may prefer to drive at night. Do not ask directions from anyone; do not stop at any restaurants; keep all contact with people to a minimum. You must keep the entire mission a secret; this is for your own sake. Maps are enclosed. And remember: one hand washes the other. Sayonara."

I was shocked at what I was being asked to do, but at the same time, I realized it would be almost impossible to prove my innocence in the murder of Kazue Kanemoto. Without an eyewitness to the murder, I would not be able to clear myself of suspicion. After all, it was my semen they had found in the victim's body. Investigators would never doubt that I killed her. I was devastated, not knowing what would happen even if I did successfully complete this job assigned to me. I had heard of the existence of secret agencies such as the Nakano School.

If the sender of the letter belonged to one of them, I felt that he would at least honour the promise of secrecy.

The assignment would not be easy. I would need a full week to carry it out, most of it at night. Attached to the letter were full directions, including the routes of travel I should take and instructions on exactly how the women should be buried. Each destination was shown on a map, but the map was less than detailed or precise. I sensed that the secret agent may never have been to those places himself.

The next day, I was so preoccupied by my fear of discovery, I could do nothing. I could have ignored the letter, but the circumstances I found myself in were not very favourable. I had had sexual intercourse with the murdered woman. If I told the truth at an inquiry, my public shame would be enormous. My immorality would be sensationally exposed in every newspaper. I would lose my job and my family would be ruined. And I would probably be convicted of murdering the woman as well. What would happen to my wife and my baby boy if I was arrested and put in prison? I made up my mind to fight for my life and for theirs. In that life-or-death situation, I was prepared to do anything.

Very few people could afford to own an automobile back in 1936. Even my wealthy friends didn't have one, and I was no exception. Nor could I fabricate a reason to borrow a police car for the several days required for the mission. I knew of only one person who owned a car and would probably be prepared to lend it to me. He was a contractor. I first met him during the investigation of a fraud case. He was tied to dirty money. Normally, he would be the last man I would ask a favour of, as it would make me beholden to him. But I had no choice.

In order to take a week off from work, I made up a story: my wife was ill, and I would be taking her to the Hanamaki hot springs, near her parents' house. As fate would have it, I did in fact have to go to that area, so I would be able to stop to buy some souvenirs for my colleagues, which would make them believe that I really had been there. My story worked, and my boss allowed me to be away from the office for a week. On the morning of 3rd April, I told my wife that I would be leaving on a business trip that evening and asked her to prepare enough rice balls to last me for three days. I packed the food, put a shovel in the trunk, and drove to the house in Kaminoge, where I found the corpses as instructed. The bodies were mutilated and resembled deformed children. I got the two corpses I was told to bury first, laid them in the trunk, and then drove west towards the Kansai area in the dark of night.

I had to move quickly, because I knew that when decomposition set in, the stench would be unbearable; it would also attract attention. Furthermore, the possibility of a reinvestigation of Kazue's house loomed. I needed to get the bodies out of there as fast as possible.

Traffic checks were rare, but I had to take every possible precaution. I had my police identification ready, just in case. I loaded three extra containers of petrol. With luck, that would be enough fuel to reach my destination without having to stop for more. I didn't want a petrol-station attendant remembering my face. As I drove, my mind raced. The order and place of burial for each body had been spelt out in detail. But what was the reason for that? Was it to make it seem like a serial killing committed by one individual? And was there any reason why each body had been cut up in such a different way?

I didn't get to Nara that first night, so I drove into the mountains at Hamamatsu and napped at the side of a road. It was spring, and the sun rose earlier than I'd expected, which made me even more anxious. My instructions mere to bury the six bodies in specific mines spread across the island of Honshu. After the Yamato mine in Nara, I was to go to the Ikuno mine in Hyogo Prefecture. Then to the Gumma mine in Gumma Prefecture, the Kosaka mine in Akita, the Kamaishi mine in Iwate and the Hosokura mine in Miyagi.

The car I had borrowed was a Cadillac. It was bigger than any Japanese car but still too small to transport six bodies at once. I would have to make two separate trips. Still, if I was stopped for any reason, it would be easier to cover my lies in a car rather than in a truck. I was determined to fulfil my end of the bargain, even though I knew the secret agency could ambush me at any time.

I continued driving the next night and arrived at the Yamato mine at 2 a.m. on 5th April. I started digging. I had never imagined that digging a hole a metre and a half deep would be so difficult. But I managed to finish before sunrise. I slept in the mountains. At midday, I was startled awake by a man with a towel trapped around his face. He was peering into the car. At that moment, I thought everything was over. But when I calmed myself, I could see that he was mentally retarded and was wandering in the woods like a lost child. I breathed a sigh of relief as I watched him slowly amble away. He was the only person to have come so close to the car. I told myself to be patient while I awaited the end of the day, so that I could leave.

The digging at the Ikuno mine in Hyogo exhausted me, but I felt great relief once it was done. Having disposed of the two bodies, I drove the rest of the night and through the day, trying my best to stay alert. I got home in the afternoon of 6th April. I ate a quick meal and collapsed, but I couldn't allow myself a long sleep.

That night, as I prepared for the next part of my mission, I told my wife not to answer the phone until I returned. I went again to Kaminoge, loaded the four bodies in the trunk, and drove off. I neared Takasaki early in the morning of the 7th. I had had no sleep, finding nowhere that I could park safely. Here I found a remote spot, so I pulled over and shut my eyes. I resumed driving in the afternoon, arriving at the Gumma mine after midnight. Compared with the previous two jobs, this one was easy. I just covered the corpse with a little soil, and then I continued along the mountain road.

I arrived in Hanamaki at 3 a.m. on the 8th. At that hour, no place was open, so I drove on to Akita. I stopped along the way to rest and I lost my way once, but fortunately I still seemed to be keeping to schedule. The digging and burial at the Kosaka mine was finished early in the morning on the 9th. The job in Iwate was done early the next morning, and I finished the next one in Miyagi the night of the 10th, just abandoning the corpse near a mountain road. I had accomplished it all in one week as the instructions demanded.

I reached Fukushima before sunrise on the 11th—I had barely eaten or slept for a whole week. I was nearly delirious; I could barely comprehend my behaviour. I wondered how I had managed to accomplish that extraordinary feat. After I returned to Tokyo that night, I slept like a log.

My excuse had worked perfectly. I had lost weight, and my eyes were sunken. I looked like I'd been through a terrible ordeal caring for my sick wife, so I got the sympathy of my colleagues. But the stress of the week took a toll on me. I was overcome by dizzy spells, I felt nauseated and I felt profoundly tired. I was only able to carry out my task because of my relative youth and high position. If I had been older, I'm sure I wouldn't have had the strength, and if I had been in a lower position, my boss wouldn't have allowed me to take the week off. After that, I never took any sick leave.

I had done what I had been forced to do, but one question started to nag at me. Had I been tricked into doing this dirty deed? The secret agency might have set me up, creating the circumstances and then blackmailing me into performing whatever it needed done. To this day, I still don't understand what happened. I only know what a powerful tool fear can be.

The last corpse I disposed of, at the Hosokura mine, was found on 15th April. When the police report came into my office, the guilt inside me started to grow. By the time the second body was found on 4th May, it was clear that the bodies I had buried were from the Umezawa serial murders. Although I knew about the case, I hadn't made the connection between the Umezawa girls and the Kanemoto woman. I was horrified to learn that they were sisters. And while it was true that Kazue had been married to a Chinese man, could her sisters really have been spies because of that? I felt like a fool. I had been a victim. My pride was deeply hurt, because I had let myself believe that my mission was for national security, when really it was because I would do anything to save my reputation.

My colleagues were busy talking about the serial murders, but I could hardly keep myself in the office. It was not long afterwards that a woman named Sada Abe was arrested for murdering her lover and cutting his penis off. Fortunately for me, her case took people's attention away from the murder of the Umezawa girls. The Abe case is still fresh in my memory. She was apprehended at the Shinagawa Inn, while staying there under the name of Nao Owada. The case fell under the jurisdiction of the Takanawa police station, and my colleague Ando distinguished himself by being the one to arrest her. Detectives celebrated the end of the case, and a festive mood lingered in our station for a while, bringing my conscience a little relief.

In June, I read a copy of Heikichi Umezawa's note, which the investigation had distributed to each police station. I couldn't see how he could have committed the Azoth murders. The killer did everything just the way he had described it, but he himself was dead by the time the murders took place. But if it hadn't been him, then who had done it? It had to be one of his followers, someone intent on making Azoth himself. My God, I had lent my hand to a maniac!

There were so many questions. Was astrology behind the elaborate plot? Was it the killer's idea to arrange when the bodies would be discovered? If so, why were the bodies in Kosaka, Yamato and Ikuno to be found later than the others? If delay of discovery was the objective, why not other mines or more distant places? Was there a pattern?

Then there was that business about Chinese spies. If there was the least bit of truth to it, I had been drawn into the picture because of my encounter with Kazue. Was that all planned out ahead of time—just as the murders of the six girls were premeditated? If so, who would be the best person to bury the bodies? Of course, a police officer! He would have a driving licence, and the transportation of victims in a murder case could be part of his job. No civilian—not even a doctor or a scientist—could do that. Nor would anyone think a policeman was capable of participating in such a horrendous deed. And so I had been chosen! And Kazue must have been involved as a conspirator, enticing me into having sex with her. But then she was killed herself—why? So that I could be threatened with blackmail? Did Kazue know that she would be killed? Or had she been betrayed, too? True, I slept with Kazue because she enticed me. But I would never have agreed to bury the bodies if she hadn't been murdered.

Suppose it was Kazue who had killed her sisters? After killing them, she decided to seduce me so that I could be blackmailed, and then she killed herself. But what would be the point of committing suicide? Besides, the fatal blow was to the back of her head. It's virtually impossible to commit suicide by beating yourself on the head from behind. And Kazue died on 23rd March; the six girls were still alive a week later. A dead woman cannot commit murder.

When Masako Umezawa was arrested, the picture got even more confused. She confessed, but I couldn't believe that she was telling the truth. I wished I could visit her in prison to talk to her, but I couldn't come up with a reasonable excuse.

I was so unfortunate to get involved in this case in this terrible way, and I have been unable to rid myself of my guilt. As time passes, the public usually forgets. Even the shock of large-scale crimes fades, and people stop talking about them. But not this case. After the war, it came to be known as "the Tokyo Zodiac Murders", when a book by that title was published. It became a fad to try to solve the mystery, and tips flooded in to the investigation. Day after day, my colleagues read these letters. I shuddered every time they yelled out, "This information is worth taking a look at!" This fear lasted until my retirement. Even today, I have not been released from it.

Back then, there were forty-six detectives in Section 1 of the Crime Investigation Department. Today, Sections 3 and 4 are in charge of fraud, arson and violent crimes, but those used to be our responsibility, along with homicide and robbery. In 1943, I was transferred to Section 1 on the recommendation of Mr Koyama, assistant director of the Takanawa station, who praised me for my persistence and logic. I was to deal especially with fraud cases. To transport the six bodies, I had borrowed the Cadillac from a suspect in an earlier fraud case. After I transferred to Section 1, he kept calling me and asking for favours. I said yes every time.

The tide of the war was at its peak, and there were regular threats of air raids by American forces. Members of the Metropolitan Police Department were evacuated in small groups to different areas in the city. My section set up offices in Asakusa at the First High School for Women. I began thinking I would like to die in battle. Many of my colleagues joined the army, but my induction was suspended, causing me to feel more guilt.

At the time of the murders, my son Fumihiko was just a few months old. Now he is a detective himself, and my daughter Misako is married to a police officer, too. Although I felt like I was a prisoner, I continued to climb up the ladder of promotion. I took examinations for the sake of my son, did well on them and got promoted. Just before my retirement, HQ generously promoted me to superintendent. My professional life must have looked like a very successful one, but for me it had been many years of incarceration. The cancer within me remained my secret. I retired as soon as I could—in 1962, after thirty-four years of service, at the age of fifty-seven. Two years after the death of Masako Umezawa, who was charged with the capital crime of killing her husband Heikichi and the six girls, public interest in the astrology murders was still going strong. I myself was reading all the material I could get my hands on, only to find nothing but what I already knew. After a year of retirement, I found myself slowly regaining energy. Then, late in the summer of 1964, I decided to dedicate the rest of my life to solving the mystery. I made an effort to interview all those still alive who were related in any way to the case.

Ayako Umezawa then seventy-five, was the only surviving family member. She had built an apartment complex and was living there. She told me her husband Yoshio had recently died. With her two daughters murdered and with no one else left, she felt very lonely.

Yasue Tomita was seventy-eight. She was living alone in an apartment in Denenchofu, the exclusive area of Tokyo that's rather like Beverly Hills. She had sold her old gallery after the war and opened a new one in Shibuya under the same name, "De Médicis". After her son Heitaro's death in the war, she had adopted the son of a relative, who was now running the gallery for her. He visited her occasionally, but she still seemed lonely.

Neither Ayako or Yasue were likely suspects, but there was no one else left from the inner circle. Heikichi's ex-wife, Tae, had died, but Masako's ex-husband, Satoshi Murakami, was still alive at eighty-two. Murakami had never been questioned—perhaps because the pre-war police were very class-orientated and he was from a wealthy family. It seemed to me that Murakami had a motive: revenge. Masako had had an affair with Heikichi and then divorced Murakami to marry him. As an ex-police superintendent, I went to visit Murakami. He was retired, and living a quiet life puttering around in his garden. He was bent, and his bald pate made him look his age. But occasionally his eyes showed clarity and strength, and I could imagine him in his prime.

Our conversation was very disappointing. Murakami stated that, contrary to what I had thought, he had been interrogated—without reason—and that the attitude of the police had been offensive. He went on at tedious length about being treated like a suspect. I apologized and left. The Crime Investigation Department had been more thorough than I gave them credit for.

People continue to look enthusiastically for Azoth, but I now have doubts about its existence. Even so, I went to Heikichi's grave to see if it was possible that Azoth was anywhere near it. The cemetery was very crowded. His grave was almost concealed by the close proximity of other family graves. I doubted Azoth could be there.

Did he have any followers? Friends? Casual acquaintances? He was not a sociable person, apparently going out only to the gallery "De Médicis" and the bar "Kakinoki".

At Kakinoki there was Satoko, the owner, who had introduced Heikichi to Genzo Ogata, the owner of a mannequin factory. At the time, Ogata was forty-six and Satoko—a widow—was thirty-four. Heikichi seemed to enjoy Ogata's company, despite their very different occupations. The police had spoken to Ogata and cleared him of any suspicion. On the other hand, Tamio Yasukawa, a craftsman at Ogata's mannequin factory, seemed like someone who should have been investigated further—Heikichi met Yasukawa at Kakinoki, too, and as Yasukawa was in the business of constructing mannequins, the two may have had matters of common interest. Yasukawa was twenty-eight at the time of the murders. He is one of the few possible suspects still alive. He served in the military for a short while and has been living in Kyoto ever since. I must see him before he dies—or before I die.

Among the other people Heikichi knew at Kakinoki, the only person I have met is Toshinobu Ishibashi, a painter who was living near the bar. He was thirty at the time of the murders—coincidentally almost the same age as me. His family ran a teahouse, and painting was his sideline. Perhaps Ishibashi worked in the family business and entered his art in competitions when he could. As his dream had been to travel to Paris, which few people then could afford, he loved talking with Heikichi about his adventures in France. I visited Ishibashi at the teahouse in Kakinokizaka, which his family still ran. He said he had fought in the war, narrowly escaping death. He no longer painted, but his daughter had graduated from an art college. And he had just returned from a trip to Paris, where he was excited to find a restaurant that Heikichi had told him about. Ishibashi was pleasant to talk with, his wife was polite and kind, and their female employee was very friendly. Ishibashi also had an alibi, and nothing would have given him reason to commit the murders. As I prepared to leave, Ishibashi invited me to come back to the tea house at any time. He sounded sincere, and I thought I would.

As regards Kakinoki, it no longer exists. Satoko, who had been cleared of any suspicions, closed the bar when she became Ogata's lover. Ogata had a wife and family, so things must have been complicated. His son took over the mannequin business, moving the factory to Hanakoganei.

Thanks to Yasue's social skills, the gallery De Médicis was a popular place for middle-aged artists: painters, sculptors, models, poets, playwrights, novelists and filmmakers. They would gather there and have heated discussions about the arts. Even though a frequent visitor himself, Heikichi didn't socialize much with those artists—he thought them snobs.

But one friendship that he did maintain was with Motonari Tokuda, a sculptor. Tokuda was a sharp-eyed intellectual who had a studio in Mitaka. By the age of forty, he was already well known. Heikichi had been fascinated by Tokuda's sculpture, causing investigators to suspect his influence on Heikichi's notions about Azoth. I saw Tokuda when he was being questioned by the police. He had long, grey unkempt hair and hollow cheeks, which made him look like a crazy artist. However, Tokuda established his alibi and was released. The fact that he didn't have the slightest idea how to operate a car was in his defence. Moreover, he had never visited Heikichi's studio, nor had he known Kazue. If anyone viewed Tokuda's artwork, it would be clear that such art could not come from the heart of a killer. He died suddenly in early 1965. His studio was converted into the Motonari Tokuda Museum.

Gozo Abe was a painter Heikichi met through Tokuda. He was a pacifist, his artwork carrying an anti-establishment message even in 1936, and he was ostracized by his fellow artists—a feeling that he and Heikichi may have shared. Abe was in his twenties then, a generation younger than Heikichi, and it seems unlikely they knew each other very well. He lived in Kichijoji, far from Meguro. He never visited Heikichi's studio.

He had no firm alibi, but he had no reason to commit the crime. During the war, Abe was dispatched to China. Military officials treated him badly, labelling him an "unfavourable ideologue", and he remained a private the entire time. When he returned to Japan, he divorced his wife, married a younger woman, and then travelled to South America. He died in Japan in 1955, having gained a small reputation among artists. His wife runs "Grell", a cafe for artists. Abe's paintings hang on the wall.

At De Médicis, Heikichi also got to know the painter Yasushi Yamada. Yamada had a gentle personality, and Heikichi related to him easily. In fact, he visited Yamada's house on two occasions, perhaps because of his attraction to Yamada's wife, Kinue. A former model, Kinue was a poet. Heikichi was fond of Rimbaud, Baudelaire and the Marquis de Sade, and it seems likely that he and Kinue shared the same tastes. She also seemed to have knowledge of the work of André Milhaud, the artist Heikichi was so inspired by. Yasushi and Kinue both passed away in the mid-Fifties. They had established their alibis, had never visited Heikichi's studio, and had no motive to kill him.

Of all these people, the one person who stands out is Tamio Yasukawa, the mannequin craftsman. However, it's hard to believe that the investigators failed to include him among the suspects. Yasukawa lived in a dormitory located within a ten-minute walk from his workplace. He spent most of his free time with his co-workers. His alibi was not firm—he said he was at a movie—but he had known Heikichi only three months before the Azoth murders. Who would commit serial murders for a lunatic after knowing him just three months? And if he did do it, where could he have done it, and when? It doesn't seem possible.

There are three separate crimes here—Heikichi Umezawa's murder, Kazue Kanemoto's murder and the Azoth murders. After so many years, the mystery may have died with the murderer or murderers. I regret that I can go no further. As the homicide department concluded, all the suspects seemed to be innocent.

Since I retired, I have been thinking about this case every day and night. Today, I find my thoughts going around in circles and leading nowhere. As I grow older, I feel my abilities declining both physically and mentally. I have ulcers from those stressful days. I won't live long. And I will die without knowing the truth.

My attitude towards life has been too moderate, never going against the stream. Being an ordinary man, I wanted to end my life as an ordinary man. I should have taken the responsibility for my actions, but, to my shame, I failed to do so. I wish someone would solve this mystery. Not just for my sake and for the part I was forced to play in it, but for the sake of justice. All I can do now is pray. It is shameful that I still do not have the courage to tell the story to my son.

Whether I burn this note or keep it will be the last decision of my life. If anyone reads this after my death, I wonder if they will find it amusing, my being so indecisive… just like Hamlet?

Bunjiro Takegoshi

ACT TWO

More
Speculation

SCENE 1

A Little Magic

"Well, do you think Takegoshi went to visit Yasukawa in Kyoto?" Kiyoshi asked me in a low voice.

"No, I think that he probably died without meeting him."

"Boy, his note certainly answers a few questions, doesn't it? Talk about something falling into our lap. And we're the only ones to know this stuff!"

"Yes, it's amazing! I'm so lucky to know you!"

"Hmm. If Van Gogh had any friends, they would have said the same thing about him without knowing his real talent. Do the books mention anything about Yasukawa?"

"Yes, but Takegoshi's note tells us much more detail."

"You know, I got the same impression from both his note and Heikichi's—that they seemed to be written intentionally for public exposure."

"I agree."

"And Takegoshi obviously decided not to burn his. I don't think he could have," Kiyoshi said, standing up. "But how sad his life was. No one could ever read that confession without feeling his deep remorse. As a fortune-teller, I've listened to all kinds of voices since I opened my office here. Do you know what the sounds of this city are? Screams! All those buildings are grey with sadness. I sometimes tell myself, 'Enough listening, now you must help.' We mustn't allow ourselves to hold back any more. It's time to move forward." Kiyoshi sat back down.

"Takegoshi wanted someone to solve the mystery, even though his reputation would be ruined. It's our duty to solve the case."

"Absolutely."

"So now that we have this information, let's start analysing the case. But there's something I didn't understand—all through your explanation, and all through Takegoshi's note—and I still don't understand."

"What is it?"

"Why people suspected those Umezawa women of Heikichi's murder. When he was killed, Masako and all the girls, except Tokiko, were at home. If they had killed him, they wouldn't have had to pretend it was a murder committed behind locked doors. If they had acted as if they didn't know anything, any conventional style of murder would have worked."

"Yes, but the investigators would have discovered their lies. And we still have the mystery of the footprints."

"There are all kinds of ways around that. The footprints could have been faked. And that idea of pulling the bed up—well, it doesn't really work. Think about it: the awkwardness, the blizzard, the strength required, and no guarantee that Umezawa would be asleep. It would never work."

"Wait a moment! You were one of the supporters of that idea in the beginning. You're really confusing me now. So how do you explain the rope and the bottle of poison that were found in the main house? Are you saying that the killer left those things to implicate the women?"

"Could be."

"Who do you think would do that? Someone they knew— such as Yoshio or Ayako, or Tae? Who?"

"It could have been a stranger—a burglar, for instance."

"What?!"

"I have no idea in particular."

"You have to do better than that, or we'll never get anywhere. It's easy for you to criticize the investigators, but we have a big disadvantage: Masako's arrest was based on investigation of the crime scene, which we can never see. So let's get back to those three people. Tae never went near the Umezawa house after her divorce. Yoshio and Ayako could have—to make sure Masako was implicated—but surely they wouldn't have killed their own daughters. There's no one else."

"Even so, it was done by a human being like you or me. How can this be so hard to figure out?"

"In my opinion, there are only two remaining possibilities. One is something that goes beyond our reasoning powers up to now…"

"Magic?"

"Come on, Kiyoshi, you know I would never say that. What I'm saying is, it was done by an outsider—or outsiders—someone outside the family. The letter to Takegoshi might not have been a fake; the secret agency could have been waiting for the chance to kill the Umezawas. If that's right, the case is out of our control."

"But we've already denied that possibility, haven't we?" Kiyoshi replied.

"OK. Yes, I guess so. The other idea is that Heikichi wasn't killed after all. He could have disappeared by some kind of trickery and left his own prints in the snow. He had a double, who had no beard. He killed him, beating him beyond recognition. Then, his family wouldn't have been able to identify him. This would explain why he spent most of his time in his studio.

Hiding himself there for days, he had a perfect plan figured out in every detail. When his death was confirmed, he could do anything, just like an invisible man—killing his daughters, making Azoth, getting a new life. Why do you think this introverted man went out drinking? To look for his double! He didn't want his wife finding out his secret other studio, so he trapped her into being arrested. Yes, that's it! It makes sense!"

"Hmm, not so bad. If Heikichi was the sole killer, the case could be more easily solved. But too many things still don't come together. For one, it's unbelievable the family wouldn't be able to recognize a double."

"What else?"

"Wouldn't he have wanted to finish his life's work? Why was the twelfth painting left unfinished?"

"In order to pretend he was killed."

"I thought you'd say that."

"Or Azoth could essentially have become his twelfth painting."

"Let me go on. Another question: why was Kazue killed?"

"Because Heikichi wanted her house to create and store Azoth in…"

"No!" said Kiyoshi vehemently. "I'm sure he would have looked for a better place near Mount Yahiko. There might have been a police stakeout at Kazue's house. This is what you told me before, so don't get lost again, please! Before her death, Kazue seduced Takegoshi. Do you suppose that was part of Heikichi's plan? What would be the purpose of that? He could have disposed of the corpses himself."

"Better to exploit a young policeman than do the work himself."

"But how did he persuade Kazue, his stepdaughter, to sleep with a stranger?"

"He could have made up a story or blackmailed her somehow."

"Two more tough questions. Why did Heikichi leave the note? If he was alive after his crime, his note would have put him in danger. And how did he get out of a studio locked from the inside? That would be the toughest question of all."

"Exactly," I replied. "I'm going to focus on that last question. I reckon it will be the key to determine whether I believe Heikichi was really murdered or not. We can't think of any other suspects. It's hard for me to believe that one family had three murder cases committed by different killers. I think that the same person did it all. You see, once he became invisible, a little magic would be all he would need. I'll figure out how he did it."

"Well, good luck!"

SCENE 2

A Rude Visit

After I returned home, I went to bed, but my mind wouldn't stop racing. No matter what Kiyoshi said, I now believed that Heikichi had *not* been killed. I was certain of it. I couldn't find any other way to explain the mystery. He must have killed his double, and then... walked out of the studio? No, he couldn't have locked the door from the outside. What if Masako and her daughters killed the double—who had already been locked up—believing that they were killing Heikichi?

Yes, that was it!

In order to build an apartment building on their property, Masako and her daughters planned to murder Heikichi, but it turned out that they killed the wrong person. Heikichi would then have threatened Kazue, who was one of the culprits, saying he would report them to the police... and then forced her to seduce the cop to buy herself some insurance.

Yes, that plot fits perfectly!

Takegoshi's theory couldn't solve the mystery of Kazue's murder, but mine could. Heikichi knew about the women's crime, and threatened Kazue! Then why did he kill her? Well, he wasn't all there to begin with, so he wouldn't have needed any specific reason to kill her. The people who didn't believe that Heikichi had died reckoned that he had used his brother Yoshio as his double. But using a stranger was much more practicable. After the murder was accomplished, Heikichi would be invisible; he could flee somewhere and continue with his creation of Azoth...

I need to find proof that he was still alive after the crime. Then I'll be perfectly ready to refute Kiyoshi's argument. Yes! From tomorrow, I'll play the part of Sherlock Holmes and Kiyoshi will be Dr Watson!

Satisfied with my conclusion, I finally fell asleep.

The next day, I asked Kiyoshi if he had thought of anything new. He just groaned. So I told him about my idea, anticipating his surprise.

"Do you still believe the women pulled the bed up to the ceiling?" he retorted immediately. "Killing his double? How could Heikichi have kept that man in the studio? The women were living right next door; they would have noticed something. According to your theory, Heikichi would have to wait until his double grew a beard, while teaching him to draw!"

"Teaching him to draw?"

"Of course. What if his double couldn't draw? What if the women saw the man drawing a cucumber while he was looking at a pumpkin? Ridiculous!"

Kiyoshi was being provocative, and I was getting irritated. "So how do you explain Kazue's case?" I challenged him. "You have no idea, have you? Takegoshi hadn't, either. I believe my deduction is correct—at least until you present me with a better idea."

Kiyoshi was silent. My response must have stunned him. So I went on. "Sherlock Holmes would have already solved this case, and gone on to the next. Look at you, lying down on the sofa all day. Why can't you be more aggressive, like him?"

"Sherlock Holmes? Who's that?" asked Kiyoshi, pausing for effect. "Oh, you mean that funny English guy—that liar, barbarian and cocaine addict who always confused the real with the unreal?"

I couldn't believe what I was hearing. I was now getting really angry and I shouted, "And what are you? The best detective in the world? How dare you laugh at him? How dare you call him a barbarian? How dare you call him a liar?"

"Oh, you're a typically misguided Japanese, Kazumi. Your sense of values is completely based on politics."

"I don't need your criticism, thank you. Please explain why you think Holmes was a liar. And why do you describe him as a barbarian?"

"Well, there are so many examples to choose from... Let me see... What's your favourite Sherlock Holmes case?"

"I love them all!"

"Just choose one."

"OK... 'The Speckled Band'. That was Arthur Conan Doyle's own favourite, and it's also his most popular story."

"Oh, that one! It's the weirdest of all his cases! It's a story about a snake, right? If you keep a snake in a safe, it will soon die from lack of oxygen. And suppose it does survive in the box: snakes don't drink milk. Have you ever seen any reptiles breast-feeding their babies? Only mammals do that. And how about a man whistling for a snake? Actually snakes can't be trained. They don't have ears, so how can they respond to a man's commands? It's a matter of common sense. Was Holmes stupid or what? Since the incidents were so unrealistic, I have to assume the story was made up by Dr Watson. He wrote it as if he had been with Holmes, but probably Holmes just picked up the idea from something he'd heard somewhere. Holmes was addicted to cocaine, and he could have told Watson any old thing that came into his head. In fact, seeing snakes is a good example of somebody hallucinating."

"Holmes was able to guess a person's occupation and personality at first glance. He was much more instinctive than you could ever be."

"Oh, I can't stand his guesswork! It's so embarrassing! For example, in 'The Adventure of the Yellow Face', the client found a pipe, and Holmes guessed whose it was. According to Holmes, the owner had treasured this pipe, because he had had it repaired, paying almost as much as the price of the pipe itself. Holmes also said that the owner was left-handed because he lit the pipe with the flame of a lamp, not with matches, holding the pipe in his left hand. Therefore, the pipe got burnt on the right side, according to Holmes. Surely, if the pipe was so valuable to the owner, he would've been careful enough not to burn it. Anyway, if you smoked a pipe, which hand would you use? You would rather not use your dominant hand, especially if you smoke while doing something else. Many left-handed men might hold their pipe in their right hand. So we can't determine whether the man was left-handed or not. Only Watson would have accepted Holmes's dubious reasoning. Well, maybe it was just a joke—or an example of bad humour.

"What else?... Holmes was a master of disguise, wasn't he? He dressed himself as an old woman, put on a grey wig and fake eyebrows, carried a parasol and went for a walk. Do you know how tall Holmes was? Over six feet! Obviously, the old woman would have looked like a man—or a monster! Everybody in London must have been rolling around on the floor laughing and crying out: 'There goes that silly Sherlock Holmes!' Only Watson didn't notice.

"Watson said Holmes could have been a very strong boxer. How did he know? Probably Holmes, who was addicted to cocaine, got violent and beat him up occasionally. Poor Dr Watson! But he could never leave Holmes, since Holmes provided him with all the material for his stories. Watson must have tried so hard to keep Holmes happy. Every time Holmes returned from a walk, Watson had to pretend he didn't know it was him. That was the way Watson made his living. What? What's wrong with you, Kazumi?"

"How dare you say such things? It's sacrilege! You'll be cursed, my friend!"

"Oh, pooh! And, by the way, you said that I am inferior to Holmes when guessing someone's personality, but you're so wrong. I have studied astrology, which I believe is the best way to know about people. I have also studied psychiatric pathology, and, of course, astronomy. To know someone's personality, it's best to ask his or her time of birth. Some clients don't know exactly when they were born. Well, I can easily guess their birthday from their personality and appearance. As you've seen, I almost always guess right. And once I get the data, I can explore a client's personality. Even though Holmes was born in England, he didn't study astrology. That's a pity. Astrology would have enabled him to do a better job."

"I know you're knowledgeable about people's personalities," I replied, "but what do you know about astronomy?"

"How can I be an astrologer if I don't know about astronomy? Oh, I see, you're sceptical because you've never seen me looking through a telescope. Well, I do have one, actually, but it's useless in Tokyo: the only things we can see here are particles of smog. However, I can obtain updated information. I'll give you an example. We all know that Saturn has a ring around it. Do you know any other such planets in the solar system?"

"There are no others."

"You're wrong. That's what they said decades ago. By the way, the Japanese used to think that a bunny was making rice cakes on the moon. You don't still believe that, do you?"

I refused to answer him.

"No offence to you, Kazumi, but every minute that passes, scientific research is making progress. Sooner or later, elementary schools will be teaching kids how electromagnetic waves travel in the universe and how gravity, time and space relate to each other. In the near future, these children will look down at us as dinosaurs. But, getting back to the solar system, Uranus has a ring. So does Jupiter. These facts were discovered just the other day. I have the privilege of being informed of such new information."

Even though Kiyoshi looked serious, his story sounded fishy to me. "I accept that you are quite knowledgeable about Holmes and astronomy," I said, "so who would you say is the best detective? Have you ever read the Father Brown series?"

"Who? I don't know anything about Christians."

"What about Philo Vance?"

"What? What kind of vans?"

"Miss Jane Marple?"

"As in maple syrup?"

"Chief Inspector Maigret?"

"Is he a policeman in Meguro?"

"Hercule Poirot?"

"Sounds like the name of a liqueur."

"I don't know what to say. You've never read any of those detective stories, but still you insist that the tales of Sherlock Holmes are foolish."

"I didn't say I disliked him. In fact, he's one of the detectives I love the most. I love his humour. We would never be interested in people who acted like computers, would we? Holmes showed us what a real human being is. In that sense, he's wonderful."

His compliment surprised me, even if it was backhanded. I was rather touched. As he saw me smiling, he hurriedly added, "But there's one thing about him I really disagree with: his involvement with the British government during the First World War. He justified capturing German spies, while ignoring the fact that Britain had its own spies. As you've seen in the movie *Lawrence of Arabia,* Britain had been two-faced regarding Arab diplomacy. And look how they treated China in the Opium War. How could Holmes justify his work for a dishonourable country? He should never have gotten involved in their political crimes. You could say that his love for his own country motivated him, but justice must rise above patriotism. His reputation was ruined in his later years. When he and Moriarty fell into the waterfall, Holmes had to have been killed. The person we knew as Sherlock Holmes after that incident was an impostor that Britain used for propaganda. As a matter of fact, we can see…"

Kiyoshi's lecture was interrupted by someone knocking loudly on the door. Before we answered, the visitor had entered the office. He was a big man in a dark-coloured suit, about forty years old.

"Are you Mr Mitarai?" he asked me.

"No, I'm not," I replied nervously.

As he turned to Kiyoshi, he pulled out his badge from his pocket like a businessman showing off his wallet. In a low voice, he introduced himself. His name was Takegoshi.

As soon as he saw the name, Kiyoshi changed his attitude. "So you're from the police! Well, this is an unexpected surprise! Did one of us get a parking ticket? May I examine your badge more closely, please? This is the first time for me to see a real one."

"You don't know how to speak to your superiors, do you?" Takegoshi said dramatically. "These days, young men aren't acquainted with proper etiquette. That's why we're so busy, I tell you."

"According to proper etiquette, a visitor waits until he is invited into an office. He does not barge in. What do you want? Tell me quickly. We don't want to waste our time, or yours."

"What? This is amazing! Do you know who I am? Do you always talk to people like that?"

"Only to socially uneducated people like yourself. Tell me what you want. And if you would like your fortune told, tell me your birthday right away."

Takegoshi was taken aback, but he did not alter his high-handed manner. "You saw my sister, didn't you?" he said. There was anger in his voice. "Her name is Misako Iida. I know that she came to see you."

"Ah!" Kiyoshi replied, suddenly raising his voice. "She said she had a brother, and that must be you! What a surprise! This gentleman must have been raised under very different circumstances from his sister, don't you think, Mr Ishioka?"

"I don't know why she visited such a cheap fortune-teller as you. She brought our father's note here, didn't she? Don't deny it!"

"I haven't denied it yet."

"My brother-in-law told me she did. That note is an important piece of evidence. I want it back!"

"Since I have finished reading it, I may be willing to return it to you, but is that acceptable to your sister?"

"She wouldn't care. I demand that you return the note to me immediately!"

"So you haven't spoken to your sister about this yet. Well, would she really want me to hand over the note to you? What would Bunjiro Takegoshi say if he was alive? I don't think I can return his note, even though you are asking me very politely."

"You rude son of a bitch! You must know that I can take certain action."

"What kind of action might that be? It must be something nice. What do you think it is, Mr Ishioka? Putting handcuffs on us?"

"Your attitude is far different from the way I was brought up. You should learn some manners, boy."

"I'm not quite as young as you might think," Kiyoshi answered, yawning.

"I'm serious. My father will not rest in peace if you keep playing private detective with his note. Criminal investigation is not a parlour game. Only legwork brings success."

"Are you talking about the investigation of the Tokyo Zodiac Murders?"

"The Zodiac Murders? What the hell is that, the title of a comic book? People jump at anything that sounds sensational, and then act like they're private detectives. They think it's easy and fun, but real detective work is serious. We're professionals— not like you—and that note is required for our investigation."

"If legwork is all that's required, then being a detective must be the best job for the son of a shoe salesman. But you forgot something very important—brainwork. If intelligence makes a good detective, what happened in your case, eh? I don't think you deserve to have this note. However, I will consider handing it over to you. But I have my doubts. You won't be able to solve this case unless you use your head—because otherwise, I warn you, you will lose face."

"Warn me, huh? You don't need to. We're well trained, professional detectives. You must know criminal investigations are not an easy stroll in the woods."

"Why are you repeating the same thing over and over again? I've never once said that investigation work was easy, have I? You were the one who brought up legwork. Funny how brainwork never occurred to you. Guess it's easier to let your shoes do the walking."

"Are you telling me I have no brain?" Takegoshi started to raise his voice. "I've never met a person as rude as you are! Look at you. You're acting like a homeless person! You and the homeless are only good for making noise and squawking like old women. Well, that might be the way you make your living, but civil servants don't have that luxury. We have a responsibility to society. And if you're so smart, tell me, have you found a likely suspect?"

Kiyoshi paused, and then said matter-of-factly, "No, not yet." He looked calm, but I could tell he was frustrated.

"There, you see. You're useless!" Takegoshi laughed in triumph. "I knew you hadn't figured anything out. I just asked because you were acting so high and mighty. Look at you. You're just a… beginner!"

"I don't care what you say, but let me ask you a professional favour. I would like some time before you expose your father's note to the public. You can have the note back today, although it may make little difference to you in the end. And since it includes an incident that is embarrassing to your father, you may want to keep it a secret. Take some time to read it by yourself and understand it."

"OK. I'll give you three days."

"That's pretty fast. And I don't think that's giving you enough time to think it over."

"One week then."

"All right, one week."

"Are you telling me?…"

"Yes, I'm telling you I will solve the case in one week. At the least, I will prove your father's innocence, so you won't have to expose the note after all."

"Even though you have no suspects in mind? That's impossible!"

"I said one week. I will solve the case in one week. Today is Thursday the 5th, so you will wait until next Thursday, the 12th, before doing anything further with the note. Is that understood?"

"I will submit this note to my supervisor on Friday the 13th."

"Thank you. We don't want to waste our time. You can leave through the same door you came in by. Incidentally, were you born in November?"

"That's right. How did you know? Did my sister tell you?"

"It's quite plain to see. I can also see that you were born between 8 p.m. and 9 p.m. in the evening. OK, here is your father's note. Take it, and please leave."

Takegoshi slammed the door as he left. We could hear him stomping down the hall.

"Are you crazy?" I said to Kiyoshi. "Do you really think you can figure everything out by next Thursday?"

He said nothing, which made me even more anxious. Sometimes his overbearing confidence made him lose rationality. "What do you have in mind?" I asked.

"As you were talking, I just felt something click. I don't know what it is, but it felt a little like déjà vu. I must know something. It's not like a puzzle. It's something very simple... I can't remember... I may be wrong... Thank God, we have one week. By the way, do you have your wallet with you?"

"Yes..."

"Can you afford expenses for four or five days?"

"I think so."

"Very good. I must leave for Kyoto right away. Would you like to come with me?"

"Kyoto? Now? But I can't go on such short notice..."

"Then I'll see you when I get back. I'm sorry, but I can't force you to come with me."

As soon as he turned his back towards me, he pulled out his travelling bag from under his desk.

"Wait! Of course I'll come with you!" I shouted.

I think that was the moment when Kiyoshi began to put all his energy into the case. Once he makes a decision, he acts very quickly, sometimes impulsively, like a lightning bolt. We grabbed a map of Kyoto and the copy of *The Tokyo Zodiac Murders* and bolted out of the office.

Ninety minutes later, we were on the bullet train to Kyoto...

161

ENTR'ACTE

Bacteria in the Bullet Train

"So how do you think Takegoshi Jr found out about his sister coming to see you?" I asked Kiyoshi, as we settled into the ride.

"I suppose Mrs Iida must have felt guilty about consulting me without getting her husband's approval. After she got home, she confessed what she'd done, and her husband called his brother-in-law."

"Her husband sounds like an honest fellow."

"Could be. Or he might just be afraid of that thug."

"Yes, Takegoshi Jr was a rude bastard. Do you think his father was like that? Surely not."

"Oh, policemen are all the same. They think because they're cops they're all-powerful, and they run around acting like shogun, as if it's still the age of feudalism. The sister didn't consult her brother before disclosing their father's secret to a stranger. That must have infuriated him—pre-war protocol violated in modern society."

"I think Japanese tend to be unnecessarily obedient to authorities, anyway."

"Well, among all the Japanese I've met, Takegoshi Jr was as arrogant as they come. You could put him on display in a museum as a representative petty autocrat."

"No wonder his sister wanted to keep the note secret from him. I can understand how she felt."

"Oh, really?" Kiyoshi said, suddenly staring at me. "Tell me, how did she feel?"

"Excuse me?"

"I'd like to know. What was she feeling when she found her father's note?"

"She wanted to protect her father's secret, and so she decided to show it to you, hoping that the case would be solved quietly."

"Come on, grow up!" Kiyoshi interjected. "Why did she tell her husband that she came to see me, then? She wanted him to solve the case. She probably showed him the note, but he couldn't figure anything out, so she brought it to me. If I solve the case, she can claim the credit for her husband—and BOOM, his career is made. I think she has everything mapped out."

"Aren't you going too far? She didn't look like—"

"Someone so calculating? I'm not saying she's malicious; it's just natural for a married woman to think that way."

"You sound like you think all women are calculating. That's not fair."

"Most men are obsessed with the idea that all women should be obedient and powerless. Is that fair?"

There was nothing I could say.

"You and I will never agree on this issue," he went on, "just like a modern person would never be able to convince a samurai of the value of air-conditioning."

"Huh? Are you still saying that women are schemers?"

"Not all of them. There could be one good woman in a thousand."

"One in a thousand? Oh, c'mon, can't you change the ratio to at least one in ten?"

"No way," Kiyoshi replied and laughed.

I remained silent for a while.

"Now, have we examined all the known facts of the case?" Kiyoshi asked, as the train sped on. "We know about Masako, Heikichi's second wife. What about his first wife, Tae? What was her background?"

"Her maiden name was Fujieda. She was born and raised near Rakushisha, in Sagano, Kyoto."

"Kyoto? Good, we can kill two birds with one stone."

"She was an only child. When she was in her teens, her family moved to Imadegawa in Kamigyo Ward and opened a shop selling Nishijin brocade. Unfortunately, business was not so good, and then her mother got ill and became bedridden. They had no one to turn to for help. Her father had an elder brother, but he was in Manchuria. Her mother died, the shop went bankrupt, and her father hanged himself. In his will, he suggested that Tae should seek out her uncle in Manchuria and ask for financial assistance. Tae chose to go to Tokyo instead. I don't know how she liquidated her parents' debt."

"She would've renounced the rights to her inheritance."

"The rights to her inheritance?"

"Yes, then she wouldn't inherit anything, even her parents' debt."

"I see. I didn't know that. Anyway, in Tokyo, she worked at a kimono boutique as a live-in employee. When she was around twenty-two or twenty-three, her boss—who might have been sympathetic to her plight—played the role of matchmaker and introduced her to Yoshio Umezawa, Heikichi's younger brother. And Yoshio in turn introduced her to Heikichi."

167

"They were married, and fortune seemed to be smiling on her, but later Heikichi kicked her out," Kiyoshi added, filling in the blanks.

"Some people have no luck. I think Tae accepted her fate in life as selling cigarettes in Hoya."

"If you study astrology, you will know how unfair life is. Anything else about her?"

"I think that's all. Oh, this may have nothing to do with the case, but she had a huge collection of *shingen* handbags—you know, those little silk bags women carry when they dress in kimono. According to her neighbours in Hoya, her dream was to go back to Rakushisha and open a boutique selling original handbags."

"But Tae inherited Heikichi's estate. After the war, she must have received a lot of money from the sale of his paintings."

"Yes, she did, but she fell ill and didn't spend it on herself. She spent it on housekeepers and gifts for neighbours who were kind to her, and she also put a bounty on the head of the person who committed the Azoth murders. She probably could have opened a boutique in Rakushisha, but being realistic about her poor health and her age, she stayed in Hoya for the rest of her life."

"I see. What happened to her estate?"

"It was amazing. One of her relatives, who had never been close to her, suddenly came to see Tae on her deathbed. This woman was a granddaughter of Tae's uncle in Manchuria. Probably she stayed and took care of Tae for a while. Tae put the woman in her will. The story is that all the neighbours cried at Tae's funeral, because Tae had been so generous to them."

"Then, someone who didn't get any money killed her!... Just kidding. What about Yasue Tomita, the owner of the De Médicis gallery? Any more information on her?"

"She came from a rich family. That's all I know."

"What about Ayako, Yoshio's wife?"

"Her maiden name was Yoshioka. She was born in Kamakura, and had one older brother. Yoshio was introduced to her by his mentor, a man whose father was a priest. Do you need any more?"

"No, that's probably enough. Ayako wasn't a woman with a past, was she?"

"Not as far as I know."

Kiyoshi sat silently looking out of the window with his chin resting on his hand. It was dark now, and the window was like a mirror, reflecting the brightness of the train's interior.

"I can see the moon," Kiyoshi said quietly. "I can see some stars, too. Ah, it's good to get away from the Tokyo smog. Can you see that star that never blinks, right next to the moon? Well, that's not a star, actually—it's the planet Jupiter. If you can see the moon, then you can always locate the planets easily. Today is 5th April and the moon is in Cancer, soon to move into Leo. Jupiter is also in Cancer at 29 degrees. The moon moves just like the planets. You know, watching the movement of the planets every day makes you realize how small and insignificant our daily lives are. We argue. We fight. We struggle. We compete to increase our wealth. Look at the universe. Its movement is so dynamic, like a huge clock. The earth is just a cog in the gears of the clock, and humans make no more difference than bacteria do. Millions and millions of bacteria living their short lives battling their petty battles. They don't stop to think that without the mechanisms of the universe, none of us would exist. Look at what people do—they kill each other for a deposit in the bank, which they will never spend before they die. It's ridiculous." Kiyoshi had been speaking seriously, but suddenly he giggled. "Well, here's one bacterium getting excited by a foolish and petty thing. He's riding this 'bullet train' to Kyoto, trying to show up another fat, arrogant bacterium."

I laughed.

"People live their lives committing one sin after another," Kiyoshi said, lightening up.

"By the way, what exactly are we going to do in Kyoto?" I asked.

"We're going to see Tamio Yasukawa. You do want to see him, don't you?"

"Well, yes, if we can."

"He was in his late twenties in 1936, so he must be about seventy now, assuming he's still alive. Time has passed."

"Yes, indeed. Anything else?"

"So far, that's the only thing I'm thinking of. We'll stay with a friend of mine called Emoto. He's a nice guy. You'll like him. He's only twenty-five, but already a fully trained chef."

"How do you know him?"

"I used to live in Kyoto several years ago. It's a great city. Each time I visit, I feel inspired. It has a kind of special energy, and, of course, it's one of the few cities that wasn't bombed in the war. So there's the new Kyoto, which is like any other modern city, and there's also the old Kyoto, with its temples, traditional houses and geisha. It's like going back in time a hundred years—like to the London of your beloved Sherlock Holmes, except that it's Japanese!"

ACT THREE

In Pursuit of Azoth

SCENE 1

Moves on the Chessboard

"Hey, Emoto!" Kiyoshi called out, seeing his friend waiting for us on the platform of Kyoto Station.

"It's been a long time!" Emoto said as he greeted Kiyoshi, shaking his hand. There was a big smile on his face. "How are you?"

"Unfortunately," Kiyoshi grinned, "I'm not very fine, but I'm glad to see you." He introduced me to Emoto.

"Wow, you travel light!" Emoto said when he picked up our bags. He was quite tall, had neatly trimmed short hair, and seemed to have a pleasant, laid-back manner.

"Yeah. We just jumped on the train."

"Well," Emoto said, looking at Kiyoshi. "Your timing's perfect. You're just in time for the cherries."

"The cherries?" replied Kiyoshi, looking confused. "Oh, yeah, it's the cherry blossom season! Kazumi will be very happy."

Besides its cherry blossoms, the city of Kyoto is famous for the way it was designed—in a grid, like a chessboard. Every street goes north–south or east–west, like New York. Emoto lived in Nishi-kyogoku, south-west of the city centre. As he drove us home, I gazed out at the city view. There were lots of neon signs and office buildings. Some parts of Kyoto looked just like Tokyo.

Emoto had a two-bedroom apartment. Apparently, Kiyoshi and I would be sharing a bedroom for the first time in our lives.

"We'll be busy tomorrow. Let's get some sleep," said Kiyoshi, slipping into his futon.

Emoto's voice came from behind the door. "Would you like to use my car?"

"No, thanks," Kiyoshi replied, already under the blanket.

The next morning, we took a Hankyu Line train to Shijo-Kawaramachi, close to the address we had for Tamio Yasukawa.

"Yasukawa's address is Rokkaku-agaru, Tominokoji. Do you know how they find a house from its address here in Kyoto?"

"Sorry, in case you've forgotten, I'm from Tokyo."

"OK, a quick lesson, then. His house is on Tominokoji Street, which runs north–south. And Rokkaku runs east–west. Where the two streets cross is the location we're looking for. '*Agaru*' means the house is a little 'up' from Rokkaku—in other words, to the north."

"Ah, I see."

"It's very simple and convenient."

We got off the train and climbed the stairs. "Shijo-Kawaramachi is the busiest area of Kyoto. However, Kyoto lovers are in unanimous agreement it's the second worst place in the city. The worst is Kyoto Tower."

"How come?"

"Because it doesn't match their image of Kyoto."

True to his word, when we reached ground level we could only see modern buildings lining the streets. Obviously this was the new Kyoto. I wondered where the old Kyoto was.

Kiyoshi walked rapidly, and I followed. Crossing the busy street, we came to an avenue that ran along a narrow, shallow stream. The water was amazingly clear, the stones at the bottom perfectly visible. Waterweed was gently dancing in the flow of the water, which was reflecting the beams of the morning sun. We certainly couldn't find anything like that in Tokyo.

"This is the Takase River," Kiyoshi said. "Really it's a canal. Merchants dug it out to transport their cargo." That was the extent of his explanation, as we continued walking. Before long, Kiyoshi came to an abrupt stop before a building.

"What's this?" I asked.

"A Chinese restaurant. Let's eat."

As we ate, not much was said. We were both lost in thought. I was trying to imagine what Yasukawa's life had been like. Since his name was mentioned in *The Tokyo Zodiac Murders*, no doubt he'd been plagued by uninvited visitors seeking interviews with him. He must have wanted peace and quiet. Sadly, the image of him I kept imagining was a lonely man who had lost himself in drink. No matter. My own interest was to prove that Heikichi Umezawa was alive—or at least had not been murdered.

Who knows what Kiyoshi was thinking.

When we finally got to Yasukawa's address, Kiyoshi was perplexed. "This is Tominokoji... and that is Rokkaku... but something's wrong. We can't go any further; that's a different street over there. This is the only apartment complex in this area. Perhaps he doesn't live in an apartment..."

On the ground level there was a bar called the Butterfly. Our options being limited, we climbed the narrow stairs to the second floor where the apartments were. It was not the cleanest or newest of buildings. We examined the postboxes in the corridor; none bore the name of Yasukawa.

Kiyoshi was starting to look frustrated, but he quickly regained his usual composure as he knocked on the nearest door. There was no answer, so he tried the next door. No luck there, either.

"This is not good," he said. "They probably think we're door-to-door salesmen. Let's try the other end of the hall."

The tactic worked. When we knocked on the farthest door, a fat old woman answered.

"Excuse me, madam, we're not selling anything. I wonder if you could help us," Kiyoshi asked, his best manners on display. "We're looking for an old gentleman by the name of Tamio Yasukawa. Does he live in this building?"

"Mr Yasukawa?... Let me think... Oh, yes, I remember him. He moved out a long time ago."

Kiyoshi turned to me as if he already knew this.

"Oh, did he? Do you happen to know where he moved to?"

"I have no idea. Why don't you ask the manager downstairs? His name is Okawa, but maybe he's out now. He owns a bar in Kita-shirakawa. When he's not here, he's usually there."

"What's the bar's name?"

"The White Butterfly."

Kiyoshi thanked her, and we left. But, as she predicted, no one answered when we knocked on the door below.

"All right, let's go to Kita-shirakawa and find Mr Okawa."

As our bus headed towards the north of the city, many temples and old buildings came into sight. The view was so pretty that I began to picture what life would be like living in that area.

The bar was right next to the Kita-shirakawa bus stop. Before we could knock, a man opened the door.

"Excuse me, are you by any chance Mr Okawa?"

The man froze when he heard Kiyoshi's voice and he looked at each of us in turn.

We explained the reason for our visit and asked our questions.

"Hmm... Let me see... Can I remember that far back?" he said, viewing us cautiously. "Maybe I have it in my records, but they're in my apartment in Kawaramachi. Are you something to do with the police?"

Kiyoshi was as cool as could be. "Well," he grinned, "what do we look like?"

"May I see your business card?"

I was a bit flustered by Okawa's request, but Kiyoshi was on a roll. He knitted his brow and said to Okawa in a hushed voice, "To tell you the truth, Mr Okawa, we're not allowed to present our business card to any civilian. I apologize. Have you heard of the Public Security Investigation Agency?"

"Um, yeah, I think I've heard of it..." mumbled Okawa. It was his turn to look nervous.

"Well..." Kiyoshi paused for a moment before continuing. "I shouldn't have mentioned it, really. Please forget that I mentioned it at all. When can you find Mr Yasukawa's current address?"

Okawa's attitude was suddenly cooperative. "I have to go to Takatsuki now, but I'll be right back. I'll get his address by 5 p.m. Could you call me around that time? I'll give you my number..."

"You were marvellous," I whispered to Kiyoshi, as we walked back to the main street. "I didn't know that you were a con man!"

"Oh, just common sense," he responded casually. "Would a private eye reveal who he really was?"

His tactic had worked well, but I was anxious. We had four hours to kill—four hours that would be wasted. And it was already Friday the 6th.

We walked along the river until we came to a bridge with heavy traffic. I recognized a tall building; we were returning to Shijo-Kawaramachi, where we'd started the day's activities. I was just thinking how good a cold drink would taste when Kiyoshi started talking.

"Something's missing... And it's probably something very, very simple," he said, his eyes to the ground. "The case was grotesque and incomprehensible, but I have a hunch that it's not so incomprehensible after all. When we uncover the missing link, we will understand the whole story. We may have to review the case from the beginning, especially the first half of it. Yes, I think it's all about that one missing link. For forty years, detectives throughout Japan have been stymied. Well, I am one detective who will not give up!"

A Profanity

We sat down in a coffee shop and passed the time sipping fruit juice slowly—very slowly. When it was almost five, Kiyoshi suddenly stood up and went to a payphone. He talked for a while, and then came back.

"I got it!" was all he said. I grabbed my things and followed him out of the door.

The street was getting crowded with people finishing work. Kiyoshi walked straight through the crowd, crossing the bridge over the Kamo River.

"So where does he live?"

"In Neyagawa, on the way to Osaka. We can take the Keihan Line train from over there."

The station was straight ahead of us.

From the platform we could see the river slowly changing colour as evening approached.

We got off at Korien Station. The Chinese characters of the name meant "garden in a fragrant village", so I had imagined a pleasant wooded area. The place was anything but that. From what I could see, it consisted mostly of small bars and nightclubs with gaudy neon signs that had just been turned on to attract the first customers of the evening. Some office workers who had clearly started drinking early came weaving down the street, and several hostesses with heavy make-up passed us on their way to work.

It was completely dark by the time we located the address Okawa had given us. The manager of the block was out, so we went upstairs and started knocking on doors again. A middle-aged woman said she'd never heard of anyone named Yasukawa.

We were luckier with another tenant. "Someone moved out just the other day," he said. "I think his name was Yasukawa. We never spoke to each other, so I don't know where he moved to. Why don't you ask the manager?"

Kiyoshi couldn't hide his disappointment. But we tried the manager's office again and, to our surprise, we found he'd just come back from an errand.

"I don't know where the family moved to," he said, trying to be cooperative. "It seemed they didn't want to tell anyone, and I didn't push the matter. They must have been depressed, because the grandfather had just died."

"Died?!" Kiyoshi and I exclaimed at the same time.

"You mean Tamio Yasukawa?" Kiyoshi asked.

"Tamio? Oh, right, it was something like that."

So Yasukawa had died here in Osaka. I felt demoralized. Now there was no way of learning what his life had been like. He had lived in Tokyo, he had been in the war, and he had moved to Osaka. And his life had ended in this old apartment with its cracked walls.

Unexpectedly, the manager was able to provide us with some new information. He told us that Yasukawa had not lived alone. He had a daughter, who was probably in her thirties. She was married to a carpenter and they had two children.

The light bulb in the corridor flickered, and the manager gave it a hateful glance every time the light dimmed.

My heart had sunk into a bitter sadness. I felt like a kid who had been caught misbehaving. We were on the trail of a poor guy who couldn't have had a happy life and had just expired. This wasn't an adventure any more. It seemed somehow profane to be poking around in this old man's personal history—a profanity against all humanity.

Kiyoshi seemed to be lost in thought, too.

"If you really want to know where they went," the manager volunteered, "you could ask the freight company. They were here just last month, so I remember their name—Neyagawa Freight. They're located right in front of Neyagawa Station."

We thanked him and left.

"What time is it?" Kiyoshi asked.

"Ten to eight."

"Then we can still make it," he said, apparently cheered. "Let's go to Neyagawa Freight!"

We walked back to the station and took the train to Neyagawa.

It was easy to find the company, but too late to talk to anyone. From a sign that read "MOVING? CALL US!" Kiyoshi took down the company's phone number. He would call the next morning. Then we headed back to Emoto's apartment.

And so ended Friday, 6th April.

Crossing the Moon

The next morning I was awakened by the sound of Kiyoshi's voice; he was talking with someone on the phone. It was late enough for Emoto to have left for work already. I got up, put the futon away in the wardrobe, and went to the kitchen for some coffee.

When I entered the living room to offer Kiyoshi a cup, he was just finishing his call. He ripped off a memo from his pad and said, "Yasukawa's daughter is in Higashi-yodogawa in Osaka. I couldn't get her exact address, but the freight company guy said it was close to the bus station at Toyosato-cho, down an alley, and near a pancake shop called Omichi-ya. Her husband's name is Kato. Let's get going!"

When we arrived at Toyosato-cho, we could see in the distance the iron bridge across the Yodo River. The area was undeveloped. Old tyres were scattered over stretches of vacant land overgrown with weeds. The road, however, seemed newly paved. We went down an alley between a cluster of shacks and soon found the pancake shop. There were several modest apartment complexes beyond. From the names on the postboxes, we soon located the Katos' apartment.

We climbed the wooden stairs, and made our way to their apartment, pushing our way through laundry drying in the passageway. Their window was slightly open, and we could hear the sound of dishes being washed and a baby crying.

Kiyoshi knocked, and shortly afterwards a woman opened the door. She had no make-up on, and her hair was unkempt. It was Yasukawa's daughter. Kiyoshi began to explain the purpose of our visit, but she interrupted him before he could get very far.

"I have nothing to say about it! My father didn't do anything. We have been bothered enough. Leave us alone!" She slammed the door, which caused the baby to wail even louder.

Kiyoshi stood in front of the door, unmoving. He looked dismayed.

I had been surprised to hear Yasukawa's daughter speak in the Kanto dialect; we were deep in the Kansai area, and all I had heard in the last two days was variations of the Kansai dialect.

As we walked away from the apartment building, Kiyoshi said quietly, "I knew that she would refuse to talk to us. Her father would have, too, if he was still alive. I just wanted to see Yasukawa on behalf of Bunjiro Takegoshi. Oh, let's forget about Yasukawa and his daughter."

"What shall we do then?"

"I don't know. Let's go back to Kyoto."

So, with barely a plan in mind, we got on a train.

En route, Kiyoshi, who'd been deep in thought, abruptly said. "Kazumi, now that you're in Kyoto, why don't you take the opportunity to do a little sightseeing? I highly recommend Arashiyama, where the cherries should be in full bloom. You can change trains at the next stop, Katsura. Here's a guidebook.

I want to be alone so I can concentrate. I'll see you back at Emoto's apartment."

I got off the train at Arashiyama and headed towards the river. Kiyoshi was right about one thing: the cherry blossoms there were gorgeous.

A *maiko*—a young girl training to be a geisha—passed by, drawing the attention of everyone. She was in a kimono and walking with a teenage boy whose hair was dyed blond. He had a camera hung from his neck. Her thick-soled wooden sandals made a pleasant, soft sound with each step she took.

I followed the crowds over the Katsura River. The bridge, according to the guidebook, is called Togetsu-kyo, which means "the bridge crossing over the moon". Supposedly, when the moon is reflected in the surface of the river, you get the feeling that you are indeed floating above the moon.

Nearby was a tiny shrine. But as I approached it, I realized that in fact it was a phone booth in the shape of a shrine. I thought about calling someone from it as a novelty, but no one came to mind.

After lunch, I took a ride on a tram. This simple activity delighted me, as Tokyo no longer has trams. I recalled reading in a mystery novel once that the detective was struck by inspiration while riding a tram. It struck me that today good old mystery novels are just as obsolete as trams!

I had no idea where the tram was going and got off at the last stop. It was Shijo-Omiya. I walked along a busy street and suddenly found myself back at Shijo-Kawaramachi. Did all roads in Kyoto lead to Shijo-Kawaramachi?

From there, I headed to the famous Kiyomizu Temple. I walked up the stone pavement of Sannen-zaka and stopped at a small teahouse for a cup of sweet *amazake* rice wine. Then I wandered on.

In front of a small curio shop, a woman dressed in a kimono was splashing water on the pavement to wash the dust away. She was careful not to splash me, and it occurred to me how much I appreciated her thoughtfulness.

I returned to Shijo-Kawaramachi. I was tired from all this strenuous tourism, and decided to return to Emoto's apartment.

Emoto was already back from work.

"Oh, you're back! Did you enjoy your sightseeing?"

"Yes, it was wonderful."

"What happened to Kiyoshi?"

"We separated on the train... Well, actually, he abandoned me!" Emoto scowled, half-amused, half-sympathetic.

As we were preparing the tempura for dinner, Kiyoshi came back in a daze, as if he was sleepwalking. Other than the barest hello, he said nothing.

Over dinner he was no different. Emoto's food was excellent, but Kiyoshi didn't seem to notice it.

"It's Sunday tomorrow," the chef said to him. "It's my day off, so how about a drive to northern Kyoto? I know you're busy, but, according to Kazumi, what you're doing here is mostly brainwork. Why don't you come for the ride? You can work in the car."

Kiyoshi nodded obediently. "All right—as long as you allow me to sit quietly in the back."

SCENE 4

The Riverbank

Kiyoshi didn't utter a word while Emoto was driving us to Sanzen-in, a temple in Ohara, north of Kyoto. He sat in the backseat like a statue of Buddha.

We stopped at a restaurant in Ohara for some fine *kaiseki* Zen cuisine. Even when Emoto was explaining the traditional dishes, Kiyoshi's mind seemed to be elsewhere.

Emoto and I got on well, and I was pleased to have the opportunity of visiting many places around Kyoto: Doshisha University, Kyoto University, Nijo Castle, Heian Shrine, the Imperial Palace and the Uzumasa film studio.

In the evening, Emoto treated us to a sushi dinner in Kawaramachi and then took us to a very attractive coffee shop that played only classical music.

It was a thoroughly enjoyable day, even though we made no progress on the case.

When I woke up the next morning, Kiyoshi and Emoto had both already gone.

I ate breakfast near the station and then started walking nowhere in particular. I went into a shopping mall, and then crossed a creek into a playground. Several groups of joggers passed by. I tried to bring my focus back to the case.

The case of the Zodiac Murders was no ordinary mystery.

It had achieved such stature that people's lives had even been ruined by it. One person had sold all his property to finance his research on the case. Another man had gone crazy and killed himself by leaping from a cliff into the Japan Sea. Was I to be sacrificed at the altar of this mystery, too?

I decided to go back to Kawaramachi. I'd been charmed by the coffee shop that played classical music and thought I'd take refuge there. Then maybe I'd stop at a bookshop to buy a book on illustration.

As I waited on the platform for the local train, an express zipped by, causing some loose litter to get blown around. Suddenly, I recalled the view by the river in Toyosato-cho—the vacant land, the weeds, the discarded tyres. I thought about Yasukawa's daughter. Not being able to talk to her had left a huge hole in our investigation. We needed her story—however much she could tell us. That did it. I stood up, went down the stairs and over to the other side of the tracks. I was going back to see her.

It was slightly after four when I arrived at Toyosato-cho. Not much was going on around the station. There were just some street concessions selling *okonomiyaki* pancakes and *takoyaki* octopus-filled dumplings, both favourite Kansai snacks. I walked towards the bridge over the Yodo River, went down the alley again, located the pancake shop, and started up the stairs of the apartment block. That was when uncertainty set in.

Would she be willing to talk to me at all? The Umezawa murders were not a pleasant thing, but she had to have had at least a slight interest in her father's involvement in the case.

Maybe I should bring up Takegoshi's note. Our connection with him surely distinguished us from the hordes of amateur detectives who'd knocked on their door. I could say I was a close friend of Takegoshi's daughter. It was a lie, but I had to do what I had to do. What I wanted was to get even the slightest clue that Heikichi Umezawa had not died. Also, I had this profound interest in what Yasukawa's life had been like after the case. If Heikichi had not been murdered, maybe they had stayed in touch?

This time, there was no laundry in the passageway. I knocked on the door. She answered, making no attempt to hide her annoyance at seeing me again.

"I'm very sorry, please excuse me, I mean no disrespect, I'm really very sorry," I said, bowing and bowing. I was trying to get a few words inside the door before she slammed it in my face. "I came here by myself. I have some new information about the case, and I wanted to tell you about it..."

I probably looked very serious—and maybe a little silly—apologizing so profusely. She smiled, and then she slowly stepped out of the door. "Let's go to the riverbank," she said. "My child likes being outside."

Once there, I started talking, barely pausing for breath. Oddly, she didn't seem as interested in my story as I expected. She did listen, though, and then she began to talk.

"Well, Mr Ishioka, what can I tell you? I was raised in Tokyo. Our house was near Hasunuma Station on the Ikegami Line, but my mother used to walk to Kamata in order to save money," she said, smiling cynically. "My parents didn't tell me about their younger days, so I don't know how much help I can give you. What I do know is, after the Umezawa murders, my father was drafted into the army. He was injured in the war; his right arm was paralysed. When he got back to Japan, he met my mother and married her. They were happy in the beginning, but then my father slipped into a rather sleazy lifestyle. We fell into poverty and lived on welfare, while he gambled. He went to the Omori and Oi racetracks every day. My mother was forced to work. Our apartment had just one, six-tatami-mat room. It was too small for the three of us, but there was no choice. My father got drunk and abused my mother daily. Sometimes he hallucinated, insisting that he saw acquaintances who were no longer alive…"

I had to interrupt. "Who were they? Did he mention Heikichi Umezawa?"

"I thought you would ask that. Yes, I heard him mention Umezawa, but how could we trust my father? Mostly, he didn't make any sense. He was probably high from alcohol or drugs. You see, he used morphine occasionally."

"If your father really saw Umezawa, then your father would have been a very important witness in the case."

Excitedly, I told her about my theory: Heikichi had killed his double and disappeared; he murdered Kazue to keep his crimes a secret; only Heikichi had the motivation to commit the Azoth murders…

Mrs Kato's interest in the case seemed to dwindle further. She bounced her baby up and down on her back, letting the wind blow through her hair.

"Did your father mention anything about Azoth?" I asked.

"Well, he might have said something, but I was small at that time… I think I heard the name Heikichi Umezawa mentioned again recently, but I have no interest in the case or that person.

I still feel disgusted when I hear his name. It only brings back bad memories. Total strangers used to badger us. Once I came home and found a man sitting inside our apartment, waiting for my father, wanting to ask some ridiculous question. We had no privacy, and I lived in embarrassment every day. Even today, I'm angry about it. That's one of the reasons we moved to Kyoto."

"I'm very sorry. You have endured so much hardship already, and I've only added to it. I'm very sorry I bothered you."

"Please don't apologize. I am sorry for the other day. You arrived at a terrible time, and I lost my temper."

"You're very kind, and I thank you for talking to me. Is your mother well?"

"She divorced my father. She wanted to take me with her, but he refused. After she left, he was a good father to me. I was sorry that he had to leave a job he liked. We were poor, but many people were very poor then, so I never felt humiliated about our living conditions."

"Did your father have any close friends?"

"He gambled and drank with different people, but he had only one close friend, Shusai Yoshida. My father had great admiration for him."

"Is he still alive?"

"Yes, he is."

"What does he do?"

"I believe he's a Chinese-style fortune-teller. He was probably about ten years younger than my father. They met in a bar in Tokyo."

"In Tokyo?"

"Yes, that's right."

"Was your father interested in fortune-telling, too?"

"I don't think so. My father liked Mr Yoshida because doll-making was an interest they had in common."

"Doll-making?"

"Yes, I think that's why they became friendly. After Mr Yoshida moved to Kyoto, so did my father."

"Did you talk about this to the police?"

"To the police? Why should I? No, never."

"What about all those amateur private detectives? Did you tell them anything about this?"

"No, no. You are the first person."

"I'd like to ask you two more questions. From what you heard from your father, do you think Heikichi Umezawa is alive? And do you think that he really made Azoth?"

"I have no idea. I didn't listen to my father seriously. He seemed to believe that Umezawa was still alive, but—let me tell you this again—my father had lost his senses. If you had met him, you would have seen that. Why don't you meet with Mr Yoshida? He would be much more reliable. My father trusted him completely. I don't think he would fabricate the truth."

"Where does he live?"

"I've only met him once, and I don't have his address or phone number. I believe he lives near the Karasuma Garage in Kita Ward, Kyoto. It's at the end of Karasuma Street. If you ask someone, I'm sure they'll know where it is."

I thanked her and said I would be leaving. She walked away, lulling her baby. She didn't turn back to look at me.

I climbed down the riverbank, and walked into the reeds, following a narrow path towards the water. The reeds were taller than me, giving me the feeling of walking through a tunnel. At the water's edge, gentle waves lapped at the black soil. I looked up. The iron bridge cast a shadow onto the river in the fading daylight, and the lights of cars were beginning to glimmer.

Speaking to Yasukawa's daughter had energized me.

So her father thought that Heikichi hadn't died… Shusai Yoshida must know something.

It was five past seven on the evening of the 9th. We had three clear days before our deadline. I couldn't waste any time.

I grabbed a train back to Shijo-Kawaramachi, and then a bus bound for Karasuma Garage. I didn't know the way at all, and it seemed the bus was taking the most circuitous route. It was almost 10 p.m. when I arrived there. The streets were deserted. I walked along, looking for a house with Yoshida's name, with no success. I asked for directions at the neighbourhood police box.

Finally, I found the house, but there were no lights on inside. Too late again! I decided I would return the next day. I just hoped he would be home then.

When I got back to Emoto's apartment, it was quiet. Kiyoshi and Emoto had already gone to bed. Kiyoshi had kindly put out my futon for me—maybe he just didn't want to be bothered by my knocking around late. Anyway, I appreciated the gesture. I quietly slipped under the blankets, thinking about all that had happened and all that lay ahead. My breath slowed, and I fell into a deep sleep.

The Doll-maker

I woke up the next morning only to find Kiyoshi and Emoto already gone—again. I had missed the chance to tell Kiyoshi all I'd learnt from Yasukawa's daughter, information I was very excited about. I was sorry to have overslept, but then it occurred to me: I could continue my research separately. And if I solved the case before Kiyoshi did, it would have an extra happy ending.

I got dressed and headed out to Karasuma Garage. I arrived at Shusai Yoshida's house at around 10 a.m. I opened the sliding door at the entrance and called out to see if anyone was at home. An elderly woman in a kimono appeared. I asked her if I could speak to Mr Yoshida.

"I'm afraid my husband is in Nagoya," she replied.

I felt deflated. "Well, may I ask when he will be back?"

"Probably this evening."

Well, that was better than nothing. I asked for their phone number so that I could call before visiting again.

Dejected, I walked south along the Kamo River until it joined the Takano River. Quite accidentally, I found myself near to Imadegawa; it was where the family of Heikichi's ex-wife Tae had lived their unhappy life.

It was now the 10th. In two days we'd have our reckoning with Takegoshi Jr. It began to seem impossible that we'd have anything by then, even supposing a strong clue emerged from

Shusai Yoshida this evening or there was some unexpected lead tomorrow.

I called Yoshida's house at 2 p.m. His wife told me he hadn't returned yet and apologized deeply. I didn't want to keep bothering her, so I decided not to call again before 5 p.m. But I could feel my frustration building.

I sat in a park for a while and then went to a bookshop. Finally, I went to a first-floor coffee shop so that I could watch the passers-by without them seeing me. At 4.50 p.m., I could wait no longer. I dialled Yoshida's number and was elated to hear that he had just returned home. I hung up the phone and ran out, barely missing a waitress with a tray of hot coffee.

Yasukawa's daughter had said that Shusai Yoshida was about sixty; but his full head of grey hair made him look older than that. He greeted me politely and led me into the living room. As I sat on the sofa, I hastily recounted Bunjiro Takegoshi's written confession and my conversation with Yasukawa's daughter.

"Mr Yasukawa seemed to think that Heikichi Umezawa was still alive. Do you think he lived? And if so, did he make Azoth?" I asked.

Leaning back in his chair, Yoshida listened quietly and attentively. His appearance was pleasing—his grey hair framed his rather narrow face handsomely, and his eyes had a strong yet gentle quality. His posture was upright and he seemed in good health. Unexpectedly, he fit my image of a lone wolf.

"I know about the case, of course," he began. "I explored it with my fortune-telling techniques, but I couldn't reach any conclusion about Heikichi Umezawa's death. I think there is a 60 per cent chance that he is dead. Concerning Azoth, I think he did create it, yes. I am a doll-maker myself, so I can understand what might have been in his mind. If he committed the murders, there would be no reason for him not to complete his creation."

At that moment, Yoshida's wife came into the living room with some tea and biscuits. I realized that I had been so absorbed in my thoughts I had forgotten to bring the customary gift. I apologized embarrassedly.

"Oh, don't worry about it," Yoshida laughed, putting me at ease.

The shelves in the living room were full of books and dolls of various sizes; some were made of wood, some of synthetic resin. Most of them were arrestingly realistic. I asked Yoshida how he developed his interest in doll-making.

"Well, really, I was interested in human beings. It's not easy to explain the connection unless one shares the same interest."

"I see. But you said you could understand Heikichi Umezawa's passion for creating Azoth."

"Let me explain. There is something magical—for want of a better word—about doll-making. Dolls are copies of humans. When we are fabricating a doll and the work is going well, we get a certain feeling of creation. We feel as if the doll is slowly obtaining a soul. I've had this feeling many times. In this regard, there is an awesome sense of power in making a doll. The feeling I get is so profound that I cannot find the right words to express just why it fascinates me so much. The word 'fascination' does not quite correspond to what I feel, either. Traditionally, Mr Ishioka, the Japanese didn't like making dolls much. In ancient times, they made *haniwa* figures for rituals;

they were substitutes for human beings who were to be buried alive as a sacrifice. Doll-making came to mean the creation of a human; it was not a hobby or an art. In fact, the ancient Japanese were afraid that a doll might steal their soul. That was why they didn't want to create them or even draw portraits; it was not because they lacked the skills. Drawing portraits—like doll-making—was a taboo. That is why there are very few portraits or statues of emperors and leaders in Japan, whereas in Greece and Rome there are statues and portraits of emperors and heroes everywhere. In ancient Japan, only the Buddha was made into statues. All this may sound odd to modern society, but that was the ancient belief. Craftsmen devoted their lives to the solemnity of their work. Doll-making only became a common hobby in, perhaps, the late 1920s."

"So the idea of Azoth was…"

"Well, it might have been of interest intellectually, but it was a completely outrageous concept, of course. Using real humans to make a doll is against the rules; it's against nature. Given history, I can well imagine where Umezawa got his ideas from. Perhaps most of the serious doll-makers of my generation would understand it. But none of them would ever follow the path he took. It's a matter of principle. Umezawa's ideas were very far from those of a doll-maker."

"That's very interesting. I begin to understand what you mean, Mr Yoshida. But you said you thought that Umezawa probably died. Why do you think that?"

"That would be my guess. As both a doll-maker and a fortune-teller, I was curious about the case. And besides, as you know, I knew Yasukawa, who was Umezawa's friend. There was a slight possibility Umezawa was alive, but in order to prove it, I would have required specific evidence, which I didn't have. My hunch was based on intuition, not logic. I would put it like this, Mr Ishioka. Suppose Umezawa had survived, he would still need to have had contact with society. Even if he hid in a mountain, he would need to eat. It's not as simple to do that as one might think. If villagers saw Umezawa hunting for food, they would think he was a vagrant and report him to the police. And if Umezawa chose to live in town, then his neighbours would want to know who he was and where he came from.

"Japanese people are very nosy—in fact, I think they pay too much attention to others. Japan is an island, and because of our island-nation mentality, any community would soon grow suspicious of someone like Umezawa, wherever he tried to live. Suppose he had killed himself after he created Azoth; his body would surely have been found. Someone else would have had to bury it or burn it. He could not have done that alone, obviously. And so it seems unthinkable that Umezawa remained alive."

"Did you talk about this with Yasukawa?"

"Yes, I did."

"What did he say?"

"He wouldn't listen to me. He was a bit fanatical about his own notions."

"Yes, I heard he believed that Umezawa was still alive… But what did he think happened to Azoth?"

"According to him, it was created and placed somewhere in the country."

"Did he mention any specific location?"

"Yes, he did," Yoshida replied, suddenly bursting into laughter.

"Where did he say it was?!"

"In Meiji-Mura… Meiji Village. Do you know the place?"

"I've only heard the name."

"It's a theme park, which the Meitetsu railway company developed in Inuyama, in Aichi Prefecture, north of Nagoya. Everything is based on life in the Meiji era (1868–1912) and it contains dozens of real buildings from that time. By coincidence, that's where I've been today."

"Really? But where in Meiji-Mura is Azoth? Buried somewhere?"

"Well, in the park there's an old post office, from Uji-Yamada, which exhibits mementos of the Japanese postal service through the years. It includes mannequins of postmen in uniform from different periods, old-fashioned postboxes—that kind of thing."

"So it's like a museum?"

"Yes. Now in the exhibition there's a single female mannequin, which has been placed in the corner. Yasukawa insisted that she was Azoth!"

"Huh?… That's unbelievable! But couldn't we trace where it came from? That would be possible, wouldn't it?"

"Oh, there's no need for you to trace its origin, Mr Ishioka. That was a project I was involved in personally. You see, I was on the team of the Owari Mannequin Company of Nagoya that travelled back and forth between Nagoya and Kyoto, making the mannequins for the village. But something mysterious did occur: on opening day, we noticed that a mannequin that we had not made had been added to the display. The craftsmen at Owari had no idea where it had come from. It was a mannequin of a woman. None of us had been asked to make a female mannequin, so we concluded that the administrators of Meiji-Mura had changed their minds and included one at the last moment. It's not entirely crazy that Yasukawa thought it was Azoth, because the mannequin did have a very strange aspect about it."

"Were you at Meiji-Mura today to repair the mannequins?"

"No. I went to see a friend, who used to be a fellow craftsman. I must confess I love that place; it reminds me of my youth in Tokyo. They transferred many old buildings there, you know: part of the old Imperial Hotel—which was designed by Frank Lloyd Wright—the old Sumida River Bridge—things like that. There are few visitors on weekdays, so it's very relaxing to be there. Tokyo's too crowded; I could never live there any more. Kyoto's fine, but I think Meiji-Mura is great. I sometimes envy my friend being able to work there."

"Is it such a nice place?"

"Oh, it's a perfect place. I don't know if young people would agree with me, though."

"But, going back to the female mannequin… Do you still laugh at Mr Yasukawa's idea about it being Azoth?"

"Well, Yasukawa was always lost in his fantasies. I never took him seriously."

"But he moved to Kyoto to be near you, didn't he?"

"I have no idea," Yoshida smiled, with perhaps a trace of bitterness.

"You must have been close friends?"

"He visited me often. I shouldn't speak ill of the dead, but, to tell you the truth, Yasukawa grew quite irrational in his later days. Trying to solve the Zodiac Murders became his obsession. As you know, it was a hobby of many people, but for Yasukawa it turned into a kind of mania. He would discuss the case with everyone he met. He was also ill. He always had a small bottle of cheap whisky in his pocket. I told him he should quit drinking, but he brushed me off. He didn't care. He would sip his whisky and launch into notions about the murders, whether his listeners had the slightest interest or not. So eventually people began to avoid him. His visits became less frequent after I expressed my uneasiness with him. But whenever he had a dream, he would come over to tell me about it in detail. Most of the time, he didn't make any sense. He'd lost touch with reality. The last straw was when he pointed to a friend of mine and said, 'This man is Heikichi Umezawa!' He then threw himself on the floor, bowing and crying and saying, 'It's been so long since I've seen you, Mr Umezawa!' My friend had a scar over his eyebrow, and that appeared to be what set Yasukawa off."

"Did Umezawa have a scar?"

"I have no idea. Perhaps only Yasukawa knew."

"Are you still in contact with that friend of yours?"

"Yes, he's among my closest friends. He's the one I went to see in Meiji-Mura."

"I see. May I ask his name?"

"Hachiro Umeda."

"Hachiro Umeda?!"

"Please don't draw any hasty conclusions, Mr Ishioka. Yasukawa strongly believed that Hachiro Umeda was Heikichi Umezawa. Their names may sound alike, but there is no proof whatsoever that they are the same person. Umeda is a very common name in the Kansai area, and in fact the largest station in Osaka is located in a place called Umeda."

Although Yoshida tried to deny any connection, my suspicion was growing stronger. I was focusing less on his friend's last name than on the first—Hachiro. *Hachi* means "eight" and there were exactly eight victims in the astrology murders: Heikichi (or his double, if my idea was correct), Kazue and the six Umezawa girls.

"As far as I know," Yoshida went on, "Umeda has never lived in Tokyo. He's younger than I am, so he cannot be Umezawa. Perhaps Yasukawa was confused because he thought Umeda resembled Umezawa in his younger days."

"And what does Mr Umeda do at Meiji-Mura?"

"He's an attendant at the Kyoto Shichijo Police Station, another genuine building from the Meiji era. He plays the part of a policeman, wearing a nineteenth-century police uniform with a sabre."

I was just thinking about how I could meet this man, when Yoshida interrupted me as if he had read my mind. "You may wish to see him, but I must insist that you should not think he is really Heikichi Umezawa. He's much younger than Umezawa would have been today, and he has a totally different personality; Umeda's a natural-born comedian, whereas Heikichi Umezawa was antisocial and introspective. In addition, Umezawa was left-handed; Umeda's right-handed."

As I was taking my leave and thanking Yoshida for his time, his wife came out to say goodbye, bowing deeply. Yoshida walked out to the street with me. "Meiji-Mura is open from ten to five in spring," he said. "Arrive early. It will take you a few hours to look around."

I thanked him again, and walked towards the bus stop. I looked at the setting sun, hoping it was not a reflection of what was to come.

—

When I got back to Emoto's apartment, I found him calmly listening to music. But Kiyoshi was nowhere in sight.

"Where's Kiyoshi? Have you seen him at all?" I asked.

"Yes, I met him just as he was going out," Emoto replied.

"How was he?"

"Well… um… he looked furious. He didn't tell me where he was going. He only said 'I'll never give up!' and then stormed out."

Very curious. But I had my own fish to fry, so I asked Emoto if I could borrow his car the next day.

"Oh, please do," he replied.

I decided not to stay up late, because I was exhausted. I set the alarm, hoping to get an early start. I didn't know whether the traffic in Kyoto was as bad as in Tokyo, but I reckoned I could probably avoid the rush hour if I left around six. I wouldn't have any time to see Kiyoshi, but it couldn't be helped. He was obviously following his own path; and so should I. I could talk to him when I got back in the evening.

I spread my futon on the floor, and set out Kiyoshi's, returning the favour. I pulled a blanket over myself and was soon fast asleep.

SCENE 6

The Mannequin

I had a weird dream. When I awoke, I couldn't remember what it had been about, but the effects of it remained.

Kiyoshi was still asleep. I heard him groan when I pulled myself out of my futon.

It was chilly outside, but the air was refreshing, and I was fully awake by the time I'd reached the bottom of the stairs.

Emoto's car started easily, and I drove to the Meishin Highway. The traffic was flowing smoothly. A billboard in a field to the left came into view. A girl was smiling sitting next to a refrigerator, her hair flying in the wind. Suddenly, the dream came back to me. A beautiful woman, completely naked, had been floundering in the middle of the ocean, her long hair undulating with the waves. Her lower chest, her stomach, and her knees all seemed unnaturally thin, as if tied up with a rope. She was looking straight at me, but I didn't recognize her. She seemed to be beckoning to me in the cold silence. And then she disappeared beneath the dark waves.

It gave me goosebumps just recalling it. Could it have been some kind of message from Azoth? I suddenly remembered the mystical charm that had haunted Tamio Yasukawa, and the man who had gone mad and jumped into the ocean...

I left the highway at the Komaki Interchange, and suddenly the traffic got heavier. I didn't arrive at Meiji-Mura until 11 a.m. I parked the car and boarded the shuttle bus that took visitors to the entrance of the park. The road was narrow, and the branches from the low trees kept brushing against the windows of the bus; it was like going through the woods. Then suddenly a patch of blue water came into sight—Iruka Pond. The theme park had been designed all round it like a huge open-air museum.

I followed the signs to the restoration of a typical town centre from the Meiji era. The thing that struck me most was how American it all looked. Apparently, Meiji architects were deeply influenced by Western-style construction. Very few buildings from that era remain today in Japan; rapid modernization has transfigured the urban landscape, leading to the ruin of many traditions. The British, on the other hand, still live in the same houses with the same furniture from the period of Sherlock Holmes. The typical Japanese city looks so boring and lacking in character; every new building looks like a factory or a prison. Surrounded by mortared walls and cut-out windows, people appear to have chosen to live in graveyards. The popularity of Western-style construction didn't last very long; perhaps it didn't really fit the Japanese climate. In summer, people preferred to leave their windows open in order to reduce the heat and humidity indoors. In order to protect their privacy, they piled concrete blocks around their homes. But as a result of Japan's post-war economic success, most Japanese households have now turned to air-conditioners. Soon, we may be able to get rid of those ugly concrete blocks.

As I strolled through Meiji-Mura, I began to wish that Japanese architecture would regain the openness it once had.

I passed the Oi Meat Shop and St John's Church, and then I came upon two traditional Japanese structures. One of them was the actual Tokyo house in which Soseki Natsume wrote his famous novel *I Am a Cat*. Several people were sitting on the porch. One of them was calling out, "Here, kitty kitty!" pretending to be the author. It made me wish Kiyoshi was there. He would have enjoyed mimicking the legendary writer.

One thought led to another, and I recalled a line from another Natsume novel, *The Three-cornered World*. I memorized it when I first read it:

"Approach everything rationally, and you become harsh. Pole along in the stream of emotions, and you will be swept away by the current... It is not a very agreeable place to live, this world of ours."

I would say that Kiyoshi fits the former image very well. On the other hand, I am more of an emotional type; I have always been easily swept away. Neither of us has been very successful in this material world. What Natsume said made even more sense to me now than when I first read it. Bunjiro Takegoshi was like me in that respect—he was a man of emotions. If I had found myself in his situation, I'm sure I would have done the same things he did. And, of course, the world was not a very agreeable place to live in at all for him.

Beyond Natsume's home, there were some stone steps. As I walked down them, a white cat casually crossed my path. It made me smile. Whoever kept a cat there must have a good sense of humour. The steps led down to a square, from where an old Kyoto tram slowly made its way around the town. Off to one side, a group of teenage girls were giggling as they had their picture taken with a middle-aged man in an old-fashioned policeman's uniform. He was wearing black trousers with gold piping down the seams, and there was a gold sabre attached to his belt. As the girls took their turns posing, the policeman rolled the ends of his waxed handlebar moustache, which caused the girls to shriek with laughter. Some other visitors smiled as they lined up to have their pictures taken.

Everything there seemed so pleasant and gentle. The attendants were all middle-aged and kind, and they seemed to enjoy their work. It occurred to me that the man dressed up as a Meiji policeman could be Hachiro Umeda. I decided I would return to talk to him later.

I climbed onto the tram. The elderly conductor punched my ticket, stamped it, and handed it back to me, saying "You can keep this as a memento of your ride." I wondered if life in Japan could ever have been so gracious. Certainly it was a far cry from the Tokyo subway during the rush hour.

"The lighthouse coming up on your right used to be in Shinagawa in Tokyo... and that house on your left was the home of the famous writer Rohan Koda..." The conductor spoke with the confident voice of a professional storyteller or a stage actor. Each time he pointed out some building or historical monument, the group of middle-aged women on the tram would rush from one side to the other to get a better view. They reminded me of buffaloes stampeding.

When the tram reached the terminal the conductor jumped out of his seat. Surprised by his quick movement, I watched him through the window. Despite his age and his tiny stature, he leapt up to grab the rope hanging from the pantograph like a frog leaping for a willow branch. His weight pulled it down. Then he ran beside the car as it turned on the turntable. He turned the pantograph in the opposite direction and then ran back to his seat. He signalled to the driver and the tram started up again very slowly; it resembled a cow just waking up from a nap.

The elderly man's brisk movements astonished me. Nobody seemed to be in a hurry at Meiji-Mura, and presumably there wasn't a timetable, but even so he seemed passionate about running the operation smoothly. I'm sure his family would have been worried if they could see how hard he worked. Working like that would suggest that he didn't suffer from either back pain or insomnia—but what if he had a heart attack while jumping around? Well, I suppose that would be his fate. In fact, he would probably be happier to die with the tram rope in his hands than peacefully in bed. I remembered what Shusai Yoshida had said about envying his friend working in the village. I could understand why he felt like that.

After the tram ride, I passed by the Shimbashi railway and the Shinagawa Glass Factory. Finally I came to the Uji-Yamada post office. I was ready to meet Azoth!

I walked slowly up the stone steps and entered. Inside there was an oil-coated wooden floor. My heart was almost in my mouth. Sunlight was streaming in through the high windows. Specks of dust were floating in the air. I was the only one there.

The exhibition was arranged in chronological order, beginning with a mannequin of an express messenger who delivered letters on foot. Next, there was the first postbox used by Japan's postal system. That was followed by several different designs, ending with a familiar red postbox in the shape of a column. Then there was an exhibition of postmen in different uniforms.

I was beginning to feel irritated. "Where is she?" I said to myself out loud. I turned to one side, and there, in a dark corner, was a female mannequin wearing a red kimono. Her black hair was in bangs.

Are you really her?

I approached the mannequin timidly, like a hesitant child. She was standing up straight. Her vacant black eyes stared at me. The dust on her hair and shoulders was a testament to her forty-year history.

Who are you? What do you want to tell me?

On that peaceful afternoon, facing this mysterious object, I felt so alone. I was suddenly full of fear. I began to shiver and wrapped my arms around myself. I leant on the guardrail to get a closer look; my legs felt leaden.

What if she begins to move?

I stood where I was—about six feet away—and stared at her. The mannequin seemed to have wrinkles around her eyes. Her eyes were made of glass. Her hands looked artificial.

Wait… wrinkles on her face? I must get a closer look…

I looked round. There was nobody in sight. But just as I was about to step over the guardrail, the door to the post office opened and in walked the janitor, holding a broom and a metal dustpan. She began to sweep, paying me no attention. Suddenly she dropped the dustpan and it clanged on to the floor.

Unnerved, I hurriedly left the post office…

I felt famished. I bought some pastries and milk at a kiosk and sat down on a bench. From there I could see the main entrance of the famous old Tokyo Imperial Hotel. In front of me there was a pond with a twin-arched bridge. Some swans were gliding on the water. It was so nice and quiet. There was not a soul in sight. A streak of smoke was trailing above the trees. A steam locomotive appeared from the woods, pulling three cars. It trundled over an iron bridge.

As I munched on the pastries I began to start wondering again. I was entirely perplexed. How could Tamio Yasukawa have possibly thought that *that* mannequin was Azoth? It seemed impossible. No, not *that* mannequin. Had Yasukawa really lost his mind? Or had someone replaced the real thing?

I walked back to take another look at it, but, unfortunately, there were several visitors in the post office. I stared at the doll briefly and then went to look for Hachiro Umeda.

The mustachioed policeman was sweeping the square in front of the police station when I returned. "Sayonara," a group of girls were shouting happily, bowing as they left. The police-man—who really did look the part—bowed back.

I walked up to him. "Excuse me, would you happen to be Mr Hachiro Umeda?" I asked.

"Yes, I am," he responded quite openly.

"My name is Ishioka. I'm visiting from Tokyo. Mr Shusai Yoshida mentioned your name to me. He thought I might want to meet you."

A curious expression appeared on Umeda's face. After I explained the situation to him—by now I had had a lot of practice—he put down his broom and invited me inside. He offered me a chair.

"Let me see… Yasukawa Tamiko… Yeah, yeah, I remember him. A heavy drinker. He died, didn't he? Poor old man, he would have enjoyed his life if he'd moved here. The air's clean, the food's great… Everything would have been perfect for him if alcohol was allowed in here!" He paused, smiled and continued, "I look good in this uniform, don't I? This was my dream, you know. For the chance to wear a uniform with a sabre like this, I would've happily done anything—even joined a parade or posed for a poster. So when I was offered the job here, I was very excited. I had several choices—I could have been a train conductor, a tram driver, anything—but I chose the policeman's job right away!"

He was pleasant and friendly, but he was a disappointment to me. From all indications, it was highly unlikely that this cheerful middle-aged man could have dreamt up the complicated Umezawa schemes and committed the horrible murders. Also, he looked like he was only in his late fifties, much younger than Umezawa would have been if he was still alive. Of course, it was likely that his lifestyle contributed to his youthfulness.

I asked him if he had ever heard of Heikichi Umezawa.

"Heikichi Umezawa? Ah, that's very amusing. Yasukawa got drunk once and started calling me 'Heikichi Umezawa'. I told him I wasn't called Umezawa, but he kept bowing and talking to me like I was. I looked like him, maybe? But Umezawa was a criminal, so I didn't appreciate it very much. Now if I had looked like General Nogi or the Emperor Meiji, that would've been different. That would have made me very happy!" He laughed loudly.

"Excuse me, but could I ask you where you lived in 1936? I know it's almost forty years ago, but…"

"1936? Hmm… I was twenty… That was before the war, so I was living in Takamatsu on the island of Shikoku. I worked at a liquor store."

"Were you born in Takamatsu?"

"That's right."

"But you seem to have an Osaka dialect."

"Oh, I lived in Osaka for long time, that's why. When I left the military, I couldn't find a job in my hometown, so I moved to the big city. I was hired at another liquor store, but they went bankrupt. Since then, I've had many different kinds of jobs. At one time I pulled a stall around selling *ramen* noodles; another time, I worked in a mannequin factory."

"Is that how you met Mr Yoshida?"

"No, no, I met him after I quit that job, when I was a security guard at a building in Osaka. That was over ten years ago... no... must have been nearly twenty years ago. I knew a sculptor who was renting a space for his artwork in the same building. We became friends, and he introduced me to a doll-making club in Kyoto. Shusai Yoshida was the person who started the club. He had just moved from Tokyo and was new to the area, so I offered to help if I could. Eventually, I became his doll-making assistant. He said that he was just doing it as a hobby, but he was too modest. When it comes to doll-making, there is nobody better than him. This is not just my personal opinion; all the experts say the same. He's almighty in the field. But his technique and artistry are especially brilliant when it comes to creating the faces of Western-style dolls. For Expo '70 in Osaka, he was asked to exhibit some of his dolls, and that was when our friendship developed. In order to have everything ready by opening day, we sometimes had to work through the night. It was tough work, but I enjoyed working with him a lot."

It was true—Shusai Yoshida did have a certain charisma. I had seen it myself. Yasukawa and Umeda were in his thrall;

others certainly were, too. What was the secret of his charisma? His ability in fortune-telling? His artistic sensibility?

On the other hand, Umeda seemed like such an easy-going fellow, someone who enjoyed life, that I no longer entertained the possibility he was Umezawa. I asked him about his family.

"Well, I used to be married. It was a long, long time ago, so it's hard to recall. My wife was killed in an air raid while I was in the army. But even though I was at the front, I didn't die... I don't know why. Our duty was to protect women, children and our country, but I lost her anyway. I loved her very much. Since then, I've been single, enjoying my freedom. It might be good for some people to wear the ball and chain of married life, but not me."

I didn't know how to respond to that, so I changed the subject. "Mr Yoshida was here yesterday, wasn't he?"

"Yes, he visits quite often, maybe once a month. I have the greatest fondness for him, so if I don't see him for a few weeks, I go to Kyoto to visit him."

"What was his family background?"

"Neither I nor the other club members know anything about his past," he said, "but we don't really care. I heard somebody say that he came from a rich family. He already had his own house and studio when he was young, so it must be true—but who cares? We all love him. He's like our guru. I feel very relaxed when I see him. He has great knowledge and experience in so many fields. I asked him about my future, and he was very perceptive, very wise. Let me tell you, his gift is something more than fortune-telling. Perhaps he knows everything... Yeah, that's right, he knows *everything*..."

Umeda was just speaking normally, but his last sentence left me stunned. This carefree, simple soul had understood something I'd missed entirely. The person I was looking for was a killer with supernatural power, knowledge, and intelligence, who was skilled in doll-making and fortune-telling... Could it be Shusai Yoshida?

Suddenly several details seemed to come together. Yoshida could be around eighty, the right age. More important than that, he knew something that the books did not mention: that Heikichi was left-handed. How did he know that? When Yoshida was talking about the life of a fugitive, he seemed to speak with almost first-hand knowledge. He also knew the history and philosophy of doll-making in Japan. It had the ring of something that could easily have been part of Heikichi's note.

Another question popped into my mind. Certainly Yoshida was a charming, attractive person, but what was the real reason that Tamio Yasukawa had followed him to Kyoto? Excitement surged through me.

Not realizing what was going through my mind, Umeda kept telling me how great his guru was. I waited until he was finished and then asked him about the mysterious mannequin in the post office.

"Oh, yes, I know those mannequins. Mr Yoshida and the Owari Mannequin Company created them... Oh, you already know that?... What? There's a mystery mannequin? I've never heard of it, never... Mr Yoshida doesn't know where it came from, either? Wow, really?... Hmm, why don't you ask Mr Muro-oka, the director of Meiji-Mura? He's at the main office near the entrance gate."

I thanked Umeda deeply and left the police station. He'd been so kind and easy, and I felt as if I was leaving a new-found friend. I looked back at him a bit wistfully, thinking I would probably never meet him again. He seemed so comfortable leading his uncomplicated life and wearing his favourite uniform. Almost certainly, however, he was not the man I was looking for.

At the office, I was led to the director's room. When I asked him about the female mannequin, at first he seemed surprised. Then he laughed, "It's nothing of a mystery, young man. We originally had male mannequins only, so I talked to the Meitetsu company, and the next day they brought in that female mannequin from their department store."

If this was an ordinary mystery I was solving, without a deadline looming, I might have followed up on the Meitetsu lead, but this mystery was far from ordinary—and after tomorrow our time was up. So I got back in the car and headed for Kyoto. Besides, I hadn't spoken to Kiyoshi in days. We needed to compare notes.

As I drove, my mind filled with thoughts about Shusai Yoshida, now the focus of my investigation. He was charismatic and smooth and smart, but anybody can make a slip. He was a man of means without a past. Had a magical trick been performed? Had Heikichi Umezawa been put in a black box and re-emerged as Shusai Yoshida?

The case was getting too big for me. I needed Kiyoshi's help.

I ran into the evening rush hour, so I parked the car at a rest area and had something to eat in the cafeteria. I gazed at the sunset, still thinking about Yoshida. It would be tough to challenge a mind like that. I would have to pick up on something that only the culprit could have known. But his friend Yasukawa, who had known Heikichi, was now dead; Yoshida could always claim he had heard it from him. Dead men tell no tales, so I would have no way of determining the truth.

I returned to Emoto's apartment a little after 10 p.m. Kiyoshi wasn't back, and Emoto was watching TV alone. I thanked him for the use of his car and gave him a little souvenir from Meiji-Mura. But I was too tired to tell him much about the place. I went into the bedroom, flung the two futons from the wardrobe on to the floor, crawled into mine, and fell once again into a deep sleep.

SCENE 7

The Philosopher's Walk

My sleeping habits seemed to have changed. I awoke early, at exactly the same time as the day before. Shusai Yoshida immediately came to mind. I needed to talk to Kiyoshi. I looked over at his futon, but he was already up and gone.

Such diligence, such commitment to the task!

Upon closer inspection of his futon, however, I realized it hadn't been slept in. Before I passed out the night before, I had thrown his bedding on the floor just like a fisherman tossing a net into the dark sea, and it still lay there in a heap.

Where is he? Has something happened? Is he in danger? And where the hell has he been? Has he found some vital clue?

Today was Thursday the 12th, our last day.

We need to talk. Boy do we need to talk!

My research had been useful, but I had solved nothing. Not yet. I desperately wanted to exchange information with him. Then maybe we could bring our investigation to a fruitful conclusion.

Why doesn't he call?

I tried to stay in bed, but my mind was racing. I got up. Emoto was still asleep. I got dressed quietly and went out for a walk. I paced around on the dew-soaked grass of the park, still thinking furiously.

—

When I returned, Emoto was brushing his teeth. Kiyoshi hadn't called. I decided I would have to stay put until he did.

Emoto left for work, and just as I heard his footsteps descending the stairs, the telephone rang. I jumped up and grabbed the receiver.

"Kazumi..." groaned a weak voice at the other end. It took me a few seconds to realize it was Kiyoshi.

"What's happened? Where are you? Are you all right?" I blurted out in a high-pitched voice.

"I feel sick," he said, his voice fading. Then, after a pause, he pleaded, "I think I'm dying... please... come and help me..."

"Where are you? What's going on?"

I couldn't stop myself from asking questions, but I needed to know exactly where he was. I could hear the sound of traffic and children's voices, so I assumed he was calling from a payphone on the street.

"What happened? I can't tell you right now... I'm too weak."

"OK, just tell me where you are!"

"The Philosopher's Walk... not the Ginkakuji side... the opposite side... at the entrance..."

I was confused. The Philosopher's Walk? What the hell was that? Was Kiyoshi losing his mind?

"What's the address? Can I get there by cab?"

"Yes, the driver will know. Just say the Philosopher's Walk. He'll find it... And please... buy some bread and milk... for me... please."

"Bread and milk? Sure, but why?"

"To eat, of course... What else can I do with it?"

He could be sarcastic even when he was not feeling well. Pure Kiyoshi.

217

"Are you injured?"

"No…"

"All right, I'm on my way. Stay where you are!"

I bolted out of the apartment and ran to the station. At Shijo-Kawaramachi, I bought some sandwiches and a couple of cartons of milk. I hailed a taxi. Kiyoshi was right—the driver knew where to take me.

I was clueless about what was going on. Kiyoshi sounded like he was on his last legs. Was he really dying? Was this another neurotic episode? Was he pulling my leg? Sometimes Kiyoshi could be totally obnoxious, but still he was my only true friend.

The driver dropped me at the bottom of a small slope and pointed me to the top. There was a small park, and, sure enough, a sign that said "The Philosopher's Walk". There was no one around.

I followed the path along a canal. Not far along, I came across a black dog wagging its tail and sniffing around a homeless man lying on a bench. It was Kiyoshi!

I called his name. He mumbled something and tried to sit up. He was so weak that I had to help him. Since I had last seen him, a few days before, he had undergone a radical change. His eyes were bloodshot, his cheeks were hollowed out and he needed a shave. He didn't look good at all. In fact, he looked very sick.

"Did you bring some food like I asked?" he said. I handed a sandwich to him, and he ripped the package open. "Ah, what a nuisance eating is! If we didn't have to eat, we could save so much time…" he mumbled, and then proceeded to wolf down the food.

I was relieved to see him eat, but still perplexed. He was clearly in distress, and although he still had some spark it was flickering dangerously. I was worried about his state of mind. I didn't want to think he'd fallen into manic depression.

"When did you last eat?" I asked him.

"I don't know… Maybe yesterday, maybe the day before… I forget…"

I waited while he ate, telling him not to eat so fast. When he was done, he seemed to have regained some of his energy.

"Have you made any progress with the case?" I asked gently.

"Squeeze an orange, and you'll get garbage!" he spat out angrily, standing up and waving his arms. "Kazumi, we are born to be deceived! Look at me. After running all over the place without sleep for days, I'm no better off than a dying grasshopper. One or two days of fasting is a good thing; it sharpens our senses. Oh, I can see it now. A vast field of rape flowers in bloom! The city is made of history and mystery! I see roofs, countless roofs, looking like half-open books. And I hear cars screeching everywhere! Aren't they sickening?… No, those were not rape flowers, they were cosmos! I used to be strong enough to walk through fields of cosmos. I could cut them down with a machete. Now, I can't even remember how I did that… Ah, where did I leave my machete? It must be getting rusty! I've got to find it. I've got to keep digging like a mole! Time is running out. It's now or never!"

This was insanity; Kiyoshi was going insane. I felt my whole body become numb. "No, no, no, Kiyoshi. You're exhausted. Calm down, calm down!" I repeated the same words over and over again. I grabbed his shoulders, and then slowly pushed him back down onto the stone bench.

He finally settled down, and I began to breathe a little easier. I was struck by the bitter irony of the situation: exhaustion and pressure had driven him insane, but they didn't seemed to have helped our investigation at all. I realized I shouldn't have let him get involved in the whole thing; I knew his mental health hadn't been good. But he was the one who had launched into the challenge with Takegoshi Jr. Now the result was clear: Kiyoshi would suffer in defeat. It was hopeless. Takegoshi Jr had to do nothing but wait for us to come bowing and scraping and apologizing like pathetic fools. The mystery had been unsolved for forty years; we were crazy to think we could solve it in a week. But I still held out the hope that Shusai Yoshida was really Heikichi Umezawa incarnated. It was only a glimmer of hope, but for some reason I felt confident. In his state, however, Kiyoshi could not be talked to rationally. I had to take immediate action, alone, even if I had to leave poor Kiyoshi alone on the brink of insanity. There were only a few hours left. I needed to catch Yoshida, for the sake of both of us.

It was now past 10 a.m. I was about to call Emoto for help, when Kiyoshi started talking again.

"I shouldn't have spoken ill of Sherlock Holmes. You were right, Kazumi, I should have known my place. I thought it would be easy for me, and in fact, I was almost there. God, it's all so simple—like dominoes. I just need to know where to hit them to start them falling. Just one tile—that's all I need—and then everything will fall into place! Shit! I've concentrated all my efforts on this, and now I'm losing it. I need inspiration. I need something, a little bit of something to inspire me." He held his head in his hands. "Ouch! This is great. You told me I would suffer for my pride, and now I can feel my lips swelling up. I can barely move them. How can I talk like this? I've lost my pace; it's hopeless. You, at least, seem to be doing very well. Tell me what you've discovered."

This brief flirtation with sanity—and uncharacteristic modesty—were very welcome, but his stability and clarity were another matter. This guy—my best friend—had had a nervous breakdown. And now he was going to have to eat crow in front of that arrogant detective. I couldn't abide the thought. Even if I had to do the job alone, I was determined I was going to make the effort to meet the challenge.

"C'mon, tell me what you've found out," Kiyoshi said again.

So, with measured sentences, I explained to Kiyoshi all the things I'd done: the return visit to Yasukawa's daughter; the meeting with Shusai Yoshida; the trip to Meiji-Mura to see the mannequin Yasukawa had talked about; and the conversation with Hachiro Umeda, whom Yasukawa had thought was Heikichi.

As I spoke, Kiyoshi lay on the bench, his arm under his head, looking up into the sky with vacant eyes, showing not the slightest interest. Either he really was insane or he had given up the pursuit. I was terribly disappointed.

Suddenly, he sat up straight. "It's about time for Nyakuoji to open…" he said in a sleepy voice.

"Nyakuoji? What's that? A temple?"

"It's a shrine… no, that isn't what I mean! I mean, that building over there…"

He pointed to the top of a small, Western-style clock tower.

"That's where I want to go! Forget about the shrine!"

From the Philosopher's Walk, we went down a slope and then climbed down some stone steps.

"What's that tower?"

"A coffee shop. What did you think? I need a hot drink."
Kiyoshi was coming back to life.

The coffee shop was in the courtyard of a famous actor's house. There was a Spanish-style well and several statues. Despite Kiyoshi's condition and the fact that time was running out, it was refreshing to be seated at a table in the morning sun. We were the only customers there, and the quiet made me feel more relaxed.

"Nice place," I said to Kiyoshi.

He nodded vaguely. "Yeah…"

"I think I'm going to see Yoshida now. Do you want to come with me?"

"Well, yes, I'd be happy to…"

"Come on, then!" I said, encouraged. "We have a deadline to meet…"

I stood up, grabbing the bill off the table. I had nothing smaller than a ten-thousand-yen bill, and as it was early in the day, the cashier took some time getting me my change. Kiyoshi was waiting for me outside. As we climbed the stone steps back to the Philosopher's Walk, I arranged the nine one-thousand-yen bills so that they would all be facing the same direction—it's an old habit of mine. One of the bills had been torn and taped back together. Making small talk, I showed the repaired bill to Kiyoshi.

"Tape? It's not opaque tape, is it?" he said, taking the bill in hand and studying it. "No, they used transparent tape. That's all right."

"What's wrong with opaque tape?"

"It's used for forgery, but usually with ten-thousand-yen bills. None of this cheap stuff."

"Why do they use opaque tape?"

"Because… Oh, it's too hard to explain. I need a pen and a piece of paper to show you. Anyway, forgery may be not the correct word. It's more like… maybe… cheating… perhaps…" His voice was fading. It sometimes happened. Usually, it signalled the onset of a deep depression. This was getting sad.

I turned to face Kiyoshi, who had come to a stop. I was astonished. His bloodshot eyes were open unnaturally wide. His mouth was wide open, too. He clenched his fists and started to scream: "AAAAAHHHHHH!"

A couple of tourists stopped in their tracks. The black dog stared at him.

I had often complained about Kiyoshi's oddity, but I never doubted his talent, his intelligence, his knowledge and his powers of intuition. Those were the good things about him. But they lingered just on the other side of catastrophe.

It's all over!

Kiyoshi had obviously passed through the gate of madness.

"Calm down!" I said. I grabbed him by the shoulders and tried to shake him.

His worn-out face was right in front of me. But he was not the one who was dumbstruck—I was. Kiyoshi looked like a lion—starved and weak, but still full of dignity. He had stopped screaming. Suddenly he shook off my hands and began to run.

What's he doing now? Hallucinating?

He headed straight towards the canal.

Is he going to leap in? Save a drowning kid?

I took off after him, but he was fast. After a hundred-metre dash, he stopped, turned around and ran back to me. Several passing tourists backed off. The black dog watched the madman from a distance.

Kiyoshi squatted down, his hands on his head, breathing heavily. Then he looked up at me and smiled. "Oh, Kazumi! Where have you been?"

"OK, so you're a very fast runner," I mumbled.

"I've been so stupid!" Kiyoshi yelled, not quite as loudly this time. "What have I been doing? I've been searching for the pair of glasses that are perched on top of my head! Damn! I should have put all my effort into it from the beginning! Thank God, I didn't victimize anyone with my negligence. We've been very lucky!"

"Well, *you* have been lucky. If I wasn't here, those people would have called an ambulance."

"It was just a little pin, Kazumi! And I found it! I pulled out the pin, and WHAM, everything fell into place! What a great magician! Such a simple trick! In fact, it was so simple, we never thought of it… ridiculously simple. What have I been doing? I've been like a mole digging for a radish from the opposite side of the earth… Say something, Kazumi! Laugh at me. Please, everyone, laugh at me! I want the world to laugh at me. I'm so stupid. How could I have been so blind? Any kid would have seen it. Now, I must hurry. What time is it?"

"What?"

"I asked you the time. Aren't you wearing a watch?"

"It's eleven…"

"God! What time's the last bullet train to Tokyo?"

"Er… 8.29, I think…"

"Right, I'll catch that one. Could you wait for me at Emoto's apartment? I'll call you later. So long!" He began to walk away.

"Wait, wait! Where are you going?"

"To meet the killer, of course!"

I was stunned. "Are you crazy? You don't even know where he is, but you're still working on it?"

"It'll take a while, but don't worry. It'll be done by the evening."

I had been on Kiyoshi's roller coaster all morning, and I felt like I was about to faint. "You don't know what you're doing, Kiyoshi," I said. "We're not talking about going to a lost-and-found office. What do we do about Yoshida? Aren't we going to meet him?"

"Yoshida who? Who is he? Oh yes, you mentioned him. No, no, there's no need to see him."

"But why not?" I said, my voice raised.

"Because he isn't the murderer."

"How do you know?"

"Don't you understand? Because now I know who did it!"

"Wait! You can't be serious?"

Kiyoshi turned the corner and disappeared.

I stood there helpless and exhausted.

What did I do to deserve such a friend? If this is fate, I must have done something very bad in my previous life.

Now that I was alone again, I had to make a decision. Should I go to see Yoshida? Kiyoshi had said to forget him, but did he really know more than I did?

Ridiculously simple? A ridiculously simple case? What is so ridiculously simple in this case? There has never been a case so ridiculously complicated! Even a kid could see it? Even a kid could see he's mad...

225

Suppose Kiyoshi had suddenly seen the light, could he possibly find the killer by the evening?

People have been trying to solve this case for forty years—forty years!—and Kyoshi is just going off to find the killer like finding an umbrella he left at a phone booth five minutes ago. If I'm wrong, I'll walk all around Kyoto on my hands...

Kiyoshi could not possibly have obtained any more information than I had. He'd been lying on that bench, starving himself. He hadn't met Yoshida and he hadn't met Umeda. And now, he was saying he knew who did it.

How dare he say that!

I was supposed to wait for his call at Emoto's apartment. That meant he expected me to do nothing and trust that he knew what he was doing.

He surely didn't know what he was doing just a few minutes ago. But what if he needs my help? What should I do? What about my intuition?

My intuition, finally, was to put all my doubts aside and try to figure out how Kiyoshi was going to solve the mystery. What had triggered this sudden realization? It had happened when he saw my taped-up thousand-yen bill. I pulled out my wallet, and looked at it. Nothing was odd about it; there was just a piece of tape on it where it had been torn. What could he have discovered from that? The tape was on both sides of the bill; Kiyoshi had just looked at the front.

What's on the front? Anything written?... Nope. Everything looks legitimate. The face of the legendary statesman Hirobumi Ito. Something about his name? Can't be. Something about it being a one-thousand yen bill? Could be. Frankly, I don't have a clue. Try again: a one-thousand-yen bill means money, financial matters. A fight over money—OK, but that's nothing new. Maybe it's—what did he call it?—forgery! Something faked, something counterfeit. Yes! Maybe the murders were faked. Maybe they were a decoy, drawing attention away from some other crime? Nope, that makes no sense either. What other crime, anyway? He said that the bill could be faked if opaque tape were used, but usually it was a ten-thousand-yen bill, not a one-thousand-yen one. So, the higher the denomination the better? That means hundred-thousand-yen bills, if they existed, would be better than ten-thousand-yen bills. But what's the point about opaque tape? Counterfeiters print fake money. They don't put tape on existing bills... Ah, I don't understand!

I gave up trying to figure Kiyoshi out. I would wait for him at Emoto's apartment as he requested. Exhaustion was one reason. Not knowing what else to do was another. I just didn't want that fine line between a madman and a genius to get blurred.

ENTR'ACTE

Message from the Author

Gentle Reader,

Unusual as it may be for the author to intrude into the proceedings like this, there is something I should like to say at this point.

All of the information required to solve the mystery is now in your hands, and, in fact, the crucial hint has been provided already. I wonder if you noticed it? My greatest fear is that I might already have told you too much about the case! But I dared to do that both for the sake of fairness of the game, and, of course, to provide you with a little help.

Let me throw down the gauntlet: I challenge you to solve the mystery before the final chapters!

And I wish you luck.

Yours sincerely,

Soji Shimada

ACT FOUR

The Storm

The Teahouse

I decided not to think about the case any more. Otherwise, I wouldn't be able to sit still waiting for Kiyoshi's call and I'd run out to see Yoshida. I needed to be where Kiyoshi could reach me, but how was I going to kill the time?

Back at Emoto's apartment, I ate lunch as slowly as I could. I placed the telephone close to me and lay down on the floor. I was still uncomfortable about waiting, but I was determined to cheer myself up. At least my best friend had risen from the grave, regained his positive attitude and was on the move again. Twenty minutes later, the telephone rang. It was much too soon to be Kiyoshi. "Hello, you've reached Emoto," I answered.

"I don't believe it! It sounds to me like I've reached Ishioka!" It was Kiyoshi.

"Is that you? What's up? Where are you?"

"I'm in Arashiyama."

"Great. That's where I saw the cherry blossoms, which you weren't interested in at all. How's the brainwork going?"

"Better than ever!" he said, sounding buoyant. "You know Togetsu-kyo, the long wooden bridge? Well, there's a telephone booth near it in the shape of a shrine."

"Yes, I know it."

"Well, that's where I'm calling you from. Across the street, there's a teahouse by the name of Kotogiki Chaya. Their rice cakes are excellent—no sweet beans inside. Come and join us. I'd like you to meet someone."

"Sure. But who is it?"

"You'll see. Just come!" It was typical Kiyoshi again—which I reckoned I should be glad about.

"Is this a social thing? Are you just killing time? Have you forgotten about the murderer?"

"Oh, no. You'll really want to meet this person. And if you don't, I guarantee you'll never forgive me. So hurry up and get over here! She is very famous and very busy. She won't be able to stay long."

"Is she a movie star or something?"

"Hmm, that's right, yes, a star—a very big star. Hey, the sky's clouding over. Looks like rain. Bring an umbrella for me, will you, and borrow one from Emoto for yourself. Hurry up! See you soon!"

I was on my way in a flash, two umbrellas in hand.

But what was going on? A movie star? I mean, meeting a movie star might be nice, but how was this going to help us?

When I got off the train at Arashiyama, the sky had grown very dark, and the wind had picked up. By the time I got to the bridge, there were flashes of lightning in the distance. A spring storm was approaching as fast as my heart was racing.

There were few customers in the teahouse. Kiyoshi was sitting near the window on a bench covered with a red cloth, which was common in traditional teahouses. With him was a woman in a kimono. He waved me over to them, and I took a seat beside him. There was a good view of the bridge.

"What would you like?" A waitress had come up behind me to take my order.

"*Sakura mochi*, please," Kiyoshi answered, ordering me the cherry rice cakes which were the speciality of the place. He handed several coins to the waitress.

Although the mystery guest kept her face down, I was able to study her closely. Her face was thin but very pleasant to look at. She looked to be forty-five or fifty years old, and must have been very beautiful as a young woman. She didn't touch the tea and rice cake in front of her. Why didn't she look up at us? Was she really a movie star?

Kiyoshi didn't introduce us, and this made me very uncomfortable as well. "We'll talk when you get your cake and tea," Kiyoshi said.

We sat there in silence.

After the waitress brought my *sakura mochi*, Kiyoshi suddenly broke the silence.

"This is Kazumi Ishioka," he began, speaking to the mystery guest. "He and I have been working together."

The lady looked up at me for the first time, smiled and bowed slightly. She seemed a bit shy, like a teenage girl. At the same time, there was a maturity and modesty about her. She was very lovely.

Kiyoshi then slowly turned to me, and said an unbelievable thing: "Let me introduce you to Taeko Sudo. She is the person we have admired for so long. She is the culprit in the Tokyo Zodiac Murders…"

I was speechless. I couldn't believe what I was hearing. I thought I would faint. The moments of silence that followed Kiyoshi's statement felt as long as forty years.

Suddenly, a streak of lightning flashed through the teahouse and the silence was broken by a massive roar of thunder. The waitress tried to muffle her scream. Then there came the sound of large drops of rain beating on the roof, and within seconds the rain was falling in torrents.

The view through the window turned into a *sumi-e* ink painting as the rain drove against it. We could see people racing for shelter; some came dashing into the teahouse, clattering the sliding wooden door at the entrance and speaking in loud voices.

I saw this all in a trance—as if all the things in the world were slowly vanishing. A great sense of exhaustion overtook me. I imagined a piece of paper burning and shrinking...

Is Kiyoshi kidding me as usual? If he is, the lady is taking him very seriously...

I returned to the moment. Taeko Sudo? I'd never heard the name. How did Kiyoshi find out that she was the murderer? Did it mean that the murders were committed by someone outside the family? But she only looked about fifty. At the time of the murders, she would have been only a child. How could a child have killed Heikichi, Kazue and the six girls?

Don't tell me those crimes were committed by a kid! Is this the woman who blackmailed Bunjiro Takegoshi? Is this the woman who sawed and sliced up the bodies of six girls to create Azoth? Does this mean it wasn't Heikichi, Yoshio, Ayako, Yasukawa or Yoshida, but this woman alone? Why? What was her relationship to the Umezawas? There was no Taeko in the family tree. Where did she come from? Thousands of people have tried to solve this mystery, but nobody knew of her existence? How could a kid have done it?

And, most importantly, how could Kiyoshi possibly have found her in such a short time? Only a few hours had passed since he ran off from me. Forty years had passed, and then the case was solved in a couple of hours? How could that be?

The rain continued to pour down, punctuated with flashes of lightning. The teahouse grew humid. Still the three of us sat there silently, probably looking like mannequins.

As the storm began to subside, it was Taeko who spoke first.

"I always expected that someone would find me," she said, her voice slightly husky, suggesting she might be older than she appeared. "I couldn't believe the mystery remained unsolved for so long, but I had a feeling that the person who solved the case would be a young man such as yourself."

"Please allow me to ask you one question," Kiyoshi said matter-of-factly. "Why did you stay here? You could have moved anywhere to keep yourself hidden. You were smart enough to learn a foreign language. You could have lived abroad."

The sky had lightened to a yellowish grey, as the rain kept falling quietly.

"It's difficult to explain… Maybe because I have been waiting to meet you… I was so lonely, you see, having never found a man to love. I believed that whoever solved the mystery and found me would have a mindset similar to mine… Oh, I'm not saying that you are an evil person like me or capable of doing the things I did…"

"I understand what you mean," Kiyoshi responded seriously.

"I am so glad to meet you at last."

"I am thrice as glad to meet you," said Kiyoshi.

"And you are a very talented young man. I am sure you will accomplish great things in the future."

"Thank you. But I wonder if I will ever have the chance to get involved in so challenging a case as this again."

"No one can know that, so don't get too much satisfaction from solving this one mystery."

"Don't worry. It was not easy because I was blind for so long. Well, we must go before I become too self-congratulatory about my little achievement. It's very regrettable, Miss Sudo, but when I return to Tokyo, I must report you to a policeman—the son of Bunjiro Takegoshi, as a matter of fact. On a dare, I told him I would solve the mystery. It may have been my pride that made me do it. He had a boorish attitude, and yet I felt a kind of obligation. If I told you why, you would understand. I must meet him tomorrow. Probably he and his fellow detectives will visit you tomorrow evening. You still have time to escape. I certainly won't stop you. It's your choice."

"Even though the statute of limitations has run out, you shouldn't help a criminal," she said very simply.

Kiyoshi turned away and laughed. "Unfortunately, I've never been to prison. I wish I could explain what it feels like."

"You are fearless. I used to be, too, when I was young."

"I thought that the squall would pass quickly, but it seems to be lingering. Please take this umbrella with you," Kiyoshi said, handing my umbrella to her.

Taeko hesitated. "But I won't be able to return it to you."

"Don't worry. It's not very valuable," said Kiyoshi with a smile. The three of us stood up to leave. We stepped outside. I was dying with curiosity, but I didn't want to destroy the atmosphere that enveloped the two of them. I felt like an outsider, so I kept quiet.

Taeko opened her purse, and with her left hand she pulled out a red and white silk sachet. "You've been most kind. Let me return your kindness with this."

Kiyoshi accepted the gift with his own left hand and thanked her, somewhat brusquely. He glanced down at it.

Taeko Sudo, under my umbrella, bowed deeply, first to Kiyoshi and then to me. I was flustered, but I bowed in return to her. And then she walked slowly away.

Kiyoshi and I, under one umbrella, headed towards the bridge. As we crossed over it, I turned back. Taeko had turned to look back at us as well, and she bowed again. Kiyoshi and I bowed, too. I couldn't believe that she was really the serial killer who had caused such a sensation. She kept walking slowly, and nobody paid any attention to her.

The rain tapered off, as the drama of the moment passed.

"Will you explain it all to me later?" I asked Kiyoshi.

"Of course I will, if you're interested."

"You don't think I am?"

"Of course you are, but I just thought you might not want to admit you lost the game."

I was silent.

SCENE 2

The Roll of the Dice

When we returned to Emoto's apartment, Kiyoshi made a phone call. He seemed to be talking to Misako Iida.

"Yes, the case has been solved... Yes, the culprit is still alive. We just met... Who is it? Well, if you'd like to know, please come to my office tomorrow afternoon. What's your brother's name?... Fumihiko? Hmm, I didn't expect that he would have such a sweet name! He is free to join us, of course, but please remind him to bring his father's note with him. If he doesn't bring the note, I won't talk to him... Yes, I'll be in all day tomorrow. Any time is OK, but please give me a call before you come... Goodbye." Kiyoshi hung up, and then dialled another number. He was calling Emoto at work.

I found a broom and began to sweep the room we'd stayed in. After the call, Kiyoshi continued to sit absent-mindedly in the middle of the room, staring off into space. I had to chase him away with the broom.

When we arrived at Kyoto Station, Emoto was already there, waiting on the platform.

"These are for you. Please enjoy them," he said, handing us two *bento* lunchboxes. "Please come and visit me again."

"Thank you very much," I replied. "You've been so kind.

I had a very good time. Please visit us in Tokyo whenever you can. Thank you so much for everything."

"Oh, I didn't do anything. My friends just come and stay and go. Feel free to use my place any time. I'm happy to hear that the case has been solved."

"Me too, but I don't understand it yet myself. I'm still puzzled. Only this unshaven genius knows the truth," I said, pointing to Kiyoshi.

"And he's still keeping it a secret?"

"That's right," Kiyoshi piped up wryly.

"He's never changed. He loves to hide things, but he never remembers where he's hidden them! If you clean his room, you'll find his stuff everywhere."

"I just hope he doesn't forget how he solved the mystery."

"Make him explain everything while he remembers."

"I wonder why so many fortune-tellers are cranks?"

"Usually it's because they're elderly," Emoto said.

"So he's already one of those stubborn old guys... at his tender age!"

"So young, yes. I feel sorry for him!"

"Hey gentlemen, it's time to leave!" Kiyoshi said, interrupting our silly conversation. "Our train will soon be taking us back to an era five hundred years ago. We shall put on Roman armour and ride on a white mule again!"

"See? He's always like this," I said to Emoto.

"It must tire you out," he replied sympathetically.

"But if and when I hear his explanation, I'll let you know. It will probably be a very long letter."

"I'm looking forward to it. Please come and visit me again soon."

—

As the bullet train ran though fields gleaming in the sunset, I pressed Kiyoshi to explain everything.

"Couldn't you give me just a hint? That wouldn't hurt, would it?"

Kiyoshi was tired, but he couldn't resist feeling superior. "As you saw, it was the transparent tape."

"How can that be? You're kidding!"

"I have never been more serious. It was more than a key; it solved the whole mystery."

I was so confused.

"So Yasukawa and his daughter, Shusai Yoshida and Hachiro Umeda didn't provide any key to the mystery at all?"

"Hmm. Well, they were related to the case, but we didn't need them."

"You mean we already had all the information necessary to solve the case?"

"Yes, of course we did. Nothing is left to circumstance."

"But, wait… we didn't already know Taeko Sudo's address, did we?"

"Oh yes, we did."

"From the information we had?"

"From the information we had."

"But you must have obtained some new information— something I didn't know—while I was running back and forth between Kyoto, Osaka and Nagoya."

"Absolutely not. I only took a nap beside the Kamo River. Actually, we could have visited Taeko Sudo right after we got to Kyoto. We were just incredibly inefficient."

"But who is she? Is that her real name?"

"No, of course not."

"Do I know her real name?... I do, don't I? Please tell me! And what about Azoth? Was she really made?"

"Azoth?... Hmm, yes, she exists," Kiyoshi replied. "Azoth stood up, moved and committed all those crimes."

I was dumbfounded. "What? But how?"

"It was magic, of course."

"So you're joking," I said, my excitement subsiding. "That's right. It would never be real... But who was that woman? I have no idea."

Kiyoshi opened his eyes slightly and grinned.

"You've got to tell me, Kiyoshi. This is intolerable! I'm dying to know!"

"I'm going to sleep for a little while, so please ponder the case and relax," Kiyoshi chuckled, leaning his head on the window.

"As a friend of mine, don't you think you have an obligation to tell me everything now? We've been working together, after all. You're putting our friendship at risk, you know."

"Oh, so now you're starting to threaten me? I didn't say I would never explain it to you, but I can't do it in an offhand way. When the time comes, I will tell you everything step by step. I am exhausted physically and mentally. I won't be able to rest if you bother me with all your questions. So, please relax and sleep. All will be revealed in my office tomorrow."

"But I'm not sleepy!"

"Maybe not. But I am. I have barely eaten for two days. I haven't slept in a clean bed. I haven't shaved for several days. My beard irritates my skin when I lean my face against the window. I would like to shave right now. Why should men have to bear such a nuisance?" Kiyoshi turned to look at me. "All right, I'll give you one more hint. How old do you think Taeko Sudo is?"

"A little younger than fifty?"

"Come on. You're an illustrator, aren't you? You couldn't tell? Well, she's actually sixty-six."

"Sixty-six?! Then, she was twenty-six years old forty years ago..."

"Forty-three years ago."

"Ah right. So she was twenty-three then?... I've got it! She was one of the six dead girls! But that means someone else's body must have taken the place of hers, right?"

Kiyoshi yawned. "That's all for today's preview. But just think: could she have found a ballet dancer of the same age that easily?"

"What? You mean I'm wrong? Shit! I won't be able to sleep tonight!"

"That's good. For the sake of our friendship, have a sleepless night, just as I did. You'll feel much better tomorrow," Kiyoshi said, closing his eyes contentedly.

"You're enjoying watching me suffer, aren't you?"

"No, I'm not. My eyes are closed."

After a few seconds of that charade, Kiyoshi, miraculously rested, opened his eyes, took out the sachet that Taeko Sudo had given him and started to study it.

The sky was aglow with the setting sun. I thought of the storm at Arashiyama several hours ago. I thought of the last seven days in Kyoto. Different places, different people, so many different things. All in one week.

"I guess all my running around was useless, then, huh?"

"That isn't true," Kiyoshi said, as he played with the sachet absent-mindedly.

"Why do you say that?"

"Because you had such a good time in Meiji-Mura."

When Kiyoshi turned the sachet upside down, out fell two dice. He rolled them around in his hand. "You know, Taeko said that she thought the case would be solved by a young man?"

I nodded.

"Was she satisfied with us?" Kiyoshi asked.

"What do you mean?"

"Oh, I'm just talking to myself."

Kiyoshi kept playing with the dice as the brilliant sunset faded into night.

"The magic show is over," Kiyoshi said.

As we raced back towards Tokyo, I sat thinking about Taeko Sudo. What would happen to her? I didn't know anything about the law, but—according to Kiyoshi—the statue of limitations for murder is fifteen years under Japanese law. So she could not be punished for her crimes. However, thinking about the sensationalism of her crime, she would never lead a quiet life again...

ENTR'ACTE

Another Message from the Author

Dear Reader,

Let us leave Kiyoshi and Kazumi speeding back to Tokyo for a moment.

Before you continue, I should just like to say that Kiyoshi was not exaggerating. By the time he and Kazumi arrived at Kyoto Station, you could have identified the murderer. I continued the story, however, because I thought you might be in need of some more hints. After all, the case had remained unsolved for more than forty years, so there was a good chance you were still confused!

Why not pause at this point and see if you can answer two very simple questions before all is revealed in the following pages:

1. Who is Taeko Sudo? Well, in fact, her identity has already been revealed.

2. How did she accomplish her murderous plan? Have you determined the type of magic she used?

I wish you luck in your pursuit of the truth.

Yours sincerely,

Soji Shimada

ACT 5

Magic in the
Mists of Time

The Invisible Killer

Early in the morning of Friday the 13th, I got off the train at Tsunashima Station. Everything was quiet in the morning mist, although that same area at night is boisterous and bright with all the neon signs of the love hotels. I hadn't slept well the night before. The more I thought about Taeko, the more confused I got. Kiyoshi had revealed very little, and I was still stuck. I realized now that none of my reasoning had risen above the level of mediocrity. I had breakfast at a coffee shop and tried to anticipate the day ahead. It would be a day to remember.

When I got to Kiyoshi's office, however, he was still asleep. So I washed the coffee cups left in the sink and prepared places for the two visitors who were expected. Then I put the stereo on low and lay down on the sofa. I dozed off. Eventually, Kiyoshi emerged from his bedroom, yawning and scratching his head. He was already dressed and clean-shaven; in fact, he looked very dapper. "Did you sleep well?" I asked.

"So-so," he replied. "You're here early. Bet you couldn't sleep last night, huh?"

"Because today is a historic day."

"Historic? Why?"

"Well, today is the day the great mystery is finally revealed. You're the one who's going to deliver the truth, so you must be as excited as I am."

"Delivering the truth to that gorilla, Takegoshi Jr? I won't enjoy that very much. The historic moment has already come and gone. But I'm willing to explain the case to you."

"However, today's meeting is official; it's not only for my sake."

"Clearing up the mess officially, huh?" Kiyoshi responded.

"Whatever. There are only a couple of listeners today, but they will soon spread the story."

"Oh, yeah, that's thrilling," Kiyoshi sniffed. "I'd better brush my teeth."

He didn't seem excited or nervous at all—if anything, he just seemed reluctant.

"Kiyoshi, today you're a hero!" I said to encourage him when he reappeared.

"I'm not interested in being a hero or being treated as one. I solved the mystery; that's all. I don't want to be decorated! What a bore! Good paintings don't need to be framed, you know… The thought that I'm going to help that thug of a cop disgusts me. If I didn't care about his father, I wouldn't tell him anything. People, huh!"

Mrs Iida phoned a little after noon. She said she and her brother would arrive in about an hour. While we waited, Kiyoshi drew some diagrams in a notebook.

Finally, there was a knock on the door.

"Hello, please come in," Kiyoshi said. He looked perplexed when Mrs Iida entered with someone else, not her brother. "Oh, where's Fumihiko? Isn't he coming?"

"He wasn't able to come today, so my husband has accompanied me. This is Mr Iida."

Iida bowed to us twice. He was a modest-looking man who looked more like the manager of a kimono shop than a detective.

"He is with the police department, too, so there should be no problem," Mrs Iida continued. "I also wish to apologize for my brother's rudeness when he met you, Mr Mitarai. I regret that very much."

"Well, I am also sorry he couldn't be here," Kiyoshi replied, trying to contain his sarcasm. "I wonder if he would have been absent if I had failed to solve the case. Well, we must understand that a man in such a high position is always busy. Mr Ishioka, aren't you fixing coffee for us?"

I hurried off to the kitchen.

When everyone was settled and I had served the coffee, Kiyoshi went over and stood in front of a small blackboard.

"I asked you to come here today," he began, "because I wanted to explain the Tokyo Zodiac Murders. But first, do you have your father's note with you?... Very good. May I have it, please?"

The legacy of Bunjiro Takegoshi was very important to Kiyoshi. The policeman had suffered his entire life, and Kiyoshi had worked passionately to redeem his honour. When he accepted the note from Mrs Iida, I noticed that the blood vessels on the back of his hand stood out.

"It's not difficult to tell you the name of the murderer. She now goes by the name of Taeko Sudo, and she sells small hand-bags at her boutique near Seiryoji Temple in Sagano in Kyoto. The name of her shop is Megumi. There are no other shops in Sagano named Megumi, so you will find it easily enough. May I end this meeting now? You will know the whole story when you ask her for the details—unless you wish for me to continue? Shall I? All right, then, let me continue. It will be a long story…"

Kiyoshi's explanation was so brilliant, so coherent and well articulated, that I wished we could have had a thousand people in that small office, listening to him.

"The case was really very simple. Taeko Sudo killed all the Umezawas single-handed. Then why, we may ask, did such a simple crime remain unsolved for forty years? It is because Taeko Sudo, serial killer, made herself invisible. As Mr Ishioka conjectured earlier, it was, indeed, the work of magic. But it was not magic performed by Heikichi Umezawa, as he imagined; the magician was Taeko. The success of her plan was based on the Umezawas' astrological background. So perhaps it should be called the magic of astrology. But I will come to that later.

"First, let's consider the enigma of Heikichi Umezawa's death in his locked studio. As you will recall, all of the windows had iron grilles, there were no hidden exits and the door was secured with a sliding bar and a padlock. Moreover, due to the heavy snow that day, visitors to the studio could not have come or gone without leaving shoe prints.

"Heikichi had taken some sleeping pills before he was killed. His beard was cut short, but there were no scissors or razor at the scene of the crime. There were two lines of prints left in the snow. One was made by a man's shoes, the other by a woman's shoes. It appeared that the man walked away from the studio after the woman. It stopped snowing at 11.30 p.m., and so the presumed time of Heikichi's death was between 11 p.m. and 1 a.m. A model was believed to be sitting for Heikichi that evening, but she was never found.

"So, how many possible scenarios can we think of? Well, I have come up with six. One: the murder occurred right after 11 p.m. and the killer left immediately. The snow covered up his shoe prints. The two lines of shoe prints were made by two other people. Two: Heikichi was killed by his model. Three: the person who wore the man's shoes killed Heikichi. Four: those two people worked together. Five: the model intentionally made two different types of shoe prints. Six: the person who wore the man's shoes was trying to trick us with the pair of woman's shoes.

"Now some people have speculated that Heikichi's bed was pulled up to the ceiling and then dropped. However, that does not seem at all feasible to me, so we will dispense with that theory altogether.

"The business of the shoe prints is very interesting. But no matter how logically we approach it, the clues lead us nowhere. This is part of the reason why the case remained unsolved for so long. However, finding no answer is actually an exquisite key to this mystery. You see, it is the pauses between the notes that make the music!"

After that dramatic statement, Kiyoshi paused for a sip of coffee.

"Now, let's look again at these six scenarios. The first has some plausibility, I admit. But if two people had witnessed the murder scene after the killer left, they never revealed themselves. Why? If they wanted to hide their reason for visiting Heikichi's studio, they could have sent an anonymous letter to the police. And if they were murder suspects, they would have wanted to claim their innocence. But no one came forward.

"The second scenario is impractical. Based on the duration of the snowfall, the person wearing the man's shoes and the person wearing the woman's shoes must have met in the studio. If the model killed Heikichi, the person in the man's shoes must have witnessed it. But there was no indication that that happened.

"The third scenario is similarly impractical. If the person in the man's shoes killed the victim, the person in the woman's shoes must have witnessed it. Again, there is no indication of that happening.

"The fourth scenario is more likely, but would Heikichi have taken sleeping pills in the presence of two visitors? Of course, he might have been threatened and forced to take them. And would the same two killers have committed Kazue's murder and the Azoth murders? There is no evidence of two killers being involved in those cases. It's always difficult for two people to keep a deadly secret. And if there were two killers, then they wouldn't have needed Mr Takegoshi to dispose of the bodies. All this would suggest that the murders were organized by a single person—a person with a cool mind and a cold heart.

"The fifth scenario seems unlikely, too. The model entered the studio after 2 p.m. on the 25th. At that time, snow had not been expected, so she wouldn't have thought to bring men's shoes for a later cover-up. She would have had to use Heikichi's shoes. There were two pairs of his shoes in the studio before and after the murder. However, the shoe prints showed the fact that the model did not return with his shoes after she left. What may have been possible was for the model to have walked out of the studio in her own shoes, and then walked back on her toes using long, man-like strides; then she put on Heikichi's shoes and stepped in her toe prints. But if so, she wouldn't have been able to return the shoes to the studio. And why did she leave the shoe prints of her first walk, even though she could have covered all her shoe prints? Perhaps her aim was to confuse the investigators, leading them to think that there were multiple killers who had pulled the bed up to the ceiling—or that the crime was committed by a man.

"The sixth scenario might at first glance appear the most plausible. A man came to the studio alone after it started to snow. He brought a pair of woman's shoes with him, and made prints with them while leaving his own shoe prints. But if so, the police would have thought that the prints of the woman's shoes were the model's and concluded that the killer was a man after all. Furthermore, Heikichi didn't have any close male friends, and the thought that he would take sleeping pills and go to sleep in the presence of a man seems very unlikely. Therefore, this scenario comes to a dead end, too.

"But having no other way to turn, we must reconsider these six scenarios. As I said, we can definitely cross the first off and the fourth off. Neither seems possible. The second and third don't hold up, either. So we are left with scenarios five and six. A man putting down the prints of a woman's shoes really does strain credibility. So I would suggest we are only left with scenario number five.

"Let's look at it carefully again: the model intentionally made two different types of shoe prints. The fact that the killer would not have been able to return Heikichi's shoes to the studio and the fact that the shoe prints of a woman were left become critical to the mystery. But one question remains. Was the person wearing the woman's shoes Heikichi's model? Assuming that the answer is yes, and that she was the one who killed Heikichi, would she come out to testify to anything? Of course not!

"Who was this model, then? She must have been close enough to Heikichi to be able to return his shoes to the studio. We can focus on only one person: Taeko Sudo.

"You see, Taeko had been planning these murders for a long time. She was determined to trap Masako and her daughters. She had decided that the 25th would be the night she killed Heikichi. She had already broken the glass of the studio skylight and had it replaced. But things didn't quite go as planned, because it started to snow while she was posing for him. As the snow accumulated, she must have grown more and more bewildered. But she was smart enough to think of a new trick. Making the prints of a man's shoes would make the police think the murderer was a man. She must already have had a precise plan for killing Kazue as well, so it would fit conveniently with that murder if it appeared that Heikichi's murder had also been committed by a man. She must have had a murder weapon in mind—such as a frying pan—so even though the snow presented an unexpected obstacle, she wouldn't have needed to change her basic plan.

"After beating Heikichi to death, Taeko put some dust in his hair to suggest that he had fallen out of his bed and hit his head on the floor. Then she cut his beard with scissors. Now why did she do that? Perhaps it was to confuse the police, since Heikichi and his brother looked so alike. She was complicating things unnecessarily, however. This was her first murder and she must have been in a panic—her methods were rather amateurish. She didn't need to put down two sets of shoe prints; a man's shoe prints alone would have been enough. That way, the investigators would have spent their time looking for a male killer—and not spent time trying to locate the model. Also, if the police had thought that Heikichi's visitor was male, they might have turned their attention to the possibility, however remote, of the group of Umezawa women climbing up on the roof once the male visitor had left. However, because Taeko had left prints of a woman's shoes, I was able to exclude any suspicion involving the Umezawa women.

"But how did Taeko return Heikichi's shoes when the studio was locked from the inside? In fact, to lock the studio from the outside is not difficult. You will remember that shoe prints were jammed near the window above the sink. She stood there, tossed a piece of string or rope in and hooked the sliding bar and the padlock into position.

"And that is how Heikichi Umezawa's murder was committed." Kiyoshi stopped briefly to sip his coffee again, and we all did the same.

"Now let's move on to the murder of Kazue. Pardon me, please, but talking about all the details is rather tiring, so allow me to give you the conclusion first. Bunjiro Takegoshi entered Kazue's house at around 7.30 p.m. and left near 8.50 p.m. The presumed time of Kazue's death was between 7 p.m. and 9 p.m. How was this possible? Again the answer is quite simple: Kazue was already dead when Mr Takegoshi entered her house. If he had opened the sliding doors to the next room, he would have seen her naked body lying on the floor. The woman who seduced him was not Kazue, but Taeko. Her plan was to trap him and blackmail him into disposing of the bodies of the dead girls. After having sex with him, she took some of his semen from her own vagina, and put it into Kazue's. That explains the difference between his confession and the investigation that suggested intercourse after the victim died."

"But," I interrupted him, "if Taeko wanted to make all the murders look like they had one male perpetrator, why did she bother to ransack Kazue's house?"

"She wanted to make the case look unrelated to Heikichi's murder," Kiyoshi replied. "She needed things to look as though both a burglary and a sexual assault had taken place. Otherwise, the police would have gone over the house with a fine-tooth comb and found the bodies of the girls in storage. However, she made another amateurish mistake: she left Kazue dressed very neatly in her kimono despite all that had supposedly happened to her. That made me curious. Besides, Taeko's basic plan was to frame Masako for the Azoth murders. Making it seem that a man killed Kazue would effectively clear the way for Masako to be accused of killing the six Umezawa girls.

"But the risk of keeping the girls' bodies at Kazue's house was still high. Therefore, Taeko had to force Mr Takegoshi to dispose of the bodies immediately. She was lucky, because rural police investigations then were very slow and unsophisticated. Her trick wouldn't work today; criminal investigation is much more advanced and precise. The same thing can be said about the newspapers. The printing of Kazue's photo was so bad that Mr Takegoshi couldn't be certain that she was not the woman he'd had sex with.

"Now, Kazue's blood was cleaned off the vase that was used as the murder weapon. Taeko then set the vase in a place where Mr Takegoshi would be sure to see it, imprinting it in his memory, so that he would think that the murder occurred *after* his visit. Knowing that the vase was the murder weapon would also raise his level of fear.

"Kazue was killed while facing the mirror. She didn't try to run away and she didn't put up a struggle, implying that the victim knew the killer. After she bludgeoned Kazue to death, Taeko also carefully wiped the blood off the mirror, and moved Kazue's body to the adjacent room. Why Taeko killed Kazue in her home is not clear, but women looking into a mirror can be caught off-guard. Either Taeko planned it this way or something occurred between her and Kazue to trigger the violence. I'm a man, so I can only imagine what was on Taeko's mind at that moment. One of her motives may have been a deep-seated grudge towards Kazue, but let's explore the motive later.

"As regards the murder of the Umezawa girls, I think Taeko killed them when they were all together at Kazue's house. It was remote and it was convenient; she could poison them at once, store the bodies and then cut them up. In the larger picture, Kazue's murder was merely a stepping stone for the Azoth murders."

Kiyoshi paused again, and sipped some more coffee.

"Now, the Azoth murders. These serial murders have bedevilled and fascinated this country just as if they were indeed an excellent magic show. When I heard of this case for the first time, I might have sensed that the key was magic, but I did not fully comprehend what it was all about and so I kept overlooking the core of the mystery. But yesterday I happened to recall a magic trick. As a result, I quickly solved the case, and two hours later I was able to meet the culprit.

"The trick itself was so simple that no one ever thought of it being used in this case. But many policemen will remember it, I'm sure. It was a technique for committing fraud with ten-thousand-yen bills that was mainly used in the Kansai area some years ago. I remember that a television news programme

I was watching in a restaurant reported it something like this: 'A ten-thousand-yen bill was found today with a missing part that had been covered up with opaque tape. The bill had been cut and taped together, so the bill was not quite as long as a normal ten-thousand-yen bill, and the serial numbers on the right side and left side didn't match. Investigators suspect fraud. It is the first case of fraud using this technique that has come to light in Tokyo.' Perhaps to prevent copycat fraud, the news did not explain any further. In fact, the young people at the next table to me in the restaurant immediately started wondering how they could make some money by cutting up bills! Since you may not be sure how it is done, allow me to demonstrate."

Kiyoshi turned to the blackboard and drew a series of rectangles.

1 2 [1]	11 [12 11]	
2 3 [2]	12 [13 12]	
3 4 [3]	13 [14 13]	
4 5 [4]	14 [15 14]	
5 [6 5]	15 [16 15]	
6 [7 6]	16 [17 16]	
7 [8 7]	17 [18] 17	
8 [9 8]	18 [19] 18	
9 [10 9]	19 [20] 19	
10 [11 10]	20 [21] 20	
	21 [22]	

"Here are twenty bills. Ten bills might do, but the risk of detection is too high because of the size of the missing parts. The safest way would be to use thirty bills, but that might hurt your profit margin! Twenty is about right. Now on each bill we draw a line, like this. Starting with the first bill, the distance of the line from the left edge increases incrementally. By the time we come to the last bill, the line reaches almost to the right edge. Then with a pair of scissors we cut each bill along the line drawn. We now have twenty bills cut into forty pieces.

"So that the exact operation is clear, I'll label each piece in this way, with L representing the left side of the bill and R the right: like this, 1L, 1R, 2L, 2R, and so on... This is where the magic—or the fraud, depending on your point of view—begins.

"All twenty bills have been cut in this pattern—with, as I said, the left side of the bill getting wider and wider until, finally, it makes up almost the entire bill and there is only a very narrow strip remaining on the right side. From bill #1, we put aside 1R, the slightly shortened right side of the bill. Then we take the narrow strip cut from the left side, 1L, and attach it—with opaque tape—to 2R, the right side of bill #2... We take the left side of bill #2, which is labelled as 2L, and attach it to 3R, the right side of bill #3... and so on, and so on. Finally we attach 19L to 20R, and save 20L as a slightly small bill, just like 1R. As you can see, we are left with what appear to be 21 ten-thousand-yen bills! The first and last bills will look severed, but if a cashier doesn't check carefully, we have succeeded. We have fabricated one new bill with the help of scissors and tape; it must be opaque tape to obscure what has been done.

"This technique for committing fraud gave me the key to this mystery. I realized that the killer had applied the same technique to the bodies. We believed that there were *six* victims in the Azoth murders, and we never doubted it. In fact, it only looked like there were six. In reality, there were only *five!*"

SCENE 2

The Vanishing Point

I uttered a cry of astonishment.

So it was all an illusion! Azoth never existed. She was like a mirage.

I was too dizzy to think. I could barely sit still. I had come out in goosebumps.

Mrs Iida and her detective husband seemed dumbfounded, too. The three of us stared at Kiyoshi, eager to hear his next revelation.

"Now, of course, body parts can't be stuck together with opaque tape," Kiyoshi continued with a tone of detachment. "Therefore, Taeko needed something that would work like glue. The concept of Azoth was so grotesque in itself that the thought of mixing and matching the body parts of different girls never entered anyone's mind. Everybody assumed that the missing head had been used for Azoth, the perfect woman of supreme beauty. The image of her mysterious smile has held people in thrall for forty years, as if the art of the Renaissance painter was the trick. In this case, the killer used perspective to draw the perfect picture of the murders. But Azoth existed only at the vanishing point. Nobody ever considered the possibility that the girl whose head was missing could be still alive. That's right—Azoth was never created, even in the killer's mind; moreover, she was never meant to exist.

"Well, I'm sure you can untangle the rest of the mystery yourselves. Thank you for listening."

For a moment, the three of us sat there, stupefied.

Then I shouted out, "Wait! You can't stop now!"

I had more questions than I knew how to ask. Kiyoshi, who was feigning boredom, simply grinned. He took his time sipping his coffee.

I was still totally bewildered. I felt as if I was standing in a forest surrounded by hundreds of trees in the shape of question marks. My emotions generated a storm that shook the trees, the questions came tumbling out.

"But who was the culprit? Why were some bodies buried deep and others so shallow? Did the placement of the bodies really have some connection with astrology? How were the locations designated? What does longitude 138° 48′ E signify? Was the order of discovery of the bodies important? What was the killer's main motive? Where did she hide herself? What was the real significance of Heikichi's note?..."

"Well, Mr Ishioka, I'm surprised you're interested in such details!" said Kiyoshi with a smile. "You don't usually listen to me when I say something of importance. Now it may seem that I am praising the killer—and in fact I suppose I am. Taeko Sudo pulled off the murders brilliantly; she deserves our admiration. If I were a killer, I'm sure I would have done it the same way. It's a pity we can't hear the explanation directly from her. But would you really like me to continue?"

Mr Iida and I nodded and Mrs Iida opened her eyes wide, urging him to go on.

Kiyoshi opened the notebook he had been drawing in earlier.

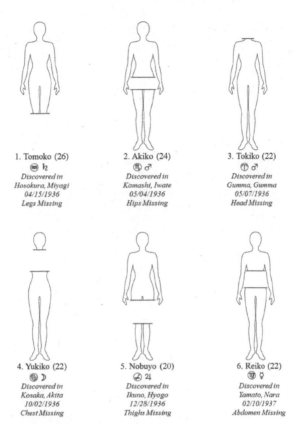

1. Tomoko (26)
♏ ♄
Discovered in
Hosokura, Miyagi
04/15/1936
Legs Missing

2. Akiko (24)
♍ ♂
Discovered in
Kamashi, Iwate
05/04/1936
Hips Missing

3. Tokiko (22)
♌ ♂
Discovered in
Gumma, Gumma
05/07/1936
Head Missing

4. Yukiko (22)
♋ ☽
Discovered in
Kosaka, Akita
10/02/1936
Chest Missing

5. Nobuyo (20)
♎ ♃
Discovered in
Ikuno, Hyogo
12/28/1936
Thighs Missing

6. Reiko (22)
♏ ♀
Discovered in
Yamato, Nara
02/10/1937
Abdomen Missing

"All right, my friends, here is an illustration of the six bodies in the order they were found, starting with the one identified as Tomoko on the left. You can see I have included their personal details and also noted which parts of their bodies were missing. Just looking at this, however, it is not easy to see how the trick works—which was the whole point, of course!

"But if we arrange the six bodies in a different order, you will see how a distinct pattern emerges." Kiyoshi went to the blackboard and drew all six bodies again as he spoke.

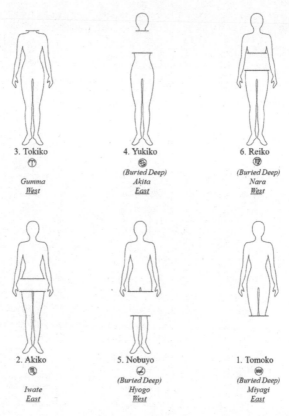

3. Tokiko
Ⓣ

(Buried Deep)
Gumma
West

4. Yukiko
Ⓢ

(Buried Deep)
Akita
East

6. Reiko
Ⓜ

(Buried Deep)
Nara
West

2. Akiko
Ⓜ

Iwate
East

5. Nobuyo
Ⓢ

(Buried Deep)
Hyogo
West

1. Tomoko
Ⓢ

(Buried Deep)
Miyagi
East

"First, on the left, let's put Tokiko, the Aries, whose head was missing; then, Yukiko, the Cancer, whose chest was missing; then third, Reiko, the Virgo, whose abdomen was missing...

"Now please look again at my first illustration that shows the order in which the bodies were found. At the time of their discovery, as you will recall, the fourth, fifth and sixth bodies were all in an advanced level of decomposition. Their faces must have been unidentifiable. However, the first, second and third bodies found were still fresh enough to be identifiable. Recall as well that Umezawa's note was being used as a guide.

272

"Moving along, let me put names on each body part discovered—to show which body part in fact belonged to whom...

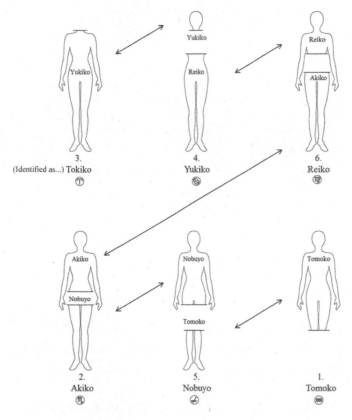

"As you can see here, with the exception of the first case, each 'body' actually consisted of the body parts of *two* different women. In each case, the combination of these body parts was identified—or misidentified—as being *one* person.

"Let me now show you how this is basically the same technique that was employed in the fraud committed with the ten-thousand-yen bills...

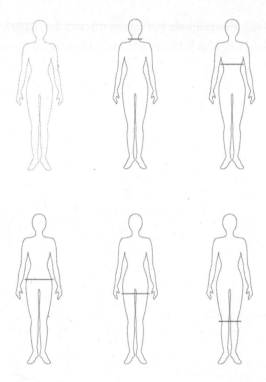

"The killer sawed through *five* bodies like this. Then the lower part of each body was buried together with the upper part of the adjacent body. At the end, you have the illusion of six bodies.

"In view of the gruesome nature of the deed and the tremendous effort involved, you may be surprised to hear it was carried out by one woman. Well, up to now, nobody ever doubted that the killer had had to saw through six bodies a total of ten times—twice for four of the bodies and once for two of them. In fact, the work was only half as strenuous because she only cut five bodies into ten pieces. Then she had to piece them together in the way I suggest here and dump them. Of course, changing their clothes might have been a little troublesome, but the killer was obviously up to the task.

"Now, how about the locations where they were dumped? Well, obviously, if the six groups of body parts had been disposed of in one location, the killer's method would have been readily apparent to investigators once they were discovered. In order to avoid this, she chose six very different places. Yes, that's right, *she* chose the locations, not Heikichi! *She* was the one who wrote his note. I don't think she believed in the astrological reasoning that she included in the note, because, as you can see, the upper and lower parts of the body of each woman were in fact buried separately in western *and* eastern Japan. But it was a very clever ploy indeed.

"As must now be clear, Taeko Sudo was one of the six women. And now I can reveal which one it was. The police were led to assume that she had died with the others and that the corpse without a head was hers. Yes, the one head never found belonged to... Tokiko. So she had to be the killer."

There was a sudden silence. For a few moments we were all speechless.

"Then," I said, "you mean that Taeko Sudo is, in fact..."

"Tokiko Umezawa."

Again, there was a stunned silence as we tried to digest this revelation.

Kiyoshi allowed us a lengthy pause and then he said, very casually, "Well my friends, do you have any questions?"

Mr and Mrs Iida obviously had not been thinking about the case as much as I had; nor did they know Kiyoshi as well as I did. So I assumed the role of leader of the small and very confused group of listeners.

"First, about the depth of the burials…" I started. "The bodies that were believed to be Yukiko, Nobuyo and Reiko were found much later than the first three bodies because they were buried deeper. So that was deliberate?"

"Yes, indeed," Kiyoshi replied. "That was exactly the point of the deeper burials: to delay the time of discovery. Here we can observe the brilliance of Tokiko. She arranged for the first three bodies to be found in the spring; the heat of summer was approaching, so the bodies would be cremated soon after. So when the other three bodies were found, the police would not have the first three corpses to compare them with. If they had had all six bodies they might have compared the surfaces of all the cuts and discovered the exact combination—although the clothing might have impaired their judgement. Needless to say, this trick would not have worked in any country where bodies are buried rather than cremated.

"Tokiko chose Tomoko's body to be found first, because it really was Tomoko's, although missing her lower legs and feet. It would be identified as Tomoko right away. That's why it was left on the ground—to facilitate discovery. On the other hand, the body identified as Tokiko was in fact Yukiko's—without her head. Tokiko knew that a headless body would be subject to very careful examination, so she arranged for it to be found later—but not the last. If Tomoko was found first, Akiko and Tokiko would probably be next, followed by Yukiko, Nobuyo and Reiko. That was the desired sequence because by the time the last three bodies were discovered, the sawed body parts would have rotted and they would be more or less reduced to skeletons.

"The segmentation and sequence would work very effectively, because either the upper or lower part of each victim would have been cremated before the rest of her body was discovered. And the investigators wouldn't realize that the combination of upper and lower body parts was wrong, even if the first three bodies found were put together in one place.

"Yukiko's body—which was misidentified as Tokiko's—was not deeply buried. But the body parts identified as Yukiko's were buried very deep. That's how the fraud was achieved."

"How did Tokiko ensure that Yukiko's body would be misidentified as her body?" I asked next.

"Well, Yukiko's feet had been disfigured from years of ballet dancing; that was one point for identification, but it wouldn't be sufficient. So Tokiko cleverly prepared false evidence. In Heikichi's note she described herself as having a birthmark; in fact, it was Yukiko who had the birthmark on the right side of her stomach. Tokiko contrived to create a similar mark on herself and presumably showed it to her mother so that she would later be able to identify her. Yukiko's body was not deeply buried so that it would be discovered while the birthmark and the disfigured toenails were still recognizable; and, sure enough, Tae misidentified the body as her daughter's.

"There was the risk posed by Yukiko's mother, Masako, who naturally would have known about Yukiko's birthmark. Therefore, it was important that Masako wasn't allowed the opportunity to identify either the body with the birthmark or the body buried with Yukiko's head—which was, in fact, Reiko's. Masako would immediately have spotted the deception. So Yukiko's body had to be buried deep.

"By the time Yukiko, Nobuyo and Reiko were found decomposed, Masako had been incarcerated as a suspect. In prison, she must have become deranged. The police would not take her ravings seriously. They would not let her see the body found with Yukiko's head for identification, certainly not when it was badly decomposed. And Yukiko's actual body was cremated as Tokiko without being shown to Masako.

"But Ayako Umezawa was more of a problem. Reiko and Nobuyo were her beloved daughters and Tokiko knew she would go anywhere to identify them; she would examine their bodies closely, no matter how horrible they looked. And if anything seemed odd, she would certainly say so. Moreover, she was also excluded from the list of suspects, so the police would probably believe what she said—or at least listen to her. Therefore, the body parts that were to be identified as her daughters were buried the deepest.

"I would say that the greatest obstacle Tokiko faced in carrying out her scheme was not the police investigation but the mothers of the victims, because a mother's intuition can be very powerful.

"It was also important that the first body—which was missing its feet—was found soon after the girls' disappearance so that the police could start relating the murders to Heikichi's plan for Azoth. If all the bodies were deeply buried, they would all be decomposed, destroying important bits of evidence—the birthmark and the deformed toes of the ballet dancers. Besides, some of the bodies might never be discovered; Tokiko needed all six burial sites to be discovered before she could feel secure."

"But wouldn't testing for blood type have revealed some funny business?" I asked.

"All of the five women were blood type A. What a coincidence that was, especially since they all had a different astrological sign! That fact had inspired Tokiko. But you're right, Mr

Ishioka—the situation would be different today. If the testing for blood type was done now, something would surely have been discovered. As I'm sure Mr Iida knows well, conventional ABO testing has several different classifications—such as MN, Q and Rh typing. That means that blood can now be classified into a thousand different types. Moreover, forensic medicine can now examine a victim's chromosomes, bone tissue and many other things for identification. Information can be obtained from blood, sputum, semen, skin, bone, and so on. Even a corpse that has been burnt or decomposed can provide chromosomal evidence. The Azoth murders were successfully carried out in 1936; but they would not be successful today. In this sense, science helps to deter crime in our society, because there are so many ways a criminal can be caught."

"But how about police stations in remote villages?" I asked. "Do they have the ability to do all that testing?"

"Well, Japan is a relatively small country with an excellent transportation system. From anywhere, within three or four hours, evidence can be sent to centres where sophisticated methods of forensic medicine can be applied. As far as I know, however, MN and Q typing were only discovered many years after the war ended. Do you know about this, Mr Iida?"

"You're right," replied Mr Iida. "Back in 1936, there was only ABO typing."

Kiyoshi nodded. "Any more questions?"

"Yes," I said at once. "I understand now just how and why Tokiko's scheme worked. No wonder you screamed in Kyoto when the truth suddenly came to you! But how did you know that Taeko Sudo—or Tokiko—was in Kyoto?"

"Oh, that was easy! Think about her motive, Mr Ishioka."

"But I'm still in the dark about that. Why did she do it?"

"Well, you have a copy of *The Tokyo Zodiac Murders*. Could you please open it up to the page that shows the family tree?... Yes, there it is. Now think about the circumstances of the Umezawa family. Tokiko was the only child of Tae, Heikichi's first wife. Among the whole family, Tae was the only one who did not come from a wealthy background, and the only one who didn't live comfortably.

"This is how I picture it: Heikichi, who was something of a womanizer, dumped Tae in the same way a child throws away a toy when he gets bored with it. He divorced her and married Masako. When Masako and her three daughters moved into the Umezawa house, Tokiko's life changed, and certainly not for the better. A child is sensitive to such things. Later, Heikichi's nieces, Reiko and Nobuyo, also joined them. Yukiko and Tokiko were related by blood, but only through Heikichi, who had betrayed Tokiko's mother. Tokiko must have felt disgusted and alienated. I imagine her loneliness and resentment grew from day to day, turning eventually into a violent rage that struck down the other family members. I didn't ask her about that yesterday, because we simply didn't have the time. It would probably have taken a long time for her to explain. Suffice it to say, she committed such a horrible and historical crime both for her own sake and her mother's sake.

"Tae had faced many difficulties since her parents' business failed. Her misfortune seemed to end when she married Heikichi Umezawa, a wealthy man; but he took a lover and divorced her. Women these days are strong and clever—they will do anything to keep their marriage intact to avoid financial ruin or social dishonour—but Tae was a very traditional, modest, obedient woman. She never complained; perhaps she didn't know what else she could do. Tokiko kept seeing her mother alone and poor and miserable while the Umezawa women were enjoying their luxurious lifestyle. By killing them off, she got vengeance for her mother and also helped her financially.

"I reckoned that if Tokiko's crimes were motivated by her love and sympathy for Tae, there was one place she would be drawn to: Sagano, in Kyoto. It had been Tae's dream to open a boutique there, because it was the only place she had fond memories of. But Tae died in Hoya without fulfilling her dream. I felt Tokiko would want to make her mother's dream come true.

"I immediately went to Sagano and visited the police station. I asked if there was a shop around there that sold little handbags or sachets and was called something like Tae's; it was reasonable to think she'd name her shop after her mother. They told me there was a bag shop called Megumi's. I went along to check it out, and, sure enough, forty-three years after the murders, Tokiko was there. She had changed her name to Taeko Sudo."

"And do you think she was the model who was with Heikichi on 25th February?"

"Yes, I'm pretty sure of it."

"What about the mystery of the locked studio?"

"Ah, that's simple. You'll recall that on the night of the murder, it started to snow while Tokiko was posing for her father. The snow gave her the idea of making the misleading shoe prints. Heikichi was close to her and took two sleeping pills in her presence. Perhaps she was pretending she was about to leave. When his back was turned, she hit him on the head with some flat object, killing him. She cut his beard, and moved his bed and his body. She put one of his legs under the bed so that it would look like he fell as it was being pulled up to the ceiling with ropes. She then went out of the door, wearing her own shoes and carrying his. She went to the window, which she'd previously opened, and with a length of string or rope looped the sliding bar, pulling it into place. She wasn't so successful with the padlock—she couldn't lock that from outside.

"Then she walked, still in her own shoes, to the street. Next, on her toes this time, she walked in long strides back to the studio door. She slipped her father's shoes on, and, stepping very carefully onto her own toe prints, she walked to the street again.

"She must have spent the night outdoors; she could have gone back to her mother's house, but it was too late for a train or a bus. Taking a cab was out of the question, since the driver would remember her. She must have walked somewhere and hid on that cold, snowy night. She probably disposed of her weapon somewhere.

"The next morning, she returned to the Umezawa house. She must have been carrying her father's shoes in a bag. She cooked breakfast for him as usual, carried the meal to the studio, looked in the window, and then screamed and ran for help. She might have thrown the shoes into the vestibule through the window. The Umezawa women came running to the studio and together they managed to break the door down. They would not have noticed the shoes. In the chaos, I would guess Tokiko secured the padlock as she was cleaning up the debris around the door."

"I see," I said. "So when she was questioned by the police, she said that the door had been locked."

"That's right."

"And her mother lied for her?"

"Correct. She said that Tokiko had spent the night at her house."

"Then Tokiko killed Kazue and trapped Mr Takegoshi?"

"Yes, that is the most detestable part of the story. Unlike the Umezawas, Mr Takegoshi had no reason to suffer. It might be too late now, but we finally know the truth and can offer up our prayers for him. Mr Ishioka, could you please bring me the container of kerosene from the next room?"

I went out and found the tank we used for lighting the heater in winter. When I returned, Kiyoshi was standing by the sink. He dropped Takegoshi's note into it and poured some kerosene on it.

"Please all come over here," he said. "Do you have any matches or a lighter, Mrs Iida?... Ah, good. May I use one?"

I volunteered that I had some.

"Thank you, Mr Ishioka, but I think it would be better to use Mrs Iida's." He took a book of matches from Mrs Iida, struck one and tossed it into the sink. The note flared up immediately.

The four of us stood around the sink as if we were at a campfire. Kiyoshi poked the burning note with a stick and black ashes flew up into the air.

"It's finally over," said Mrs Iida in a very low voice.

The Basic Structure

After the departure of Mr and Mrs Iida, Kiyoshi went straight back to his normal routine. I returned to my apartment still buzzing with excitement. In fact, for me the case wasn't closed—not until I saw Kiyoshi's achievements recognized publicly. I was looking forward to that.

And I still couldn't comprehend the whole story. My mind was full of questions:

How had Tokiko obtained the toxic substances?

Where and how had Tokiko hidden over the past forty years as Taeko Sudo?

How did she dare to risk being a nude model for her father?

Was Tae involved in the plot from the beginning?

How did Shusai Yoshida know that Heikichi was left-handed?

I decided that last question was one I could answer myself. I called Yoshida and asked him. His answer was very simple: Tamio Yasukawa had told him!

I opened the paper the following morning, eagerly anticipating coverage of the big news that the Tokyo Zodiac Murders had finally been solved by the master detective Kiyoshi Mitarai. But there was nothing.

I did find one shocking item of news, however: a woman in Kyoto called Taeko Sudo had committed suicide. She had been found dead on the night of Friday the 13th in the back room of her shop in Sagano. Probably the police had gone there after Iida reported back to his office. She had died from arsenic poisoning. She had left a brief suicide note and some money and an apology addressed to her two female employees. Her relationship to the Zodiac Murders was implied but not explained.

I grabbed the newspaper and dashed off to see Kiyoshi. My head was reeling with more questions:

Had Taeko been keeping some of the same arsenic she used on the Umezawa women?

She must have lived a very lonely life for over forty years. Had she been contemplating killing herself all that time?

But if she had waited this long, why did she have to die without telling the truth to the public?

Apparently the newspaper delivered to me was an early edition, because at the station the kiosk was piled high with newspapers blaring the headlines: ZODIAC MURDERS SOLVED and THE KILLER WAS A WOMAN! I bought a couple of copies before they sold out.

The articles were entirely unsatisfying. Along with a brief explanation of the case, they mentioned only that it had been solved thanks to the constant effort of the police investigators.

There was nothing about how the culprit had cut up the five bodies to make them look like six. And there was no mention of the man who had been central to solving the case.

When I got to Kiyoshi's office, he was still asleep in his bedroom. I went up to him, pulled his blanket off and announced, "Taeko Sudo is dead."

His eyes popped wide open.

Kiyoshi sat silent for a while. I waited for him to say something.

Finally, he said, "Kazumi, do you feel like fixing some coffee?"

As he drank his coffee, Kiyoshi read the papers intently, and then put them down on the table.

"'Constant efforts led the police to success.' Did you read that?" he said, chuckling. "What would Takegoshi Jr have learnt if he had continued his investigation for a hundred years? Well, he would have spent a lot of money on shoes and made the shoe companies happy, I suppose!"

Kiyoshi seemed to be in a relaxed mood, so I decided to bring up the questions I still had about the case.

"Tokiko was only twenty-two when she committed the murders. How on earth did she get all the toxic substances she used?" I asked.

"I have no idea," Kiyoshi answered.

"But you had some time to talk to her in Arashiyama, didn't you?"

"Yeah, but we didn't talk very much."

"Why not? She was the one person we'd been looking for."

"Well, Kazumi, I didn't want to get emotionally involved with the culprit. Anyway, my approach is different from a detective's. When I saw her, I didn't feel like I had gone through any great hardship to find her. I didn't care about what it took to get there. I didn't care about details."

I thought he was lying. Kiyoshi liked to behave like a genius, concealing his suffering when he talked to me.

"I'm sure you know how she got the poisons. Please tell me!"

"You're beginning to sound like a policeman! All those things, such as the seven—or was it six—different substances and the longitude–latitude business were merely dressing. She was so talented, we were distracted by those lifelike decorations on the pillars. But the most important thing is to see the basic structure. No matter how well you examine the decorations, you must be able to grasp the structure of the building. How she obtained the substances is not a mystery at all. She needed them, so she found a way to get them. What good is it to discuss it at all now?"

"OK, point taken. But here's another question. Could Tae and Tokiko have planned the murders together? Or maybe Tae had planned them and Tokiko carried them out?"

"I don't think so."

"You think Tokiko did it all by herself?"

"Yes."

"I guess it's possible, but how can you be so sure?"

"Just a hunch."

"You can't do this to me, Kiyoshi! Please tell me why you believe that."

"I can't really explain it logically. But if the crime had been planned by Tae, I don't think Tokiko would have gone anywhere near Sagano. However, she moved there, waiting to be discovered eventually. In fact, she even killed herself there. And if Tokiko and Tae were in on it together, you'd think they would have shared the money Tae inherited from Heikichi's death. But, as far as we know, there were no money transactions of any sort. And if Tae had been involved in the plan, surely she would have moved to Sagano right away and fulfilled her dream? But even though she had money then, it seems she didn't do anything to improve her circumstances. That must have been a disappointment to Tokiko. So she moved to Sagano herself—as I told you—to keep her mother's dream alive. And maybe that's why she stayed there, despite the risk of being found by somebody."

"I see…"

"On the other hand, Tokiko could have left Sagano for the same reason. But now that she's dead, we'll never know."

"We missed the chance of a lifetime!"

"No, we didn't. We just let it go."

"Do you think Tokiko might have mailed you a final letter?" I asked hopefully.

"She couldn't have. I didn't give her my address or properly introduce myself. Also, I didn't want to ruin the historic moment with my funny name."

I let that pass without even smiling. "But did Taeko, or Tokiko, tell you where she went after the murders?"

"Manchuria."

"Manchuria?… I see. Just like British criminals fleeing to the US."

"She told me about when she came back to Japan and rode a train. She said that after the vast landscape of the Asian continent, everything seemed so close that the mountains looked like they were jumping into the train. I thought that was very poetic. Don't you agree?"

"Uh-huh…"

"Ah, the good old days! Today, many Japanese never even get to see the horizon."

"Japan is rather small; and so is our vision. But look at what she achieved! That bold plan was carried out by one single woman, who was only twenty-two years old at the time!"

Kiyoshi looked up towards the ceiling. "Yes, she was great. She had the whole nation fooled for forty years. I've never met such a woman. I take my hat off to her."

"I do, too, but how did you see through her trick? I know that the taped-up bill gave you a clue, but you must have had some other clues. In the beginning, I told you all I knew about the case, but there wasn't enough there, was there?"

"You're right. You told me about the case from an incorrect assumption: that Azoth was created. When I considered all the facts, I couldn't find anyone who had enough time or space to do that. But whether or not Azoth was created didn't matter. The crucial key was Heikichi's note. Many descriptions in it didn't quite make sense to me, so I got suspicious."

"For example?"

"There were lots of things… First of all, one thing was fundamentally wrong. In the note, 'Heikichi' said it was not for publication and it should be placed with Azoth in the centre of Japan. On the other hand, he said that if Azoth made money, it must go to Tae. That proved he really wanted someone to read the note.

"Second, the killer ought to have taken the note with him, but he didn't. Without it, how could he give directions to Takegoshi? If Heikichi really had written the note, the killer would have needed to have copied it or memorized it. Anyway, to conceal his crime, the killer wouldn't have left it. The killer obviously left the note so that the public would see it.

"Third, the author said something about Azoth making a fortune. That struck me as odd. Azoth was going to be created to save the Japanese Empire, not to benefit a specific individual.

And then the author said that part about the money going to Tae. I should have noticed that earlier.

"There were other things. Heikichi was a chain-smoker, but the note said he didn't like going to nightclubs because he didn't like the smoky air. Tokiko was writing about herself there!

"What else?... Oh yes, the music. The author said he liked 'Isle of Capri' and 'Orchids in the Moonlight'. They were hit songs in 1934 and 1935. I used to collect music from that period, so I know them very well. Another big hit was 'Yira, Yira', by Carlos Gardel—well, it doesn't really matter. The year 1935 was the year before Heikichi's death. By that time, he had already locked himself up in his studio, and we know he didn't have a radio or a phonograph. So he had no way to listen to the latest hits; he could never have sung them. But the songs would have been familiar to Tokiko, because Masako loved to play music in the main house."

Everything Kiyoshi said made sense. Why hadn't I thought of any of those things?

"So why did she kill herself without telling anybody about her crimes?" I asked. "What was her intention?"

"Her intention? What do you want me to say? What do we see in the newspapers? Just stereotypes and preconceptions! When a diligent student commits suicide, they always say that it was the overheated competition in entrance exams that killed the kid. That's such bullshit! People never think about what the truth might be. Most people lead such boring lives, they try to justify themselves by putting everyone else in neat little categories. Taeko Sudo lived for sixty-six years, and then decided to end it all. For all we know, she might have had many

sleepless nights, with her thoughts going around in circles...
How could she explain why she wanted to kill herself? And
why should she? She chose death, that's all. You say you're
concerned about the reason she committed suicide, but surely
you know why by now, don't you?"

Still confused, I went quiet.

SCENE 4

A Knock on the Door

Kiyoshi didn't reveal any more of his thoughts about Taeko's suicide. Apparently, he believed it was not motivated by the exposure of her crime but by something else. Whenever I tried to find out what was on his mind, he became evasive.

"Think about the dice she gave me, and then you'll know," was all he would say, with a grin.

Speaking of dice, it struck me that investigating the Zodiac Murders had been like playing a game of Monopoly. I'd roll the dice and stop at "The Mystery of Heikichi's Bed" or "Longitude 138° 48′ E" or "Numbers 4, 6 and 3", and so on. Kiyoshi and I playing the game had resembled those comic nineteenth-century characters Yajirobei and Kitahachi in Jippensha Ikku's chronicle of adventures and mishaps titled *Tokaidochu Hizakurige*. But as things were winding up, my game had ended when I lost all my capital in Meiji-Mura. Pretty foolish, really!

I did have some good memories from the adventure, though. The people I'd met had all been interesting and kind, except for Takegoshi Jr. It's odd to say this, perhaps, but the person I had the most pleasant impression of was the culprit, Taeko Sudo.

The news that the Zodiac Murders had been solved provided huge excitement. Newspapers and magazines went crazy with the story for a week or so. There were television programmes galore, each network trying to outdo the others. Takegoshi Jr and his quiet brother-in-law Iida were interviewed, although the media were not too keen on the gorilla's appearance or attitude.

There was also a new boom in books on the case. The same writers who had put forward their theories on cannibalism or abduction by aliens now re-emerged from the woodwork with new books on the subject.

Iida got a promotion because of his contribution to solving the case, but Kiyoshi didn't get anything, except a brief thank-you note from Mrs Iida. His name wasn't mentioned anywhere. My dear friend, the man who had actually solved the case, was completely overlooked. I felt it was really unfair. But at least it was good for one person: the late Bunjiro Takegoshi. His note was never exposed to the public, and that made me feel good; it was a feeling that Kiyoshi shared. Still, I was not fully satisfied.

"Aren't you frustrated at all?" I asked Kiyoshi.

"With what?"

"Getting no credit for solving the mystery. You did it all, and you've been totally ignored. You could have appeared on TV; you could be famous now. You could have made some money. I know you're not that kind of person, but fame can make a business operate better. I don't think yours is an exception. You could have moved to a better place, bought a nicer sofa, made your life more comfortable…"

"Yes, maybe. But then I'd be plagued every day by a bunch of curious, stupid people," Kiyoshi replied. "My office would be so full, I'd have to yell your name to find you in the crowd in my waiting room. You might not be aware of this, but I like my present lifestyle. I don't want people to bother me. Look what I'm doing now. I can sleep as late as I like. I can relax in my pyjamas any time I choose. I can spend my time studying whatever I want. I only accept clients I like; I don't have to compromise. All of these things I treasure. I don't want to change anything. And I can overcome any loneliness I may feel because you are here!"

Kiyoshi's warm words were unexpected, and they made me so happy. Now was the time to reveal my plan to him. I tried to say it with all seriousness, but I couldn't help smiling. "What would you say if I told you I wanted to write a novel based on this case?" Kiyoshi stiffened as if he'd been caught with his hand in the biscuit jar. "Bad joke, Mr Ishioka!"

"I don't know if any publisher will like it, but I think it'd be worthwhile trying."

"I would endure almost anything, my friend," Kiyoshi said quietly, "but please, keep this quiet. No book!"

"But why?"

"I just explained it to you. I have other reasons, too."

"Oh, do you? Please tell me what they are."

"I don't want to."

Considering his response, Emoto would be the first reader of this book, and Kiyoshi would be the last. But from my work as an illustrator, I had some good contacts with publishing houses. I had every intention of going through with the idea.

"You could never imagine how nervous I get when people ask me my name," Kiyoshi muttered weakly, sinking into the sofa. "Would I be in your book?"

"Of course! You would be central to the story—a man with a strong and unusual character."

"Well, could you give me a better name? Something that sounds like a movie star."

"Sure I will," I replied, laughing, "of course you should be allowed to appear incognito."

"The magic… of an astrologer…"

But the case was still not really finished for the two of us.

One sunny afternoon in October, six months after all the excitement, we heard a very tentative knock on the door.

"Yes," Kiyoshi said, but the visitor didn't presume to open the door. It was probably a hesitant woman, I thought. There was another knock.

"Come in!" Kiyoshi repeated loudly.

The door slowly opened to reveal the figure of a large, tall man. Guess who it was… the gorilla!

"Oh, my goodness! Is that you, Mr Takegoshi?" said Kiyoshi, jumping up from his stool with a smile. "Mr Ishioka, please make some tea."

"Oh, no thank you. Please don't bother. I won't be staying long," Takegoshi Jr said, taking a large envelope from his briefcase and handing it to Kiyoshi. "I just came by to give you this," he continued tentatively. "I apologize that it took such a long time… And please excuse us for not giving you the original… but it was an important piece of evidence, you see… and it took some time to figure out who the letter was meant for…"

I had no idea what he was talking about.

"It was for you, Mr Mitarai," he said, and turned to leave.

"Thank you. But are you going? We have so many things to talk about. It's been such a long time," Kiyoshi said, unable to contain his sarcasm.

Takegoshi Jr did not respond. He was already through the door and closing it. But then he stopped and slowly opened the door again.

"As a man, I must say this," he mumbled, looking down at our feet. "Thank you very much for your help. I'd like to say thank you on my father's behalf also. He must be happy in heaven... And I apologize for being so rude to you the last time we met. Well... goodbye... and thank you."

He closed the door quickly, but politely. He hadn't looked into our eyes once.

"Hmm, maybe he's not such a bad person after all!" Kiyoshi said with a grin.

"No. I think he learnt something from you."

"Hmm, you may be right. At least he's learnt how to knock on a door!"

Just as I had hoped, the envelope contained a letter from Taeko to Kiyoshi. I would like to finish the story by printing the whole thing, because it completes the explanation of the extraordinary Tokyo Zodiac Murders.

EPILOGUE

The Voice of Azoth

To the gentleman I met in Arashiyama,

I have been waiting for you for a long time. That may sound odd, but it is true. I have been suffering from very strong anxiety, which may be only natural, considering what I have done. Every night since I came to live in Kyoto, my mother's favourite place, I have had the same nightmare, in which the story goes on nonstop: a terrifying man approaches me, scolds me in a loud voice, grabs me by my arm, and drags me to jail. It really scares me and leaves me shivering. But, strange as it may seem, I have always wanted to meet that man.

Finally, he came out into the real world, and stood in front of me. It was you. You were young and gentle, and you never asked me to tell you the terrible details of my crime. I appreciated your thoughtfulness. I want to thank you, so I'm writing you this letter.

I have never done anything good in my life. Thanks to your discretion, the truth of my crime could remain unknown for ever. But I would now like to explain the details of what I did, and confess my sins.

My days with the Umezawas, all those years ago, were very

299

difficult. Masako, my stepmother, and her daughters were very cruel to me. Even though I murdered the girls and trapped Masako, I have never regretted what I did. When I lived with them, it seemed like nothing could be worse. That is maybe why I have been able to live until today.

My father, Heikichi Umezawa, dumped my mother, Tae, when I was only a year old. Tae wanted to have custody of me and implored Heikichi to let me live with her. But he wouldn't allow it, insisting that she was too weak physically. If that was true, how could he have dared to let that poor woman live alone?

Soon after Tae left the Umezawa house, Heikichi married Masako. She was a devil. It may not be fair to speak ill of the dead, but Masako treated me with great malice. She never bought me anything and never gave me any pocket money. All my clothes, toys, and books were hand-me-downs from Tomoko or Akiko. Yukiko and I went to the same primary school. I was one year ahead of her, but being in the same school with her made me feel second-rate. I had to wear moth-eaten sweaters and stained blouses and skirts, while she was always dressed neatly with new clothes. In order to forget my misery, I studied fiercely. I began to get higher scores than Yukiko. So Masako and Yukiko employed every trick they could think of to interrupt me when I was studying.

If Masako didn't like me, why did she keep me in her house? Perhaps she was afraid of looking bad in front of the neighbours, or perhaps she enjoyed using me as a maid. All the household chores were mine from the time I was small. I asked if I could go and live with my mother, but Masako wouldn't allow it. Neither our neighbours nor my classmates knew what was happening inside the Umezawa household; they concealed the facts so well.

Every time I was getting ready to visit my mother, Masako and her daughters would do nasty things to thwart me. But it never stopped me from going out. The real reason was not so much that I wanted to see my mother, but that I had found a job secretly. I had to help support my mother and myself. She could not make ends meet from just selling cigarettes.

My mother, who understood my situation very well, helped me keep my job a secret. Sometimes the Umezawa women asked her if I was really visiting her in Hoya. She always evaded their questions. Back then, women couldn't get a job, even at night-clubs, without references. I was lucky; I met a kind gentleman. With his help, I started to work once a week at a university hospital. I can't mention his name or the name of the hospital, because I don't want any harm to come to him or his family.

I learnt a lot from that job, but at the same time I became nihilistic. It was at the hospital that I had a chance to see autopsies performed. My ideas towards life changed drastically. Death became very close to me. It struck me that people in the medical profession have a lot of control over people's lives. Eventually, I was attracted by the idea of committing suicide. I don't know if young girls feel the same way these days, but back then many girls were fascinated with the idea of killing themselves before they lost their virginity.

One day, I had the opportunity to visit the pharmaceutical department. A colleague showed me a bottle of arsenic, and it was then that I made up my mind to commit suicide. Later on, I sneaked into the pharmacy, stole a spoonful of poison and put it into an empty cosmetic bottle. I went to see my mother to say my last goodbye. When I looked into her shop from the street, she was sitting beside the coal brazier as usual. She smiled and held up a paper bag. She was expecting me, so she had bought some waffles. While we were eating them together, I looked into her eyes, questioning the meaning of life. I could find nothing good about mine, but I realized my mother's situation was even worse. I knew that I would have to do something good for her before I died.

My mother always looked so sad and lonely; she was like an empty can that someone has crushed and thrown into a vacant lot. Every time I saw her, she was sitting in the same position in the same place. The knowledge that her life would never change was very painful to me. The Umezawa women enjoyed a life surrounded by luxury. Every time I heard them chatting, laughing or playing music, my resentment and hatred towards them grew. I could feel my blood boiling; my heart was filled with rage.

One day, Kazue came to visit the Umezawas. She was the queen of complaints: she would pick on anything she disliked and grumble about it all day. On that occasion, she complained that the chair she was sitting on was uneven. Masako said, "Here, put this bit of rag under the leg to make it even." She tossed to Kazue a sachet that had belonged to my mother. It had been part of her collection. I had no idea how Masako had got hold of it—maybe it had dropped from my mother's suitcase when she was moving out of the house. Anyway, the incident made me furious—my patience was exhausted. Then and there I decided that I would take revenge on them for my mother's sake, even if it meant killing them all. I began to put all my energy into planning my act of vengeance—yes, I started planning the Azoth murders.

I sneaked into the pharmaceutical department at the hospital every so often, stealing a little bit of arsenic each time.

Then, at the end of 1935, I quit my job without giving notice. There was no way they could have contacted me because I had given them a fake name and address when I applied for the job.

I had always thought my face was rather nice, but I had never been very satisfied with my breasts, hips and legs. That's why the idea of Azoth came to me, I think. You may laugh at me, but that's a woman's nature.

I knew that I would have to find someone who could dispose of the girls' bodies once I had killed them. I kept thinking and thinking, looking for a suitable person who would do it. And then, I noticed Mr Takegoshi, the detective, who regularly passed Kazue's house. I really feel sorry about what I did to him. I wish I could have explained the whole situation and apologized to him. But I couldn't do it at the time because I would rather have killed myself than be arrested.

My father was not the real target; he was just selfish and childish. I killed him with a box made from very hard wood, which I brought home from work. I filled it with a mixture of cement and straw, which I had heard was the way carpenters made walls solid. I nailed a handle onto it, but it was a bit too heavy. When I hit my father on the head with it, it broke. That was the worst moment I have ever experienced. Although he was a selfish man, my father had never been cruel to me. A week before his murder, I told him that I was willing to be a nude model for him and I wouldn't tell anyone. He looked so happy and excited to share the secret with me. Emotionally he was like a child.

On the day of his murder, I posed for him as usual, waiting for the chance to kill him. Then it suddenly started to snow, and the snow accumulated in a very short time. I realized that my plan might no longer be effective. I thought God might be telling me to stop. I couldn't make up my mind what to do. "Tonight isn't good; better to do it tomorrow," I kept telling myself as my father took his sleeping pills. However, the situation wouldn't allow me to postpone the murder. His painting was almost finished, and he would be adding my face to the canvas the next day. Then anyone who saw it would know the identity of his model.

I struck him on the head with the box. The police determined that he died instantly, but that wasn't quite true. I couldn't kill him with a single blow. He fell and suffered terribly. I finally had to smother him. I covered his nose and mouth with several sheets of wet *washi* handmade paper. Later, I couldn't understand why the police hadn't discovered the real cause of his death.

Once he was dead, I started cutting his beard with a pair of scissors. After that, I was going to use a razor to make his face clean-shaven, which I thought would confuse the investigators. But blood started running out of his nose and mouth. I became frightened, and had to stop. I tried to be careful not to drop any of his whiskers on the floor, but I failed.

Then I went outside. After putting my handbag under the eaves, where there was no snow, I threw a rope I'd prepared to the sliding bar from the window and managed to hook it and then pull it to lock the door. Then I walked to the street, carrying Heikichi's shoes with me. My shoe prints were in plain sight in the snow; I intended to create a second set of prints on top of them using his shoes. Stepping carefully on my toes into the set of prints I'd just made, I walked back to the studio. But when I looked closely, I could see indentations in the centre of my original shoe prints. I had to disguise them somehow.

I put my father's shoes on and tried my best to walk over my first set of prints normally. When I got back to the street, I changed shoes again and put my father's shoes in a bag. If it hadn't snowed so much, and again in the morning, the whole trick might not have worked.

I hid in the woods in Komazawa that night. There was a place I knew well near the creek; it was a low spot covered with thorny vines. The thorns pricked me painfully, but it was the perfect place to hide. If my plan failed, I decided I would kill myself there. I had already dug a hole ready and covered it with old branches and grass. That's where I buried the box, the scissors and the whiskers from Heikichi's beard. I waited for morning to come, sitting in the middle of the bushes. If I walked around, someone might see me, which would be the worst possible thing that could happen. A few cars passed during the night, but I was lucky not to be seen by anyone.

It was so cold that I thought I would die. While sitting there, I was seized with regret and uncertainty. Should I go home while it was snowing? I decided I shouldn't—I had to avoid being seen by anyone. I had told Masako I would be spending the night in Hoya. If I went home then, it would seem suspicious if anyone heard about it. If I didn't go home and if Masako asked Tae if I was with her, I knew my mother would lie for me. So I stayed where I was, shivering.

Heikichi's note was my invention. I left it in his studio after I killed him, but I was not sure if it would work. I became very anxious, and started thinking I shouldn't have done it. I could have kept the whole thing simple and just used poison to kill everybody. I didn't mind if I was caught, but I didn't want Tae to suffer because of me—she would be known as the mother of a serial killer. I needed to commit my crime secretly so that she would be protected. And I liked the idea of letting Masako suffer for the rest of her life.

I tried to get rid of my negative thoughts. I felt sure that nobody would think Heikichi's handwritten note was a fake, because he hadn't written any letters or postcards to anybody since he was twenty years old. I had seen Heikichi's handwriting in his drawing book from his time in Europe. It looked very much like mine. I thought it was funny that the handwriting of a father and his daughter should look so alike. To disguise my handwriting further, I used a drawing pencil so that the characters were a bit blurred.

While I was writing the note, I thought about Heikichi. It was strange, but I could only remember the good things about him. He had been so nice to me... I thought I would go crazy from my feelings of guilt. Heikichi talked about himself a lot to me, because he trusted me. He had very few friends—probably Miss Tomita and I were his only friends. That's how I could put such feeling into that note. And then, of all the things I could do... I killed him!

Nights are long in winter. While I was hiding, I felt the morning would never come. When the eastern sky started growing light, I became scared that one of the Umezawa women would find Heikichi's body before I returned. I needed to return the pair of shoes; Masako and her daughters may well have been aware that he kept two pairs in his studio. I wanted to go back right away. But if I went there very early, Masako would grow suspicious, since I was supposed to be staying in Hoya. And if I went straight to the studio to return the shoes, my shoe prints would be left in the snow.

Having to carry Heikichi's shoes back with me was not part of my original plan. It was an unexpected complication that made me very anxious. Wouldn't it be better if I buried them or threw them away? They were wet from the snow. If the police compared the shoes with the shoe prints, they would figure out the trick. I was at a loss for a while, but I finally decided to return them to the studio. Again I was very lucky; the police never considered the possibility that the man's shoe prints had been made by Heikichi's own shoes. It's likely that they never even tried to compare Heikichi's shoes with the shoe prints. And it snowed again in the morning, making it difficult to see the shoe prints well anyway.

The police interrogation, however, was quite brutal. I was well prepared, of course, but all the other girls were hysterical, which made me feel good. I had caught a cold from staying in the woods, and I was shivering. But the investigators must have thought that it was a natural response for a young woman who had just discovered her father's dead body.

My mother was questioned about my alibi. She believed I still had that hospital job, so she insisted I was with her all night. Her intention was to protect me from the Umezawa women. She had a heart of gold.

Now I shall explain Kazue's murder. I killed her shortly after that because I didn't want her to have time to compare notes with Masako. I had previously paid her a visit alone to check out the house. I had experienced incredible fear and anxiety when I killed Heikichi, but killing Kazue was more like walking on a tightrope. I murdered her, and then waited for Mr Takegoshi to get off work. I was afraid he might not show up or would take a different route home that night.

I had wanted to wear the same kind of kimono that Kazue wore, but I couldn't afford it. So once she was dead, I had to take hers off and put it on myself. While I was waiting for Mr Takegoshi on the street, I found some bloodstains on the collar. So I looked for a dark place for the planned encounter. Fortunately he turned up. I led him back to Kazue's house. I could smell the pungent odour of blood, but he seemed oblivious to it. I asked him not to turn on the lights. He thought I was being shy; in fact it was a ploy to keep the bloodstains hidden.

When the investigators said Kazue must have died between 7 p.m. and 9 p.m., Mr Takegoshi must have been horrified—but it was lucky for me. In fact I'd killed her just after 7 p.m.

When I attended Kazue's funeral, I hadn't finished putting her house back in order. I had washed the bloodstains out of the cushion covers and hung them to dry in the house. I wanted it to look like there was still work to do—that would be a good reason for the Umezawa women all to go to the house on the way back from Mount Yahiko.

By that time, I was already getting used to killing. I even enjoyed it, as if I was playing some kind of game. I never liked spending time with the Umezawa women, but going to Mount Yahiko with them was part of my plan, and I was looking forward to it. Fortunately, the police hadn't released Heikichi's note, so nobody knew about the Azoth story. This time, everything worked smoothly. When I proposed the trip, Masako immediately agreed, and then, during our visit to the hot springs, the girls all wanted to stay longer—which I was going to suggest if they hadn't. Just as I had expected, Masako left us and went to Aizu-wakamatsu to see her parents. I knew she wouldn't go out to see anyone while she was there because she knew everyone would be curious about the Umezawa family. My only obstacle was that Masako told me and her nieces, Reiko and Nobuyo, to go back to Tokyo separately. But it was important for my plan that the six of us should travel together. We ended up taking the same train, but Tomoko, Akiko and Yukiko sat together, away from Nobuyo, Reiko and me. Nobody saw the six of us together.

I suggested we might all go to Kazue's house to finish the cleaning up, but Tomoko and Akiko said that I could do it by myself. How could they say a thing like that to me? Kazue was their blood relative, not mine. They were not only selfish, but had ugly dispositions, too. We lived in the same house and took ballet lessons together, but they were terrible dancers. Among all of them, Tomoko and Yukiko were especially bad. When I danced well, they would walk out of the practice room. When my time on the floor was over, they would all come back in and start to dance, laughing and chatting away.

To get them to go to Kazue's house, I acted like I really needed them. "Please come with me. I'm scared to go into that house alone," I said. "You don't have to do anything. I bought some fruit; I can make some nice fresh juice for you."

We arrived at Kazue's house just after 4 p.m. on 31st March. I immediately went to the kitchen, squeezed the fruit, and put the poison in the juice. I did it quickly so that they would be dead before dark. If they were still alive and it got dark, they would turn the lights on, and the neighbours would know that somebody was in the house. All five of them drank the poisoned juice, and died instantly.

I was going to take the antidote beforehand, in case they asked me to try the juice first, but I had had no chance to

309

obtain it. However, my worst-case scenario didn't come true, because the girls didn't have the slightest thought of coming into the kitchen to help or watch what I was doing.

I stored their bodies in the shower. It was not really safe to leave the bodies there, but the shower was the only place I thought secure. And I couldn't store five bodies somewhere else and bring them back the next day. If the police found the bodies, I would give up the whole plan and kill myself with arsenic; the police would have thought the killer was trying to make Azoth with six bodies. If the killer remained unknown, my mother would never be involved. Fortunately, nobody noticed the bodies in the shower.

I went back to the Umezawa house alone. I put a piece of rope and a bottle of the poison in Masako's room. Then I spent the night in my room alone. The next day, I returned to Kazue's house. The muscles of the girls' bodies had begun to harden. In the moonlight coming in through the bathroom window, I began to saw and slice through the bodies. It was very lucky for my idea of Azoth that all the Umezawa women, including myself, were blood type A. It was something I had found out when we went to donate blood one day. Then I wrapped the body pieces in oilpaper, took them to the storeroom in the garden, and covered them with a cloth. I had cleared up all the dust and straw in there on the day of Kazue's funeral, so that the bodies could not easily be traced back there.

The problem was the girls' travel bags. How was I going to get rid of them? They were not so large, but there were six pieces altogether. I couldn't tell Mr Takegoshi to take them with him. I put some rocks in them and threw them into the Tama River. I got rid of the saw and the knife in the river, too.

I had already prepared the blackmail letter to Mr Takegoshi. I killed the girls on 31st March and mailed the letter on 1st April, the same day I cut their bodies up. Everything had to be done quickly, because of the decomposition setting in. Also Mr Takegoshi needed time to carry out his mission.

I don't have a birthmark; Yukiko did. In Heikichi's note, I described Yukiko's birthmark as if it was mine. In order to complete the fiction, I hit myself on the side of my stomach with an iron rod to make a bruise and I mentioned to my mother that I had a birthmark. She was so surprised, she tried to rub it off! So when she saw the real birthmark on Yukiko's torso, she identified the body as mine.

After the murders, I changed my hairstyle and clothes and stayed in cheap hotels in Kawasaki and Asakusa, working wherever I could. My heart ached when I thought of my mother being so sad and alone.

I could have continued to live that way with my savings, but there was no guarantee that I wouldn't be traced and captured. I thought the best thing would be to flee from Japan for a while, and return later. Of all the Japanese colonies, I thought Manchuria would be the best place to hide. It was hard for me to part from my mother, but even if I stayed in Japan, I wouldn't be able to see her for a while anyway. And if she knew what I had done, I felt sure she wouldn't have been able to keep it a secret. So for her sake and mine, I made the decision to leave.

While working in a hotel, I had met a woman who was going to join a settlers' unit in Manchuria with her brothers. I begged her to let me accompany them. It was said that Manchuria was a prosperous, wonderful place to live, and many Japanese were moving there to work on the land. I was one of the dreamers; I later found the dream was far from perfect. There was no shortage of land in Manchuria, but we had to endure a very harsh climate. The temperature went down to minus 40°C.

After a while, I quit working on the farmland and got a job in the city. It was extremely difficult for a single woman to make a living there. I can't describe what happened to me. Let me just say that I understood why my mother didn't want to go to Manchuria. When I suffered, I always thought it was God's punishment.

At the end of the war, I returned to Japan. I lived for a while in Kyushu. The Umezawa murders were still famous, and I learnt that my mother had inherited a lot of money from Heikichi's estate. I was ecstatic with the news, because now she'd be able to fulfil her dream of opening her own boutique in Kyoto. I couldn't stop myself from visiting her. So in 1963, I went to Sagano. I searched the area in vain but came up empty—no mother and no shop. I can hardly describe my disappointment. There was nothing for me to do in Kyoto, so I went to Tokyo.

Tokyo had changed completely. The streets were crowded with automobiles and many highways had been constructed. There were colourful signs and banners everywhere announcing the upcoming Olympic Games. I went to Meguro, where the Umezawa house was located. Among the trees, I could see a new apartment building on the Umezawa property. Then I went to Komazawa to see my favourite creek and trees and the spot where I had buried the murder weapon. I had heard there was now a golf course in the area. When I got there, I was shocked. The woods and creek had completely disappeared. There was just a vast open stretch of land, with the characteristic red soil of the Kanto area. Bulldozers and trucks were running around, holes being dug, and earth was being hauled away. There were some huge cement pipes, which were going to be used for the sewage system. Perhaps that was where the creek had been. The construction workers told me they were building an arena and a park for the Olympic Games. It was a hot summer day, and I was sweating under my parasol. Everything was so different. I couldn't believe it was the place where I had spent a night shivering in the snow. Even the sun seemed to be shining differently. The serenity which had surrounded me that winter day was gone.

Then I went to Hoya to see my mother. I felt sure she would be there. She would have been seventy-five years old at that time. When she inherited the money, she was already over sixty. I had neglected to think of that. How could she have started a new business alone at that age? I loathed my thoughtlessness. On the way to the cigarette shop, my knees were trembling. When I turned the corner, I expected to see her sitting in her shop window as she always used to… but she wasn't there. The shop was still there, but not her. All the stores on the street now had modern aluminium windows and doors, making my mother's old, worn cigarette shop look very pitiful. No one was minding the shop. I slid the window open and called out to see if there was anybody there. A middle-aged woman appeared, and I told her I was a relative of Tae's from Manchuria. The woman let me in the house and then left.

My mother was lying in bed in the living room. She looked like she was on her last breath. I sat down beside her. Her eyes were so weak, she didn't recognize me.

"Thank you, ma'am," she said. "You're always so kind."

I couldn't stop the tears from running down my cheeks. What a fool I had been! I realized that my revenge on the Umezawas hadn't done any good. I hadn't been able to make my mother happy after all, nor had I changed her life for the better. I had been completely mistaken.

I stayed to look after her, waiting patiently in the hope she would recognize me. Several days later, she suddenly called out my name. "Oh, you're Tokiko... Tokiko!" she cried with delight. She didn't seem able to comprehend the situation, or how long it had been since we had seen each other. It was just as well. I didn't want her to know anything more than that I was back.

The Tokyo Olympic Games were going to be held the following year. I bought a colour television, hoping to please her, but she was almost comatose, her life dwindling. Her house became the television haven of the neighbourhood. Few people were able to afford a colour television back then. On the day of the Opening Ceremony, the house was filled with people from the neighbourhood excitedly watching the spectacle on TV of the acrobatic planes creating five interlocking circles of smoke. The Olympic Games represented a new era for Japan. But for me, all it meant was that my mother had completed her own circle of life; like the smoke from the planes, she drifted away peacefully, surrounded by her neighbours.

I felt I had many obligations to my mother, and one of them was to open a boutique in Sagano. Fulfilling her dream was the only reason left for me to live. I had no regrets about the murders. If I had thought I would one day feel regret, I would never have done them. I am sure you can understand that.

Running my shop with two young employees brought pleasure, but it seemed too good for me. So I decided to make myself a bet. Because you are an astrologer, you will understand this. I was born in Tokyo at 9.41 a.m., on 21st March 1913. In the first house, I have Pluto, the symbol of death and reincarnation. My inclination for bizarre things must come from the influence of this planet. Also, I have Venus, Jupiter and the moon making a triangle in my horoscope. I was born lucky. Probably my plans worked so well because of my luck. However, the fifth house—which means family and a love relationship—is diminished. At the same time, the eleventh house—which controls friendship and desire—is also diminished. In fact, I have no friends, no lovers and no children.

I was not interested in having property or money or status. My only desire was to find a man who would spend his life with me. I decided that if I ever met that man, I would devote my body and soul to him for ever. I stayed in Sagano, betting that he would come... waiting for him. He would solve the mystery, and he would find me. It was strange, but even though I knew I wasn't blessed with love or romance, I believed that my fortune would change after middle age. I was born under a lucky star, so if I stayed there, something wonderful would happen to me. No matter who it was, I knew he would be a smart person, and he would be someone to love. I wouldn't care what kind of family he came from. I would love him. I thought that was to be my fate. That was my bet.

But now I think I was just being stupid. Time passed, and I grew old. Suppose a man did find me: I would be too old for romance. My murder plans had been so perfect that I couldn't satisfy my desire. I lost my bet. It was a real punishment for a woman like myself.

I don't have any bad feelings towards you. When I met you, I thought the result of my bet was not so bad after all. It's just that the roll of the dice came up empty. I had decided to end my life when I lost the bet. I have a good sign in the eighth house, which controls death and inheritance. I won't need much effort to die peacefully.

I wish you good health and a bright future.

Goodbye.

Tokiko Umezawa